Peggy,

I'm looking forward to

Through the Eyes of a Woman

Brenda Latourelle

getting to know you. You have raised a wonderful, kind and loving son and I can only imagine he got that from you. So thank you.

Brenda Latourelle

First Page Publications
Livonia, Michigan

First Page Publications
12103 Merriman • Livonia • MI • 48150
1-800-343-3034 • Fax 734-525-4420
www.firstpagepublications.com

To my boys CJ and Dominick, with all my love.
For my parents who have always stood behind me
and continue to love unconditionally.
To my best friend, Pam, who has always been there for me.
And to John, the man of my dreams.

Thank you all, for making my life brighter.

Library of Congress Control Number:
2005927260

Through the Eyes of a Woman/
Latourelle, Brenda
ISBN # 1-928623-61-1

Summary: After escaping from an emotionally and physically abusive relationship, Amber finds hope and confidence through counseling, loyal friendships and new love, until her ex-husband stalks her and attempts to murder her.

Chapter One

The café was nearly empty. Early evening sunlight slanted through the gauzy curtains, illuminating the table Amber wiped quickly with a rag, her movements precise.

"Amber, it's past five. Why haven't you gone home yet?"

Amber looked up, interrupted from her thoughts. "I'll leave after I finish up with a few things. Guess how much money I made in tips today?" she asked Carol, as she pulled a wad of bills from her apron.

"Fifty dollars?" Carol placed a slim finger alongside her face

"Nope. Eighty," Amber said with a satisfied smile, tucking twenty-five dollars in her shirt pocket and putting the rest back in her apron.

"What a good day!" Carol exclaimed, putting her arm around her friend. They smiled warmly at each other, the fatigue of their long day visible around their eyes. "Amber, make sure you put it in the safe before you go—so he doesn't find it, like the last time. I bet you almost have enough now."

Amber collapsed into a chair with a smile. "Yeah, about two more months of saving should do it." She looked out of the window dreamily. A cloud crossed the sun and cast a shadow across her face as she turned back to Carol. "But I'm really going to miss you. You are the best boss—and friend—anyone could ever have."

"Yeah, yeah, run along now before you get yourself into trouble with Jim. That will do you no good," she said, gently pulling Amber onto her feet and leading her toward the door with an arm around her shoulder. "You need every ounce of energy you've got to get through the next few months. I just wish I could talk you into living with me." At the door, she turned to Amber and took both of her hands in her own. "I don't want you to move away," she said, her brow furrowed as she peered straight into Amber's eyes. "You can get a restraining order. I have an alarm system. I have a gun."

"Now Carol," Amber said, untying her apron and handing it to Carol. "You know how I feel about guns. And anyway, I hear that, much of the time, the guns people have are what criminals use on their victims."

"Oh, Amber you read too much. Please think about it. Remember, Chuck is a police officer, so he could put extra patrol where we live and work." She held the door open. "This isn't right—you shouldn't have to leave because of him."

"I know. I appreciate everything you do and have done for me, but I'm afraid to stay." She stepped through the door and turned to face her friend. "Dr. Dahl says it's not right either, but I need to do what I feel is best, and I really think this is it. I guess I better get home. I only have an hour to make dinner before Jim gets back." She hugged Carol quickly. "My money's in that front pocket," she said, nodding toward the apron. "Please put it in the safe for me. I've gotta run." Her eyes grew dark as she looked down the sidewalk toward her house. "I'll see you tomorrow."

"See you tomorrow, Amber."

As she hurried home, Amber fought against the cool, sharp wind that cut through her thin jacket. The smell of rain was in the air. Today was different; there were no children outside playing. The air was filled with silence. Her mind raced with the same thoughts that she'd been considering for weeks now. *Do I have to leave? Could I live with Carol and Chuck? I would be so scared. He would kill me. He could find me and kill me if I moved far away too. Maybe a restraining order? What would that really mean though? Would that protect me? I have two months. I have two months to figure out what to do. But now, I need to concentrate on tonight. On Jim. I need to make him happy.*

As she turned the corner, she saw her little white house with her white picket fence, and all her beautiful flowers she had spent so many hours planting. But as she looked around, she noticed that some of her flowers had been pulled out and scattered throughout the yard. Her face grew chalky, her eyes widened in alarm, and she began to tremble. He was already home. *Home early! Oh God, I'm late. Think, think! Act as if nothing is wrong and everything will be okay.*

Chapter Two

She walked through the door. "Hi honey, I'm home!" She fought to keep her voice even. She had to sound normal. "Where are you? I made twenty-five dollars for you today." A frightening silence served as a response. *Where could he be? Maybe he's in the garage. Find the strength, keep walking. Go to the kitchen. Two more months. Pull yourself together, he can't know you're afraid! Start dinner. Then to the bedroom to change. Act as if nothing has happened. Everything will be fine.* With trembling hands she began dinner. She peeled potatoes and carrots and put a small roast in the oven. With all the strength she could muster, she slowly walked to the bedroom.

She cautiously entered the room and saw Jim cutting up her clothes with a knife. He lunged at her.

"You bitch! Where in the hell have you been? You've been out whoring around again." His eyes twitched as he brandished the knife at her, a lock of greasy, dark hair obscuring his vision.

She screamed with all her might, but her scream was cut short when he hurled her around and held the knife to her throat. She gasped for air. He pressed the knife against her throat and she could feel how cold the steel was. Then she felt a sharp, excruciating pain, and the sensation of warm blood running down her neck.

Suddenly, everything was unclear. The room turned fuzzy and obscure. The pictures on the wall and the windows passed before her, but she could barely comprehend their meanings. Slowly, everything went dark, like someone turning down the brightness on a television set. That was the last thing she remembered: her world gradually being drained of all color.

She woke up to Jim's face above her, panicked and concerned. He rambled quickly to himself, his voice low and trembling slightly. "I really did it this time. I killed her. Now what do I do? How could this be?" His wide brown eyes caught on hers and, startled, he reared back. "Honey, are you okay? I'm sorry, I'm really sorry. I promise I won't do it again. I was so scared! I didn't mean to do it, you have to know that." He grabbed both of her hands tightly in his own cold, shaking ones, pressing his dry lips to her palms.

Amber lay still and closed her eyes. His voice sounded muffled, far away.

She could hardly understand the words coming out of his mouth, but one thought rang clear: *He is going to kill me. I need to get away.* She opened her eyes and looked at Jim's terrified, sweaty face, still close to hers. *When he sleeps tonight, I'll go to Carol's,* she thought, her mind foggy but focused.

She extricated her hands from Jim's grasp and gingerly touched her neck. It was bandaged. He had actually cleaned and bandaged her. *The pain.* She breathed deeply, and began to feel dizzy again. "Help me. I need help, Jim. You need to take me to the hospital."

Jim stood and began pacing back and forth, shaking his head like a madman. When he spoke, it was as if he was talking to himself. "No, we can't go to the hospital. They will know I did it. You've been there too much and they will put me away. We can't, we can't go," he stuttered, "we can't go to the hospital. We can't."

"Jim, I really need to . . ." Her voice trailed off. Jim stopped pacing and turned his fiery gaze on her, his jaw clenched, a deep red color creeping up from his neck. He looked right at her, but Amber could tell that he could barely see her through his rage.

"Jim, you're right. Please Jim, we don't need to go. I don't know what I was thinking. I don't want you to get into trouble. I'll be fine. I just need something for the pain." Amber's pleas came out in a steady stream that seemed to temper Jim's anger.

"I have something." Jim hurried into the bathroom. She heard him frantically dig through the medicine cabinet. She hauled herself up, wincing at the sharp, throbbing pain in her neck and shoulders. She made her way precariously to the mirror, her head spinning, and gently pulled the bandage down. She had to do a double take. There was a gaping laceration. He had cut her from one side of the throat to the other. Blood still drained from the wound. She turned her head in disgust and winced from the horrible pain. She felt sick to her stomach, too weak to run, and flooded with determination. She did not want to run far away as she had before; she wanted to stay and fight. He would not control her as he had for so long. She felt *lucky* to be alive, and this feeling brought with it a newfound determination to *stay* alive, on her own terms. *I never expected this. Hitting me? Yes. But if I leave, I will spend the rest of my days looking over my shoulder. I don't want to have to run away, start all over, knowing that he will never give up. If I stay, I don't have to leave the people I love and I'll have protection. I must stay.*

He had just missed her jugular. She would be grateful for that centimeter of uncut tissue—that detail that allowed her to still be here, standing in front of her mirror—for the rest of her life.

"Found it!" She heard the medicine cabinet click shut. With great effort, she pushed the bandage back up, and cringing, gritting her teeth, managed to settle herself in the bed just as he entered the room. "Here you go. Two of these and you'll feel better."

"What are they?" Amber asked nervously, looking up at Jim.

"Never mind, just take them." The pills were round and blue. Swallowing them caused great agony. It took a few sips of water before she could even get one down. By the time she got the second pill down, she was nearly in tears, lightly holding her throat. Before he left the room, Jim bent down and kissed her forehead.

I will leave with only the clothes on my back. As long as I get out of here, I won't need anything . . . I won't need anything . . . just the clothes on my back. Oh God, what did he give me? I feel so tired, so tired. It's like that other time, I felt so funny when I woke up. Not good. Not good at all, not right.

Chapter Three

The sun shown through the window; she had to shield her eyes from the brightness. It was ten o'clock. Her stomach turned, and she felt as though she might vomit. Her head pounded, and the corners of reality were soaked with a grogginess she couldn't shake.

That was the least of her problems. The deep cut on her neck throbbed so badly it brought tears to her eyes. When she moved her head, the wound felt like it was on fire. She held her throat warily, but it did not do anything to ease the pain. She felt as if she had a horrible hangover.

I need to get up and see where Jim is. I need to get out of here. "Jim," she yelled hoarsely. "Where are you?"

No answer.

She made her way to the window. His car was not there.

She went to the bathroom. She looked into the mirror and saw, with horror, how much blood was on her clothing. Her face had turned ashen; she looked twice her age. She couldn't believe her eyes. Her heart started to race, her mouth turned dry, and she became very disoriented. She sat down on the toilet as her stomach turned. The room started to pass before her.

She could no longer handle it. Between the vision—now etched eternally in her mind—of her wound, and the sight of all that blood, she lost it. She wept openly, staring at her distorted, horrific image in the mirror, an image she could no longer recognize as her own. When she was done, she sat on the toilet for a little bit longer and gathered her thoughts. Her life was in shambles, her reflection not her own.

Amber thought then of the story of the phoenix rising up from the flames, and knew that she had to muster the courage to rise up out of the ashes of her own life, to transcend this place and find something better.

She cleaned herself up and made her way to the bedroom to change her clothes. *Oh God, help me*, she pleaded to herself. *Get me out of here before he gets back. Thank God I came home before he was able to shred all my clothing.* Each movement was a struggle that caused incredible pain. She finally made her way out the door, tormented by her pain and weakness. *I can't walk along the street*, she thought. *I need to go a different way.*

Her short walk to work, only a little over a block, seemed to take forever. She cut through people's yards, praying fervently for no one to see her. Finally, she found herself at work, so disoriented she could hardly remember how she had gotten there. She made her way in through the back door. She didn't want any of the customers to see her. When she came out of the kitchen, she was relieved to see that there was not a soul in the place. It was their down time, the lull between breakfast and lunch.

When she slowly staggered in, Carol looked dumbfounded and stared at her momentarily before she went to her.

"Amber, please let me help you. Here, sit down. Amber, what happened?" she asked, concern written all over her face.

"Jim. He did this," Amber said haltingly, her sentences short as she gasped for breath. "He cut my throat. With a knife. I need help." Her eyes darted around the empty café and out of the windows in a panic.

Carol ran and dialed 911. "We need help here at Carol's Café. My friend Amber Labell is here . . . and her husband, Jim Labell, cut her throat with a knife." Carol paused as the dispatcher spoke. "No, he's not here . . . Thank you, and please hurry."

"Where's Jim?" Carol asked as she rushed to Amber's side.

"I don't know. When I woke up he . . . he was gone. I asked for something. For the pain. What he gave me knocked me out. I don't know what it was." She began to cry. She leaned into Carol's chest, and Carol wrapped her arms around her.

"I'm going to close the restaurant and lock the doors, just in case. You're safe until the ambulance arrives." Carol frantically locked the door, put up the closed sign, and hurried back to Amber.

"Carol, I can't believe this." She sobbed harder, so Carol held her even tighter. "I left here yesterday and headed home. When I got around the corner, my flowers had been ripped out. Thrown around the yard. Carol, his car was home. He had come home early. I went in. I started dinner. He cut up my clothes with a knife. He was yelling. Calling me a whore. He grabbed me. Pressed the knife against my neck. I didn't know what to do. Then he cut my throat." She looked into Carol's eyes, searching for answers.

Carol began to cry. "Oh Amber, I'm so sorry he did this to you. What are you going to do?" She gently stroked Amber's hair.

"If you still want me, I would like to stay with you and Chuck. I need to stay and fight. I can't run away. I don't want to look over my shoulder. For the rest of my life," Amber replied, still struggling to get the sentences out.

Carol helped Amber to the floor so she could lie down. Amber lay her head on Carol's lap. "Honey, don't talk. It's taking too much out of you."

"I'm sure this is what I want. I don't want to live in fear. I need to stay where I am loved." Amber rubbed Carol's hand.

"That's right, Amber, you can stay here with us. We'll help protect you." She smoothed Amber's hair back from her forehead, which was damp with sweat. "I have an idea; Chuck has a friend on the police force named Tim. He has no family. I bet he would take you in. Jim wouldn't know where to find you—" The sound of sirens cut her off. "The ambulance is here. We can finish talking about this later." Carol bent down and hugged Amber again. "Everything's going to work out just fine, Amber. I can feel it. And I'm so glad you're not leaving."

Chapter Four

Amber looked around dazedly at the machinery in the ambulance. The paramedics got to work immediately, checking her blood pressure, temperature, pulse, and respirations. She couldn't believe this was happening to her, and the reality of it had yet to sink in. Her mind was still foggy from the drugs she had been given. She looked at her friend. Carol's face was pale and she watched Amber with wide eyes that were flooded with worry.

As she lay there, her mind started to wander. *Carol always tells me I'm so beautiful. She covets my long, strawberry blonde hair and big green eyes. She always says she wishes she could be thin like me, with my voluptuous hips and bosoms and long legs. But I never see myself that way. Carol has told me she is jealous of me. I can't understand it because Carol is a very attractive woman. And I have so many reasons to be jealous of her. She has everything going for her. Her own business, a wonderful husband, a beautiful home. She always used to say, "Look at all these men always asking you out. And it's not just because of the way you look. It's your personality, your sense of humor, and how loving and giving and kind you are."*

And now I lie here with my throat cut, which will turn into an ugly scar. She has no reason to be jealous now. She always wondered why I had to suffer so much. In my own way, I guess I always wondered if I was being punished for something I did. But I could never figure out what it was.

"Amber, honey, are you okay?" Carol said, gently shaking her best friend. "We're at the hospital. Do you feel faint?" Amber was pulled out of her reverie by Carol's concerned face looking down at her.

"I'm fine, just thinking. And the pain . . ." Amber blacked out as her stretcher was unloaded from the ambulance.

When Amber came to, she was in a room with a nurse helping her into a gown. "Where's Carol?" Amber tried to look around but the pain was excruciating.

"Don't worry about that. She'll be here in a minute," the nurse said with a smile. "Lay down and rest. The doctor will be in momentarily."

Amber settled herself into bed and was just about to nod off when a tall man in a white lab coat strode in.

"Hi Amber, I'm Dr. Miller," he said kindly, reaching over to gently grasp her hand. He pulled a chair over and straddled it backward, bending his long legs so that they stuck out from either side of his lanky frame like a grasshopper's. "I have some questions for you."

"Okay. I'll answer them the best I can."

"What happened?"

"My husband Jim cut my throat with a knife. And I believe he drugged me with something. I have felt this way before, in the past when he had given me a few drinks."

Dr. Miller pondered this for a moment. He made some notes on her chart. "What makes you think he drugged you?"

"I feel different. Real groggy and weak. I can't remember anything after taking the pills, and I feel like I have such a hangover. I just don't feel like myself." Amber fidgeted absentmindedly with the blankets on her bed.

"How's your neck feeling?" he asked.

"It's an excruciating, sharp, throbbing pain. It hurts to turn my head, or even move."

"I need to remove the bandage to take a look at it." He removed the bandage and Amber groaned from the pain. Though he quickly recovered, Amber saw horror flash across the young doctor's face as he looked at her wound. "Amber, we will need to take some blood, and then Dr. Sheila Anderson from OB/GYN will need to examine you."

"Why?" Amber's eyebrows furrowed. *What does a gynecologist have to do with my neck?*

"In cases where patients are drugged, this is standard procedure. For now, Amber, you're going to need a lot of stitches. I'll give you some morphine through your IV to help you with the pain. We will make you as comfortable as we can. Amber, you are very lucky he didn't kill you, very lucky." Dr. Miller patted her arm, shaking his head slightly. "Are you feeling strong enough to talk to the police?"

"I will talk to them now."

The doctor left and shortly thereafter an officer strode in. "Hi, Amber. I'm Officer Mike Johnson. I just have some questions for you about what happened." He turned around the chair the doctor had sat in and plopped down.

Amber explained the situation, her voice shaking.

The officer shook his head. "Unbelievable. Do you know where Jim is right now?" he asked in a tight voice.

"He was gone when I woke up this morning, but I assume he's at work."

"Where does he work?"

"He works over at Joe's Garage in St. Paul."

“We will be going over to pick him up. You will be safe here. There will be a detective outside your door the whole time.” He stood abruptly from the chair and stuffed his notepad into his shirt pocket.

Amber managed a smile, feeling relieved. “Thank you, I appreciate that,” she said, her voice raspy and as she squirmed restlessly, trying to get comfortable.

“Not a problem. You've been through a lot, young lady. If there's one thing we can give you, it's peace of mind.”

Chapter Five

"Amber, we're ready for you in surgery," a round-faced woman said, gently shaking her awake. "This is Judy, the nurse anesthetist. She will be working with Dr. Thiel, your anesthesiologist. I'm Nancy, one of the surgery nurses assisting Dr. Wagner today. Judy just has a few questions for you before we go back."

Judy smiled kindly at Amber. "Have you ever had surgery before?"

"Yes, on my appendix."

"Any other surgeries?"

"No."

"Did you have any problems with the anesthesia before?"

"No."

"Okay, then we're going to get this surgical gown and cap on you and head back. We'll be giving you a little something in your IV to relax you. When we get back there, we'll put you under. You should wake up in about an hour, and we'll take you into recovery. Any questions?"

"Nope, I think you've explained everything." Amber's mind raced with fear.

Focus, focus, she thought to herself. *Pull yourself together. This is your first step to recovery. These stitches will pull together the fragments of your life. These stitches will start the healing process.*

When they got back to the surgery room, the nurse covered her with heated blankets, then started the anesthesia. Within seconds, Amber was asleep.

Amber woke up in recovery about an hour and fifteen minutes later with a different nurse watching over her.

"Hi, my name is Maureen," the petite, brunette nurse said in a soft voice. "Don't try to talk. Just get some rest. I've given you some pain medication."

Amber was in agony, but the medicine was doing its job; it wasn't as intense as it had been earlier. "Maureen, is Carol here?" she asked groggily.

"Yes. But it will be about a half an hour before she can see you. So for now, you just rest."

Amber drifted off to sleep again.

Chapter Six

When Amber woke up, Carol and Chuck were sitting next to her bed. Carol's eyes were bloodshot and she held a crumpled tissue in her hand.

"Oh Amber, how are you feeling? You had me so scared." She rushed to Amber's bedside and hugged her.

"Right now, grateful for morphine; it really is helping me with the pain. They want to keep me in the hospital for a few days for observation and to see their psychiatrist to see where I'm at emotionally, and then I will be able to leave." Her voice was hoarse and she spoke softly and slowly.

Chuck sat with both his feet flat on the floor and his elbows resting on his knees and looked at Amber with concern. He spoke in a low tone. "I'm happy to see you alive. When Carol told me what happened I could hardly believe it, even though part of me expected it, if that makes any sense at all. I have great news. They have Jim in custody. He denied what he did to you, but we were able to get a search warrant and we have a lot of evidence against him. As soon as we told him that, he admitted to everything. He will be going away for a long time." Chuck paused and looked at Carol, who smiled weakly at him. "Carol and I talked, and we would still like it if you would stay with our friend Tim. He's a wonderful police officer and you might feel more comfortable and safe with him. You don't have to stay long if you don't want to." He looked at Amber sympathetically, and when he smiled, there was a sadness about him.

Amber was silent for a moment before she turned to look at her friends. "Carol, what do you think about it? I mean, staying with another man. I don't even know him. I'm not sure that's such a good idea." Amber said, wringing her hands.

Carol moved closer to Amber and took her hand. "I understand your apprehension, but I think for now it's our best option. You don't have any family to speak of. If you stay with us, Jim could figure out where you are. I don't think that it's safe. I know you've had a rough past with men, so this may be very hard for you at first, but I assure you he's different. He's not like the other men you've been with. He's just here to help out. Our main goal is your safety, and we feel this is the safest place for you. Jim would never know you were there. And we feel that's very important."

"You're right. I don't have anyone else, Jim made sure of that. You two are all I've got. I trust your opinion. One thing that makes me feel comfortable is that he is a police officer. That would make me feel safer. One thing is for sure, I don't want to be alone." Amber breathed deeply, collecting her thoughts. "I guess I could go along with this, until I'm back on my feet again. But you'll come visit me, right?"

"Of course we will," Carol and Chuck said in unison.

Amber was quiet for a minute. When she spoke, her voice was soft. "I have to tell you guys, I trust your opinion, but I really feel nervous about this. When will I meet him? It would make me so uncomfortable to just move in without ever meeting or talking with him first."

"He's going to be coming down soon; I hope you don't mind that we didn't talk to you before we invited him here." Carol stroked the back of Amber's hand.

"Are you going to be here?"

"Of course," Chuck said reassuringly.

"Good, that will make it a little easier for me." She bit her lower lip and looked into the kind eyes of her friends. She knew they only wanted what was best for her. "I don't feel quite as nervous now."

"Amber, you will really like him; he's very nice, sincere, and easy to get to know. You won't feel uncomfortable at all around him, you'll see." She patted Amber's hand as if to settle the matter. "Do you mind if Chuck and I get some coffee?"

"No, go ahead."

"We'll be back. We're going to take our time so you can get a little rest while we're gone." Chuck and Carol both hugged her before they left.

"Okay," Amber said, smiling after her friends as they walked hand in hand out of the room.

If ever there was a time I wish I had a family, this is it, Amber thought as she stared out of the window. *Growing up in foster care wasn't easy. Moving from one foster home to the next wasn't any easier. If only I could have been adopted and had a family to love that loved me back. I could go stay with them. Then I wouldn't have to worry about where I was going to stay.*

Chapter Seven

The hospital hallway was empty and their footsteps echoed off the walls. Chuck and Carol walked in silence until they reached the coffee machine. Chuck dug in his pockets for change and Carol turned to face him, putting her back against a vending machine filled with snacks. "Chuck, did you talk to Tim about sharing his past with Amber? So she could feel more comfortable with him."

"I did."

"I think that will also help her to understand that he's had a rough past too. Do you think that will make her feel more at ease?"

"I hope so. Do you want hazelnut or regular?" Chuck plunked some quarters into the slot.

"Regular's fine. Was Tim okay with sharing his past with her?"

"You know Tim, he's very open. He was just fine with it. He thought it would be a good idea." Chuck hit a button and a cup dropped and began to fill with steaming brew. The rich smell of coffee permeated the small vending alcove.

"Let's just sit here for awhile and let her rest." Carol sat down on the bench across from the machines. Chuck handed her a styrofoam cup and then got one for himself. He sat down, his leg touching Carol's. They sat in silence like this for a long while.

Amber was sleeping when the nurse came in to take her vital signs, change her bandage, and put some ointment on her wound. Maureen smiled at Amber as she efficiently went about her duties. Her long, dark hair was tied into a sleek ponytail, which she pushed over her shoulder with a flick of her hand when she was done.

"How are you feeling?" Maureen asked, her forehead creased with worry.

"Tired, and my neck has a sharp throbbing pain in it," Amber said, gingerly touching the side of her neck with her fingertips. "I feel kind of hungry too."

"Let me see if you can have anything else for the pain, besides your morphine. And as far as food goes, you can't have any solids today, but I can get you some chicken broth and see how you hold that down. I'll be right back." When she returned a few moments later, she explained to Amber that she could have a pain pill on top of the morphine. The doctor had left it in his orders.

She placed a steaming bowl of soup on Amber's tray and moved it up. "Here's some broth. If you're able to hold that down and you want anything else, just let me know. Would you like your pain medicine now?"

"Yes, please," she said, her voice quiet and raspy.

"You can have it every four hours. Just let me know how you're feeling. And let me know how the broth works out for you. If you need me, just push that button," Maureen said, pointing to the call button. She then set the cup containing the pill on the tray and left the room.

Amber managed to get the pill down with small sips of water, then set slowly to work sipping on the broth. It wasn't too painful; the medication was helping.

Soon after Amber finished her broth, she fell asleep.

When Amber woke up, Chuck and Carol sat before her with a tall, handsome man, with green eyes and dark hair flecked with silver. His jaw was chiseled, his skin was golden brown, and he had a muscular build.

Amber sat up with some difficulty. "Hi, how long was I sleeping?"

Carol answered first. "About a half an hour, that's all. Amber, this is Tim."

"Hi, Tim."

Tim stood up and went over to shake her hand. "Hi Amber, nice to finally meet you. I've heard so much about you, I feel as if I already know you."

"Yeah, well, they've been filling me in on you too," Amber said with a shy smile.

"So, I guess it won't take long for us to get acquainted then. Are you up for staying at my place until you're on your feet again and feel comfortable enough to be on your own?"

Amber hesitated. "Yes, I am. I really appreciate you doing this for me. It means a lot. Chuck and Carol told me you were very nice, and I guess they were right about that. I'll try not to get in your way."

"Don't worry about it. I look forward to having the company. You won't be in my way at all." When Tim spoke, he looked directly into her eyes. She felt instantly at ease with him. "Treat my home as if it were yours, that's the only thing I ask of you. I have set up some safety measures for your comfort. We can go over them when you move in."

Amber smiled shyly at Tim, their eyes holding contact. *I can't believe a stranger would go through all this trouble just for me,* she thought.

"So Dr. Wagner says you may get to come home in a few days, huh?" asked

Chuck, standing from the chair and walking over to fiddle with the magazines on Amber's nightstand.

"Yeah. I can't wait to get out of here." Amber sighed pensively and rubbed her eyes. "I've only been here for the day and already it seems like I don't get any sleep around here, or at least not as much as I would like."

"What do you think Chuck and Tim, should we get going so Amber can get some sleep?" Carol asked as she set about gathering up her coat and purse.

"I think that's a good idea," they both replied.

"It was very nice meeting you, Amber," Tim said, reaching over to shake her hand again. "I hope you feel better. If you wouldn't mind, I'd like to stop and visit you tomorrow to see how you're doing." He held her hand for another moment, then gently set it down.

"No, I don't mind at all." Amber felt suddenly flushed, and absentmindedly stroked the hand Tim had just touched. "See you tomorrow."

Chuck and Carol gave Amber hugs and kisses and said their good-byes.

"Chuck and I will be down after work tomorrow. See you then."

"Good night."

After they left, the nurse came in to put ointment on her wound and change her bandage. "How are you doing? What's your pain level on a scale of zero to ten, ten being the worst pain you could have?"

"It's about at a seven."

"Do you want something for the pain? It's been over four hours since the last time you got your pain medicine."

"Please," Amber replied quickly, taking in a quick breath.

"I'll be right back with it." A few moments later she returned with Amber's medicine. "Here you go, honey. Go back to sleep. Tomorrow will be a better day."

"I hope so." Amber managed a wan smile and paused before continuing. "Before you go, I was wondering if I could have something for my stomach. I feel nauseated."

Maureen looked down at her sympathetically. "Let me go check your chart. I'll be right back."

She returned with some Compazine. "This should make you feel better."

It wasn't long before Amber was asleep for the night.

❧ Chapter Eight ❧

The next morning, Maureen woke her. "Your breakfast is here. I hope you still have your appetite."

"Believe me, I do," Amber said, sitting up.

"After you finish eating, Dr. Anderson will take you for your exam. From zero to ten, what's your pain like this morning?"

"About an eight. Can I have something else for the pain?"

"Sure." She handed Amber a little plastic cup with two pills in it.

Amber choked a little as she tried to swallow them.

"Are you okay?"

"Yes, I'm just really sore today. The pills didn't go down so easy this morning."

"I think I'll leave a note for the nurse to wake you up in the middle of the night to give you your pain medicine so mornings aren't so difficult. They will be taking you off your morphine pump, since you will most likely leave the hospital in another day. Do you think you're going to be able to eat your eggs?"

"I don't think so. Do you have some applesauce or something like that?"

"Yes, we do. I think you should stick to a soft food diet for a while."

"I think so too."

"I'll be right back with some applesauce," she said with a smile.

When Maureen returned, she had applesauce and red gelatin. "How's this?"

"Wonderful. Thank you."

The nurse waited to make sure Amber could eat. When she knew it was okay, she left the room.

Amber watched television for about an hour until Dr. Anderson came to her room. Dr. Anderson was a short, round woman with glasses which barely covered large, inquisitive eyes. She walked confidently into the room and held out her hand for Amber to shake. "Hi, I'm Dr. Anderson from OB/GYN. I have come to do your exam. Do you have any questions before we start?"

Amber shook her head.

"I'm going to take you to another room for the examination."

Amber was nervous. She smiled at the doctor and nodded, but couldn't hide the fact that the corners of her mouth were noticeably shaking.

Dr. Anderson put her hand on Amber's shoulder. "Amber, everything will be fine. Just try to relax a little. I know this is hard, but it will be over soon, and the information this exam could provide will be invaluable in terms of pressing charges."

The exam room was right down the hall. As they walked toward it, Amber began to feel more and more anxious.

"Why don't you climb up on the exam table, slide your bottom down, and put your feet in the stirrups," the doctor said gently.

During the examination, Amber's thoughts drifted to the idea that Jim might have raped her. *How sickening*, she thought. *I wonder if that is why, when we attempted intercourse, he was not able to achieve an erection—because he could only do it if I was asleep. Oh, I feel so sick.*

Amber wondered how many times this had happened. *How many times were we actually able to have sex? Maybe two times out of ten.*

"We're all done, Amber," the doctor said, taking off her latex gloves. "Are you okay? You look awfully pale."

"I don't feel so good. I feel very nauseated," Amber said, clutching her stomach with both hands.

"We can get you some Compazine for that. How does that sound?"

"Good. Thank you."

"I'll be right back. Then we will need to talk about your exam. We will talk more later when your tests come back."

A few minutes later, Dr. Anderson came back into the examination room with the medicine. "Here, why don't you take these and hopefully that will help. Amber, when was the last time you had sexual intercourse?"

"It's been over a month. Why?"

"Well, sometimes we can't tell that you've been raped. Only that you've had sexual intercourse. But if it's been over a month since you've had sexual intercourse, then all evidence would be gone." She looked up, searching Amber's eyes. "But Amber, I do find evidence that you were raped. When the tests come back, I will be able to see if there is any semen. Do you have any questions for me or would you just like to talk?"

Amber stared blankly at her. She couldn't believe what she was hearing.

"Amber, are you okay?" Dr. Anderson approached the bed cautiously, laying one hand on top of Amber's. "Do you want to talk?"

"No, thank you. I would just like to be left alone to think for now. I can't believe this. How stupid can I be? I knew something wasn't right but I just couldn't figure it out." Amber hung her head, her strawberry blond hair hanging in long strands, obscuring her face.

"What did you feel that was different?"

She stared blankly at her hands. "Many times, when I got up in the morning to go to the bathroom, it would sting when I urinated. You know how you feel when you're done having sex for a long time, and you get vaginally sore? Well, that's how it felt. Several times. Why didn't I put two and two together?"

"Amber, you're not stupid. This isn't something you or anyone would expect from her husband," Dr. Anderson said, her head tilted sideways, trying uselessly to look Amber in the eyes.

"Thank you, Dr. Anderson. But I'd like to go back to my room now." Amber withdrew into herself.

Amber stood shakily and headed to her room. When she got there, she immediately pushed the nurse button and sat on her bed to wait.

"Hi Amber. Can I help you?"

"Yeah, I was wondering if I could take a shower or a bath?" she asked in a downcast voice.

"You can't take a shower. But if you're careful not to get your neck wet, I'll let you take a bath. Let me go get a towel and washcloth and I'll be right down."

"Do you also have a toothbrush and a comb?"

"Yes, I'll grab everything."

"Thank you." Amber stared at the wall while she waited, her mind racing.

Maureen walked in several minutes later. "Here you go. Here's a new gown, robe, and slippers too."

Amber headed down the hall to the community bathtub. When she got in, she scrubbed everywhere except for her neck. She tried not to get that part wet. She scrubbed until her skin was red. When she got out and dressed and finished grooming, she felt a certain sense of relief. A cleanliness, as if she had washed some of him off of her.

She walked back to her room and settled into bed. Ten minutes later, Dr. Miller came in.

"Amber, I don't mean to be the bearer of bad news, but your blood tests came back and we found that you were given the drug Rohypnol. The street name is roofies. You might have heard of them. They're one of the most common drugs used in date rape cases." He stopped to look into Amber's eyes, which were completely blank. "I'm so sorry, as if you haven't been through enough already. There should be no more surprises, Amber. Dr. Dahl will be in to talk to you in a while, okay?"

"Okay." Amber stepped out of bed and went to look out of the window. Dr. Miller was still talking, but she couldn't listen to what he said. All of the sudden, Dr. Miller's voice became very small and the room began to spin. She felt sick to her stomach. When she came to, Dr. Miller and a couple of nurses were standing over her.

"Amber . . . Amber, can you hear me?" asked Dr. Miller.

"Yes . . . I . . . I . . . don't feel so good. It's just a lot…to take in."

"I know. We'll help you into bed, and you need to stay there until you're doing better. Dr. Wagner will also be coming in a little bit. Maureen will stay with you for a little while to monitor you. If you need anything, just ask." With help from Amber, they stood her up and walked her carefully to the bed.

Once she was settled in, Amber spoke. "I need to talk to Carol." The doctor nodded and left the room. As she picked up the phone and dialed, she wondered if she should make the call. Too late.

"Hello."

"Hi Carol. How are you?"

"Just fine. How are you?"

"Not doing too well. I just fainted. There's a lot going on."

"I'm coming down there right now," Carol said, and before Amber could argue, she had hung up the phone.

When Carol arrived fifteen minutes later, she looked flushed and concerned. "What's going on, Amber?"

"I was examined today, and the doctor says that there's proof that I have been raped." Amber's tone was even and she showed no emotion at all. Her voice was monotone, without any inflection.

Carol gasped and both her hands instantly went to cover her mouth. "Oh Amber, I'm so sorry."

"That's not all. They found the drug roofies in my system, which is a date rape drug. That's the drug he's been giving me all along. Carol . . . he's been drugging me and raping me." The compassionate, pained look on Carol's face broke through her resolve. She could feel the walls starting to come down inside her. "It's just too much to take," she said, and began to cry. Then she immediately pulled herself together, wiped her face, and turned her head to look out the window.

Carol came over and hugged her and then Carol began to cry also. They held each other tightly for a long time.

Carol sat back and looked at her friend, red with rage and sadness. "I hope he burns in hell."

"Carol, I don't want to sound like I don't appreciate everything you and Chuck and Tim are trying to do for me, but I've been doing a lot of thinking, and I'm still not sure I should stay with Tim. He's very nice, but after everything with me and Jim, I'm just not sure. What if I go stay with Anna from the café? I would say Mary Jo, but we don't get along as well as Anna and I. What do you think?"

"I can't believe I didn't think of that before. I still would feel safer with you at Tim's, but staying with Anna might work. But you know how you two go head to head sometimes. You're right about one thing, though, you'd be better living with Anna than with Mary Jo. You two never see eye to eye. Do you want to talk to Anna? She's working right now." Carol pulled a wad of tissues out of her purse. She handed one to Amber and blotted her face with the others.

"Yeah. I hope she says yes."

"Well, let's call her," Carol said, handing Amber the phone as she dialed the number at the café.

Anna answered on the second ring. "Carol's Café, how can I help you?"

"Anna, it's Amber. How are you?"

"Amber! How are you feeling? I've been so worried about you. But didn't want to bother you in the hospital."

"I'm in pain, but happy that Jim's in jail. Anna, I have a huge favor to ask of you."

"Anything, just ask."

"I know this is a lot to ask, but I was wondering if I could come stay with you, just for a little while, when I get out of the hospital. You know, until I can get on my own two feet?" Amber twisted the phone cord around her hand as she spoke, her eyes never leaving Carol's.

"Sure, I guess so. I suppose we can work that out. When will you be getting out?"

"Tomorrow morning."

"Wow, that's real soon, but I think we can still make it work."

"Thank you, you're a life saver."

"Don't worry about it; you would do the same for me. I got to get back to work. Talk to you tomorrow," she said, her voice monotonous.

"Thanks again. Bye." Amber hung up the phone and gave Carol a weak smile. "She said yes."

"Good," Carol said, putting her arms around Amber again. "I'll talk to Tim, he'll understand."

"Oh thank you, Carol." Amber yawned and put her head back on the pillow. "I'm so tired."

"Why don't you get some rest," Carol said, tucking the blanket in around Amber. "I'll go to the cafeteria and eat something."

"Really, you don't mind?" Amber said, her eyes already beginning to shut as she drifted off.

"No, not at all. You need your rest." She patted her knee and left.

The nurse woke her up an hour later, at lunch time.

"Here's your lunch and pain medicine. When you're finished eating, I'd like to change your bandage. Just press the button for me when you're done. Are you still feeling faint?"

"No, I'm feeling much better now." Amber sat up to eat.

Amber was happy to eat, even if it was a soft food diet. Eating soft food was still painful, but not half as painful as it would be to eat solid foods. When she finished her meal she called for the nurse, then laid back down in her bed.

Maureen walked briskly into her room and smiled. "I'm going to take your bandage off and put ointment on. It's not seeping as much as it was. So that's a good sign. But you still have a lot of healing to do."

"Say, have you seen my friend Carol?"

"She told me to tell you that she had to leave. One of the girls needed to leave work so she had to cover for her."

"Oh, okay."

"I have to check your vitals, and I need to know what your pain level is right now," the nurse said, flipping quickly through Amber's file.

"About a five. That's the best it's been so far," she said with a slight smile.

"Good, I'm happy to hear that," Maureen said enthusiastically. "I'll leave you alone now."

Fed and rested, Amber felt better than she had in days. She stared out of the window at the gray, cloudy scene unfolding outside. *I don't understand where everything went so wrong. It started off so wonderful. He was so charming. We used to do such fun things together. Camping, fishing, swimming, and hiking. We used to travel. We did everything together. He used to open doors for me. Then . . . it all changed . . . so suddenly.*

I married a loving, charming man. We had dreams of children. Then he changed. He had so much anger in him. He abused me. He killed my baby.

What am I going to do? I can live without Jim; that's a blessing. But I can't work for awhile. I'll have to use the money I've been saving. Why has my life been this way? How can I change it? Deep in thought, Amber didn't even notice when Dr. Wagner walked in. "How are you doing, Amber?" he said, startling Amber, who looked up with a dazed look on her face.

"I've been better. I'm a little emotional right now."

"I would imagine so," he said, walking to her bedside.

"The only good news that will come out of this will be Jim in jail."

"Yes, I agree."

"They told me that Dr. Dahl will be coming in a little bit."

"Yes, pretty soon, I would imagine. She's a wonderful psychologist, and funny too."

"Yeah, I know. I could use some humor in my life right now." Amber smoothed her hair back and smiled at the kind doctor. "Dr. Wagner, I appreciate you rounding on me, and I was wondering, since I don't have a family doctor, if I could come see you when I get out of the hospital?"

"Sure you can. I would like that very much." He smiled broadly, and Amber knew his words were genuine.

"Good, because I feel very comfortable around you. And now you know my history and all that . . ." she said, her voice trailing off.

"Thank you. Well, I need to get going. Dr. Dahl will be in to see you later."

"I will see you tomorrow then?"

"Yes, and I think if you feel ready, you will get to go home."

"That's the best news I've heard all day. See you later."

When he left, Amber decided to read a magazine, but her mind was too cluttered to pay attention. She sat with the magazine open on her lap and her thoughts drifted to the past. *I never thought about what happened to all my friends. Jim was the reason I didn't have any. Slowly, one by one, they went away. The way he treated them was horrible.*

As Amber's mind replayed the past, she remembered a day she had pushed out of her mind long ago. It was a dark, stormy day. There were tornado warnings all over the area. *I was on my way home from the corner market, where I had gone to get some milk. I was worried about going because of the weather, but Jim made me. He was in such a frightful mood that day. I knew I better watch myself or else there would be hell to pay.*

Bills were piling up and he wasn't making enough to pay them. I offered to get a job. He said, "No woman of mine is going to work outside the home. Your place is in the home, doing chores and making my meals. Working outside the home is a man's job." I shouldn't have pushed the issue, but I did.

We were eating breakfast, and he reached across the table and punched me right in the jaw. I remember the sharp pain, and when I came to, I was lying on the floor. Jim was gone.

He came home a few hours later, drunk. His eyes were filled with rage. I knew I better keep my mouth shut. He told me to go get some milk. I didn't want to, but knew the repercussions if I didn't.

On my way home, my girlfriend saw me walking, and she stopped to give me a ride. She told me she didn't want me walking in weather like this. When she dropped me off, I went in and Jim was standing there with a whiskey bottle in one hand and a cigarette hanging out of his mouth. He was swaying. He was wearing his steel-toed boots and blue jeans with a white muscle shirt on. His hair was slicked back. Instantly, I knew I was in trouble. He had been watching the whole time.

He grabbed hold of my arm and said, "What did I tell you about having friends?" Without giving me a chance to say anything, he said, "You are to have none." He went to say something else, but stopped. Then he said, "You're not going to leave me or I will kill you."

"I'm not going to leave you," I said, begging him to let go. "You're hurting me. I won't talk to my friends anymore, just don't hurt me." He let go of my arm and began to punch me. I was doing my best to cover up, but he was so much stronger than I was. I fell to the floor and that's when I saw the whiskey bottle coming at my head.

When I woke up, I was in the hospital. He had almost killed me. He was arrested and did some jail time. After that, I didn't have any more friends, nor did I want any.

When he got out of jail, he came up to me and hugged and kissed me and told me how much he had missed me and how our lives would be different and I believed him.

Maureen put her hand on Amber's arm, drawing her back to reality. "Amber? Dr. Dahl just called. She'll be up to your room in a few minutes."

"Okay, thank you." Amber lay down and tried to read again.

Chapter Nine

"Hi, Amber. How are you? I suppose you're getting tired of being asked that?" Dr. Dahl asked, settling into the chair next to Amber's bed.

"Yeah, kind of. Considering everything I've been through, I'm doing pretty well. I am feeling a little emotional right now, overwhelmed with everything. It's all too much to take in right now." Amber already felt a weight lifting from her shoulders just sitting next to Dr. Dahl.

Dr. Dahl was an old friend of Carol's, who had introduced the two of them. Amber had gone to talk to her a couple of times, in secret, at a reduced rate that she and Dr. Dahl had worked out. Amber had not seen her in several months; she had become too nervous that Jim would find out. Dr. Dahl had been instrumental in giving Amber the courage to start to sort through all of her emotional baggage.

"This is to be expected. You've been through a lot. You look like you're totally wiped out."

"I am. But I also feel so relieved that it is finally over and Jim is in jail where he should be. Thanks for coming in here to see me. It always feels so good to talk to you," Amber said, smiling.

Dr. Dahl was tall and rail-thin with very fine features. She wore small-framed glasses and had intense, beady brown eyes. Her nose came to a sharp point. Her hair was brown, and she always wore it in a sleek, chin-length bob.

She sat next to Amber with one hand crossed under her left elbow, her left hand sticking straight up near her face, and an air of focus and concentration surrounding her. She leaned toward Amber and looked into her eyes, as if to gauge what she was thinking. "I thought I would stop by to see how you were doing and see if you were ready to talk."

"Yeah, I'm ready to talk. I keep thinking about my past. I don't mean to, but thoughts keep flooding my mind," Amber said, finally closing the magazine and setting it back on the nightstand.

Dr. Dahl nodded, her eyes squinting slightly. "What kind of things are you thinking about?"

"Friendships lost because of Jim. Not having any family to turn to. I'm very thankful for the few friends I do have now."

"Yes, Carol and Chuck are good people."

"I was very fortunate that Jim finally decided to let me work outside the home. We couldn't make it on his income alone. If not for that, I never would've gotten the job at the café, and never met Carol or Chuck." She paused and thought for a moment. "We became best friends right away. Carol was the first person I was able to talk to about my home life. We never did anything outside of work, but at work we talked a lot. I am so thankful for her and her husband. They are such loving, understanding people."

"That's good to hear. What else have you been thinking about?"

"Pain . . . all the years of pain and suffering at the hands of him. I can't help but feel like I've been held captive in my own home. It wasn't always that way, you know? In the beginning . . . he was so loving and passionate. That's one of the things that made it so hard to leave, the memory of what was. I did love him. I cared for him deeply. It just held me there. Also, the fear of leaving. You know, toward the end, I knew he would kill me. I just wanted things to be the way they were in the beginning. He kept promising a better life, and I wanted it so bad that I believed it, but deep down I knew it wasn't going to change. In between his streaks of madness, he had moments that reminded me of years ago when everything was good. So it wasn't like he didn't have a good side to him, he did. But toward the end, the times when the good side came out were very few and far between." Amber stopped abruptly. It always amazed her how easily the words came pouring out when she was with Dr. Dahl. "Why do I keep mulling over the past?"

Dr. Dahl scooted her chair closer to Amber's bed. "There are a lot of painful memories that aren't so easily forgotten, but everyone has his or her own process for dealing with these types of things. I guess you could say it's part of the healing process. Everyone experiences these things in a different way. Your past is a part of who you are, and so it *shouldn't* be forgotten. If anything, you need to learn and grow from it, regardless of whether the experiences are good or bad. Do you understand what I'm saying?"

"Actually, yes, I do. When you say it that way, it makes sense, and boy do I have a lot of healing to do." Amber began to laugh in an effort to lighten the mood.

"The way you're feeling is to be expected. You have a long history with abuse in it," Dr. Dahl leaned back in her chair and sighed. "These things take time. You just need to commit yourself to the healing."

"Lately, I've been feeling a lot of fear, but I need to focus more on the relief I'm also feeling now that it is finally over and Jim is in jail where he should be." Amber's mood had turned pensive again. Her head hung down as she talked, and she was unable to look up and make eye contact. She was too embarrassed, too ashamed.

"Amber, it's okay. We've talked before; you have nothing to be ashamed of. You can look up at me. Remember to always hold your head high." She straightened her glasses and leaned forward, gently pushing Amber's chin up and looking her in the eye. "There are so many things that you need to overcome. And with a person such as yourself, it will take a long time. You've been through a lot, starting from childhood, but I think that together, and with a lot of hard work, you're going to be fine. In fact, I don't *think*, I *know* you're going to be fine."

"Yeah, me too," Amber said, still holding her head up and smiling.

"Amber, how is your self-esteem?"

Amber fidgeted with her hands. "It's been up and down. For a long time I felt hopeless, that I was nothing, but when I started working at the café, things started to change for me."

"How's that?"

"Well, like I was saying before, my best friend Carol—we just hit it off. I started telling her things slowly, and we began to talk a lot. I guess you could say she was like my psychologist. When I was at work, I felt like a person again. When I went home, I was nothing all over again. Well, Carol and I put together a plan, and I started putting half my tips in her safe, and lied to Jim about how much I made in tips." As she told Dr. Dahl of her and Carol's secret plan, her face brightened and she became more animated.

"Wow, it has been such a long time since we've talked! The old Amber wouldn't have done that. What were you going to do with your saved money?" Dr. Dahl asked, leaning forward conspiratorially.

"I was going to run away, as far away as I could. I had about two more months of saving and I was out of there. Carol tried talking me into staying with her and Chuck, but I was too afraid." Amber paused to collect her thoughts, then continued. "I started to change my mind about running away and thought maybe I would stay and fight. Then everything happened, and here I am. But Carol and Chuck have both been saviors to me. Whatever he ripped away from me, they gave it back, and now I am starting to realize what a good person I really was, and am."

The two women sat in silence for a few moments, mulling over these last thoughts, allowing them to sink in.

Dr. Dahl gently placed a hand on Amber's arm before she spoke again. When Amber responded by looking confidently straight into her eyes, she continued. "What about him raping you? How are you doing with that?" she asked.

"I'm not sure yet. There was a part of me that wondered what was going on, because whenever he gave me a couple of drinks, which he wouldn't let me refuse, I always passed out, and when I would wake up, I always had vaginal irritation. I've heard of date rape, but I didn't think my own husband would do that to me. How stupid. Why *wouldn't* he? He beat me. He put himself in control of every aspect of my life. When it comes to Jim, though, my thought process is messed up. So I do know that I need to work on that." Amber had, without realizing it, twisted the bed sheet around her index finger so tightly while she talked that it had turned purple. She quickly unwound her finger and flexed it a few times to get the blood flowing again.

Dr. Dahl quietly looked at Amber's finger, and then her face. "Amber. That's enough talk about Jim today, but I would like to know more about your past. Those few times we met, we never really got a chance to totally hash out your past before you had to quit coming. How was your life with your parents growing up?"

Amber instantly began to cry. "My parents were both drunks, and they abused me physically and mentally. They also ignored me, which I liked best. My father beat up my mother all the time, and he would make me watch and tell me that if I got out of line, I would be next. You know, I never did anything wrong because I was so afraid of him. But they still found things that I didn't do right. My mother tried to protect me once," she said, trying to hold back the tears.

"What happened when she did that?" Dr. Dahl asked, looking up momentarily from her furious note taking.

Amber looked down at her hands. They were shaking. She turned toward the window. "He beat her so badly, she lay in bed for two weeks. That was the last time she ever protected me." Her chin started to quiver. "She wasn't always abusive to me. It was just, the more she drank, the more she acted like my father. They died in a car crash when I was twelve. They had too much to drink, as usual, and hit a tree head on." Amber's face flushed with anger, her voice turning bitter. "You know, I never cried for them, and I never forgave them for what they did to me. In fact, when the police officer came to the door to tell me what happened, I felt so happy inside. I was finally free. We talked about the foster homes last time we met, and you know how the rest of my relationships have gone. I chose the wrong people. But not anymore. I vow to never live like that again." Amber stood and walked to the window, staring silently out of it for a moment before she spoke again. "How about next time we talk about my past boyfriends?"

"That's fine. We've talked enough for today. You've done very well; it's not easy talking about such painful things in such an open manner. When you're ready, call and set up an appointment." She closed her notebook and tucked it into her briefcase. "Thanks for talking so openly," she said, smiling at Amber as she stood and pulled on her coat.

"Thanks for listening."

"Amber, try to get some rest."

"I will." She turned to see the doctor off, then turned back to the window. She could see the parking lot, wet and dotted with puddles. *All those years of abuse, first from my parents, then from my boyfriends. No more. I will put up with it no more. I can no longer live in fear, as I've done my whole life. I have to break the cycle.*

Amber climbed back into bed and covered up. Despite all the emotions swirling around her, she was soon fast asleep.

Chapter Ten

Carol gently shook her. "Amber, Amber, wake up."

Amber opened her eyes and saw Carol and Tim smiling down at her. "Hi guys. How long have you been here?"

"Two hours."

"You should have woken me a long time ago," she said, stretching.

"No, you needed your sleep."

"Hi Amber," Tim said, stepping forward.

"Hey Tim, how are you?"

"I'm doing really well. I was wondering if you wanted me to go to your house to get your clothes or anything," he said as he pulled up a chair.

"No, that's okay; he cut up most of my clothes anyway. I was thinking, tomorrow, when you pick me up, could we go to the store so I could pick up a few things? I don't want anything from that house. That was *his* house." Suddenly, Amber became very irritated. "He can figure out from jail how he's going to get rid of it. He can call his family. I had nothing of personal value there." She took a deep breath, instantly calming herself down. "I'm starting over. A fresh start with new things, new *everything*. Carol, I was wondering if you could get that money out of the safe for me."

"I sure will, honey," Carol said, smiling happily at her.

"Where's Chuck?"

"He had to work. He sends his love. We can't stay long, Amber." Carol took her hand and held it tightly. "Besides, you look like you could use some extra rest."

"I definitely could."

"Anyway, you get out bright and early tomorrow."

"I know. I can't wait." Amber's smile glowed as she briefly contemplated the new life before her.

"We just wanted to stop and see how you were doing, and find out how things went today," Tim said.

"Well, it was a very emotional day. I found out a lot, but I don't have the energy to talk about it anymore today. We'll talk about it tomorrow."

"Understandable. What time should I be here to pick you up?"

"Nine A.M. *sharp*," she said, gesturing with her index finger, an expression of mock seriousness on her face.

Tim and Carol laughed. Carol stood, still smiling. "Amber, we have to leave now. I'll send some clothes along with Tim tomorrow so you'll have something to wear. And I'll stop by and see you at Anna's. I'm sorry I can't pick you up myself, but duty calls at work," Carol said as she patted Amber's knee.

"That's okay, don't worry about it. It will give Tim and me more time to get to know each other, right, Tim?"

"Right," he said enthusiastically.

Carol and Tim gave her a big bear hug, and she was so overwhelmed with love and emotion that she began to cry happily.

"Thanks guys, that felt great. See you tomorrow."

Chapter Eleven

By the time morning came around, Amber was so excited she could hardly sit still, but then again, she had no choice; her neck still didn't allow her to move around too well. All her doctors visited her with well wishes. Dr. Dahl reminded her to make an appointment. Dr. Anderson came to say good-bye and give her the final test results; Jim's semen was found. Amber already knew that would be the case.

By the time Amber got her stuff together, Tim was there and they were on their way.

The drive was wonderful; she felt a sense of freedom that she had never felt before, as if the world was hers.

"It sure is beautiful out today," she said as she pressed the button to roll down the window.

"Yes, it is."

The sun was shining. An unseasonably warm wind blew through the trees, gently shaking the leaves. People were out riding their bikes and walking.

"Is Anna working right now?" Amber asked, her arm hanging out of the window, her fingers playing in the breeze.

"No. Carol said she gave her the day off. Mary Jo is working instead."

"That's good."

Tim looked over at Amber and smiled. Her excitement about leaving the hospital was obvious. "Have you been to Anna's house before?"

"I haven't. I know where she lives, but I've never been inside. Have you been there before, Tim?"

"No. I don't really even know Anna," he said, stopping the car at a red light.

"She's just up around the corner," Amber said, pointing out of the window in the general direction of Anna's house. "This is a nice neighborhood." Amber couldn't stop smiling. Her whole body hummed with a giddiness she had never felt before. The sun looked brighter than usual, the sky more blue. She felt as though she could smell each flower, each blade of grass on the warm breeze that tickled her nose.

"Yeah, it is. I don't live too far away from here myself."

"Really, where do you live?"

"Just a couple blocks up, on Edgerton Street."

"Oh, I know where that is. Yeah, then you aren't too far away at all. You'll have to come over and visit."

"I most definitely will. You can come over and visit me too. You know, if you need some time away from Anna." The light turned green and he accelerated through the intersection.

"Thanks, I may just take you up on that offer." She turned to face him. "Tim, I hope you understand why I didn't come stay with you."

"Don't worry about it. I completely understand." Tim's eyes were trained on the road, but he glanced at her briefly as he spoke. "After the relationship you just got out of, coming to stay with a man you barely know probably sounded pretty dangerous to you. Don't worry, I understand. But I would still like to build a friendship. Hell, everyone can use a friend." He turned the corner.

"Thanks for being so understanding. I'd love to build a friendship with you. Everyone *can* use a friend, especially me. Aside from Carol and Chuck, I don't have anyone." She pointed to a little brick bungalow on the left side of the street. "There's Anna watering her vegetables."

Tim carefully maneuvered his car up the narrow driveway. *"Freeze,"* he said to Amber with a smile when she reached for the door handle. "Oh no you don't." He quickly got out of the car and ran around to open her door. He took both her hands in his and helped her gently out of the front seat.

Anna walked over, still holding the watering can in one hand. "Hi Amber. I don't know how you do it."

"Do what?"

"Manage to always look good."

Amber laughed. "You humor me," she said, lightly punching Anna's arm. "Anna, this is Tim."

"Hi Tim," Anna said, holding out her free hand.

"Hi Anna. Nice to meet you." They shook hands. He turned to Amber. "Amber, I'm going to have to agree with Anna. You do look good. A little tired, but good."

Amber blushed. "Well," she said, clearing her throat to change the subject, "your garden looks fabulous. Do you want to show us around the inside of your adorable little house?"

"Yeah, come on in."

Tim and Amber followed Anna into the house.

"This is the porch, where, as you can see, I keep all my plants."

"Wow, you sure do have a lot of them! Flowers too. How pretty," replied

Amber, reaching out to touch a pink blossom.

"This is the first year I've planted flowers, otherwise I usually just have a vegetable garden."

She held the front door open and followed them into the house. "This is the living room." The living room was decorated with all sorts of knick-knacks. On the wall, she had mounted framed pictures of what appeared to be family and friends. There was the smell of apples and cinnamon in the air.

Anna led them down a narrow hallway into a large room. "This is my bedroom. I love angels. Can you tell?" Both Tim and Amber nodded. Amber had noticed some out in the living room, but nothing like the bedroom. They were everywhere. Even the borders on the walls were decorated with angels.

"It's absolutely beautiful," Amber said, looking around in wonder.

They resumed their tour. "Here's the bathroom. Nothing special about that," Anna said, opening the bathroom door and flicking the light quickly on and off. She walked around them and led them to a small kitchen containing a wooden table with four chairs. "Here's the kitchen."

"That's where the wonderful smell is coming from," Amber remarked.

"Yeah, I'm making apple pie for dessert. Let's go check out your room."

It was a small room. Decorated in different shades of blue, everything right down to the sheets. "It's perfect," Amber said, excited at the prospect of having her own room, even if it was only a temporary arrangement. "Anna, you have wonderful taste."

Anna smiled. She was small, about five-foot-three and just over a hundred pounds. She had dark brown hair that she always wore up in a ponytail or a bun. She had brown eyes and a long face. Her arms didn't seem to fit her body; they seemed to be too short for her frame. When she talked, she always used her hands. Amber looked at Anna's small, delicate hands. *I can always tell when Anna is upset with me because she speaks in a monotonous tone and doesn't gesticulate at all, just locks those tiny hands on her hips,* Amber thought. *And when she gets really upset, she spits out her words.*

"Last but not least," Anna said, drawing Amber out of her thoughts. "This is my office. This is where I pay my bills, play on my computer, and keep my books."

Anna's bookshelf was huge, and full of hundreds of different books. Amber knew she would be able to keep her mind entertained here; she loved to read. This was her favorite room of the house so far. "You have a beautiful house, Anna," she said, tracing her fingers lightly over the spines of the books.

"Yes, you do," added Tim.

"If you'd like, you can go get your stuff and bring it to your room."

"Well, I really don't have much. Just a couple of things Carol loaned to me. I was hoping, if you don't have plans, we could go shopping. That way Tim wouldn't have to take me."

"Oh shoot. I have a doctor's appointment I have to keep," Anna said. "I'm sorry."

"Amber, I can take you shopping. I have nothing better to do, and besides, I don't mind," Tim said, stuffing his hands into his pockets.

"Are you sure you don't mind?" she asked, shrugging her shoulders.

"Not at all. I'll go bring in your stuff, and then we can go shopping."

"Thanks Tim."

Anna held out her hand. "Amber, here's a key in case I'm not home when you get back. Sorry I couldn't take you shopping. But I hope you know that if you ever need anything, just ask. And if you need to talk, I'll be here for you."

"That's very sweet of you, Anna," Amber said, genuinely glad that she'd agreed to let her stay.

After Tim brought in Amber's stuff, they headed off to the mall.

Chapter Twelve

"I don't think I can do much shopping today, just enough to get by until I'm feeling better. Then I can go out and get the rest of it done."

Tim held the door to the mall open and Amber walked through it. "That's a good plan; you don't want to wear yourself down too much. You're looking tired. How are you feeling?"

"Not great," she said, holding her neck. "Hopefully I'll be better soon. But that's enough about me. What about you? Do you like being a police officer?"

"I love it," he said with confidence. "I never wanted to be anything else. What about you? Do you like what you do?" Tim stopped and turned to look at Amber.

"Yes, I do. I know people may not think it's a wonderful career, but I love being a waitress. I love being around people. As a waitress, I get to meet all different kinds of people. And it's great working for Carol. She's a wonderful boss on top of being my best friend. In the future . . . who knows? I may want to do something else, but it has to involve helping people."

"Chuck and Carol are great. Chuck is my best friend. There isn't anything they wouldn't do for anyone." He paused. "Carol told me you're really good with people, so it sounds like you're headed in the right direction." They stood in the foyer of the mall next to a huge fountain. "Is there a favorite store where you like to shop?"

"Not especially. I just like to hit the sales. Let's just look around. But not for too long. Just enough for a couple of outfits."

"I can get a wheelchair for you so you don't have to walk around. Would you like that?"

"No, that's okay. But thanks," she said, feeling flattered that he cared enough to ask.

"Amber, look over there! A *sale*," he said animatedly, gesturing excitedly with his hands.

Amber had to laugh. "Let's go," she chuckled, mocking his gesture.

As they looked through the racks, they continued to talk. "So, do you do a lot of stuff with Chuck?"

"Yeah. I go over to their house or they come over to my house a lot," he said, holding up a purple sweater with tiny beads sewn all over it. "How do you like this?"

"That's beautiful," she said, taking it from him and draping it over her shoulder. "Do you have family around here?"

"Actually, my parents died when I was eight."

"Oh, I'm so sorry," Amber said, momentarily looking up from the sales rack and pressing a hand on Tim's forearm.

"That's okay."

"If you don't mind me asking, how did they die? If it's too hard to talk about it, you don't have to answer." She kept her hand on his arm.

"No, I'll answer. My father murdered my mother and then killed himself."

"I'm sorry, I should have never asked," Amber said, flushing, her hand absentmindedly going to her neck. "Sometimes I just don't think before I speak. Sometimes my mouth gets me in trouble."

"No harm done. You didn't do or say anything wrong. What about you? Do you have family around here?"

"My parents died in a car accident when I was twelve years old."

"I'm sorry to hear that," Tim said, looking into her eyes, his head tilted slightly. "I guess we both have miserable pasts."

"Yeah, it's okay. They were both drunks and very abusive, both physically and mentally. It was rough," Amber said, her eyes vacantly peering over his shoulder.

"Sounds like it. It must have been very hard for you."

"Yeah, it was." She turned back to the rack and began quickly flipping through the hangers. "What about you? It sounds like you didn't have it very easy either," she said as she put another outfit over her arm.

"No, it was very hard on me. I spent a lot of time in counseling. In fact, I went for most of my life. I've found it to be very helpful in all parts of my life. Have you ever gone to counseling?"

"I've gone a couple of times. But I had to sneak, so that Jim wouldn't know, and I got nervous and stopped going. But now that he's in jail, I plan on going regularly. I know I have a lot of issues to work out." She grabbed a cute navy miniskirt and a top to match.

"Looks like you've got a lot of stuff there. Here, let me carry that for you." He took the clothes from her and headed toward the dressing room. "I think it's time to try this stuff on."

"Thank you. And if all this fits, we're done shopping; I'm exhausted."

Amber came out ten minutes later with a slight smile on her face. Tim stood, raising his eyebrows. "Well?"

"We get to go home! *And* I got three outfits out of it."

"Excellent. I've never been shopping with a woman and been done after only one store. That's impressive."

"Well, believe it or not, I'm not much of a shopper. I like to get what I need and then get out of there."

"That's how I shop too." They walked to the register and put the clothes on the counter. "Amber, I don't mean to pry, but I know you're not working right now, and I know you had some money saved, but do you need help paying for this?"

"That's very nice of you, but I have enough saved to last me for awhile. I appreciate the thought, though. Carol and Chuck said you were nice, but I think that's an understatement."

Tim's face turned red with embarrassment. "Thank you. Now let's get you home so you can take a nap."

"That's the best thing I've heard all day," Amber said, paying the cashier and taking the bag. "But if you don't mind, I just remembered we need to make one more stop. I need to get a few things from the grocery store."

"I've got an idea," Tim said, gently taking the bag from Amber and slinging it over his shoulder as they walked out of the store. "Why don't I bring you to Anna's and you can make a list, and then I'll go get what you need. You shouldn't be doing all this running around. You need to rest," he added sympathetically.

"Normally I would say no, but I can't refuse your offer. I'm really not feeling too well." She put her hand on his shoulder. "But you really don't have to do this, you know."

"I know, but I want to."

Chapter Thirteen

When they got home, Amber went straight to the kitchen. Anna was still at her appointment. She made her list, mostly soups and other soft foods. "I know it may not look too appealing, but that's all I can eat right now. Is there anything on the list that needs clarifying?" She handed the grocery list to him.

He scanned the list quickly. "Looks just fine. But I bet you can't wait to be eating solid foods again."

"Yeah. The doctor told me to give it another week, then I can go to solids. By then, I know I'll be ready. You can only eat so much soup."

"I know what you mean," he agreed, heading for the door. "Well, I'm going to get going."

"Why don't you take the key? That way, I can lock up. I don't like the thought of being left alone with the door unlocked." Amber began to shake a little. She suddenly felt very nervous.

Tim looked at her with concern. "If you would rather, I could wait until Anna gets back to go shopping. Then you won't be alone."

"That's too much to ask."

"No, I insist," he said, shoving the list into his pocket. "You've been through a lot. I understand your fear. It's settled. You go take a nap. I'll watch some television or read a magazine. And when Anna gets back, I'll go shopping."

"You don't have to do that," she said, somewhat embarrassed.

"I know I don't. But I'm going to. So off to bed you go."

Amber headed off to bed hesitantly, but not before thanking Tim.

Amber woke up with horrible neck pain. She staggered to the kitchen to take her pain pills. Anna stood at the stove stirring something in a silver pot.

"How was your nap?" she asked.

"Good. I was exhausted," Amber responded, shaking slightly as she poured a glass of water.

"Amber, you remember my boyfriend Pat, don't you?"

"Sure," she said, swallowing the pills quickly.

"He's coming over tonight. I hope that's okay with you."

"That's fine. It's your house; you can do whatever you want. Act like I'm not even here. How long has Tim been gone?"

"He left about twenty minutes ago. He seems like a really nice guy," Anna said, turning back to the stove.

"From what I can tell and what Chuck and Carol tell me, he is. Do you mind if a borrow a book?"

"Help yourself."

Amber went into the office and picked out a novel. She read until Tim returned, then she put away the groceries and thanked Tim for everything. After he left, she ate some soup, read for a while, and headed off to bed.

Amber woke up to the sound of rain pounding on her window. There was a chill in the air. She knew she had to set up some appointments and take a bath, but she just felt like staying in bed. Her mind began to drift back to her past relationships. *Where have I gone wrong? I've never had a relationship work, not one. I move too fast. I end up in an abusive relationship every time. Always looking for love. I just want love. To be loved, and to love someone. I've never had love of any kind before. I thought I had love with Jim, but I was wrong.*

"Amber, telephone. It's Carol."

Amber got up and went to the kitchen. "Hi Carol."

"Hello, how are you?"

"Not very good."

"What's wrong?"

"I feel so depressed," Amber said with a sigh as she plopped down into one of the chairs at the kitchen table. "I was just thinking about my past. Do you know I've never had any kind of love in my life, not even from my parents? Why am I thinking about these things?" She stood, poured herself a cup of coffee, and went to the window.

"You know, all the talking you and I have ever done, I guess it never dawned on me that you have never had love in your life. You've had a rough life, and after what just happened to you, I can understand why you're thinking about all this. Amber, don't be so hard on yourself. I think you need to get in and see Dr. Dahl."

"You're right. That was one of the things I needed to do today. You know, Carol, I'm even afraid to be alone by myself now," she said, nervously wrapping the telephone cord around her finger.

"That makes a lot of sense to me. Amber, everything you're going through right now is understandable. Do you mind if Chuck and I come over later?"

Amber brightened immediately. "Not at all! The only love I've ever known is you and Chuck. And for that I'm so grateful. Come on over. What time?"

"Five o'clock."

"See you then."

Chapter Fourteen

A week later, Amber was finally eating solid foods. The pain in her neck was still there, but less severe. Chuck, Carol, and Tim visited off and on, taking shifts so that she wouldn't be left alone. And she was finally going to see Dr. Dahl.

"Thanks for coming over to bring me to Dr. Dahl's office," Amber said as she opened the door to Carol's smiling face.

"Not a problem. Too bad they couldn't get you in last week."

"Yeah, I know. But I guess I can't complain too much. At least I didn't have to wait a month. I'm kind of nervous about today's visit."

"Why would you be nervous? You've seen her before."

"I don't know, just talking about things makes me nervous sometimes." Amber grabbed her purse and stepped out onto the porch, squinting at the bright sunlight.

"It will help you in the long run."

"I know," Amber said, closing the door behind her.

"You ready to go?" she asked as she put her hand on Amber's shoulder.

"Yeah."

The ride over was pretty quiet. Amber was preoccupied worrying about what they were going to talk about. They had agreed to talk about her past relationships, a very painful subject. She knew she would need to be brave to dredge up all the details, and silently mustered her courage.

They walked into the waiting room, which was small and private. There was a coffee table covered with magazines, and two watercolor paintings of beach scenes hanging on the wall. A large metal stand holding pamphlets on wellness leaned against a beige wall. Amber quickly scanned the titles, picking up pamphlets that applied to her and stuffing them into her purse.

"Can I help you?" asked the receptionist.

"Yes, I'm Amber Labell. I'm here to see Dr. Dahl." She fought to keep her voice steady.

"Go ahead and have a seat. She'll be with you shortly."

As Amber looked around, she felt a little more comfortable. There was nobody else there. She focused on the paintings on the wall.

"Amber, you can come back now," the receptionist said, holding the door open.

"See you in a little bit Carol," Amber said over her shoulder, taking a deep breath.

"Good luck."

Amber followed the receptionist down the hallway and into the office, where Dr. Dahl was waiting for her at a large wooden desk. "Hi Dr. Dahl."

"Hi Amber. How are you doing?"

"Not so great."

"Why don't you go ahead and have a seat."

Amber looked around. There was a straight-backed wooden chair that looked hard and uncomfortable, a recliner, and a couch. *Do people really lie down when they're here?* Amber thought to herself as she chose the recliner and looked around Dr. Dahl's office. There was the desk, locked filing cabinets, and reproductions of modern art hanging on the walls. A stack of files teetered precariously on the floor next to her desk.

Dr. Dahl opened Amber's file and leafed through it. "So Amber, what's been going on since you left the hospital?"

"I'm staying with a girl I work with named Anna."

"How's that going?" Dr. Dahl said, looking up from the file and studying Amber's face carefully.

"Good so far. I have three friends that come and visit me, so I'm never alone."

"Do you not want to be alone?"

"I've been afraid to be alone. Ever since . . ."

"That's very understandable," Dr. Dahl said, nodding. "What's your mood been like?"

"I've been feeling depressed."

"Explain depressed. What does depressed mean to you?"

Amber was silent for a moment, considering the question. "I've just been feeling down, very low spirited, and gloomy. It just doesn't seem to go away. I have better moments, like when Chuck, Carol, and Tim are around. But it always creeps back."

"What about Anna? You don't mention her."

"I like her, but we kind of go head to head. I don't know why. We're just two very different people. Her boyfriend comes over every night, and she gives me this look like, 'Okay, you can go to your room now.' I understand she wants her privacy, but I don't want to hang out in my bedroom all the time."

Dr. Dahl made a note on her pad. "How did you end up staying with her?"

"I didn't have a lot of choices. I don't have family. Chuck and Carol and I decided that, since Jim knows where they live, it wouldn't be a good idea to stay there. I was going to stay with Tim. In fact, we had it all set up, but I haven't known him that long, so I felt kind of uncomfortable. But the more I think about it, I don't know why. He's one of the nicest people I've ever met." She looked toward the window. "Basically I had one other option, and that's Mary Jo. We work together, and I like her, but we don't always get along very well. It wouldn't have worked out at all."

"I see. You have quite a dilemma on your hands. Well, for now, I think you should make the best out of staying with Anna. And we'll just have to see what happens. Sounds like you thought things through pretty clearly." She glanced at her notes, then flipped back a page. "Back to your mood. It does sound like you're in a funk. You've had a lot of upsetting things happen to you in your life. What would you think about getting on an anti-depressant?"

Amber furrowed her brow, thinking. Her hand absentmindedly went to her neck. "I've never been on anything like that before, but I would be willing to try just about anything to feel better."

"Okay. Why don't we start you off on some Paxil. And of course we'll continue with counseling. Things will get better. The beginning is always hardest." She looked up at Amber and smiled reassuringly. "Now, I'd like to talk about your past boyfriends. Do you feel up for that?"

"Yeah." Amber looked out of the window, trying to hide her shame. "I didn't really date until I was eighteen. I met this man who was twenty and he swept me off my feet. Boy, did I have a crush on him. Not unlike Jim, everything in the beginning was wonderful. We went out dancing all the time—that was our thing to do. But he became very possessive. If someone looked at me, he would get into a fist-fight over it. He was jealous and controlling. It got to the point where he was telling me where I could go and when." Amber took a deep breath and exhaled slowly, her eyes still fixed on the piece of blue sky she could see through the window. "Well, I was with him for about a year. Shortly after we broke up, I started dating someone else. This time, the man I dated was an alcoholic. It wasn't long before he became physically abusive to me. I dated two more guys before meeting Jim. The other two were the same story. I was always giving my all and never getting anything back. I had friends who helped me out with my relationships. They would listen, give me advice. My friends and I used to go out dancing all the time. We used to have such a blast." She looked away from the window briefly to stare at her hands, then looked back to the window again.

"When I met Jim, that all changed," she began. "At first we used to go out dancing a lot. We did so many fun things together," Amber said, smiling distractedly, her eyes distant. "My friends thought Jim was so wonderful. He had them fooled in the beginning too. By the time they tried to get me out of the relationship, it was too late. I was totally in love with him. I thought we were perfect for each other." She stopped abruptly and looked up at Dr. Dahl. "I kind of got off track. There isn't really much else to tell, except that I've only been with four men before Jim, and that was just dating. And each relationship was abusive in its own way. It's been like that my whole life. I guess that's why I kept ending up in those kinds of relationships. Like you said before, I was looking for love from a father figure because I didn't get any love from my own father, but I ended up with someone just like him. And that's not what I meant to do. You know, Jim and I were together a little over ten years." Amber got up and walked to the window. She watched the traffic go by. "He slowly made me get rid of my friends until that first time he put me in the hospital. Then I had to get rid of *every* friend."

Amber and Dr. Dahl were silent for a while. After Amber had a little time to settle her thoughts, they talked more generally about Amber's ex-boyfriends. When their time was up, Dr. Dahl placed her notes in Amber's file and said, "Amber, you did a great job opening up today. I'd like to see you back in two days. We'll be seeing a lot of each other in the beginning, but when things get better, you won't have to see me as much."

"Thank you, Dr. Dahl."

"You don't have to thank me. See you at your next appointment."

Chapter Fifteen

"Amber, how did it go?" Carol said, standing up when Amber came back into the waiting room.

"Good. She gave me a prescription for Paxil to help me with the depression. She said between counseling and medication, I should get better in time."

"I'm happy to hear that. I was wondering if she was going to put you on something. I'm glad she did," Carol said, putting her arm around her friend and leading her slowly toward the door.

Amber stopped her. "First I have to stop at the front desk and make some appointments. She wants to see me more than once a week."

"How often?"

"Twice a week. After I make the appointments, can we stop at the pharmacy so I can get this prescription filled?"

"Sure."

When they got home, Amber took her medication.

"Carol, would you like to stay for lunch?"

"Sure, what are we having?"

"How about soup and sandwiches?"

"Sounds good to me. How have you and Anna been getting along?"

"Not great," Amber said, obviously upset.

"How come?"

"She has her boyfriend over every night. Which I don't mind, but she gives me a look like, 'Go to your room.' So I do. And there are other things too. She acts like I'm in her way all the time. And that I'm putting her out. She makes snide little comments like, 'Oh, I wasn't using that.' You know, when we're both out in the kitchen cooking. I like her, but I don't understand her." Amber pulled everything out they would need for lunch and set it on the counter.

"I was wondering how it was going to work out between you two. I know how Anna is. She's not easy to be around all the time. She likes to have her own space. And if things don't go exactly her way, she lets you know. If it gets too hard being here, let me know. You can always go and stay with Tim."

Amber poured the soup into a pot and placed it on the stove. "I'll keep that in mind. Would you do me a favor? Have a talk with Tim and let him know what's going on. That way, if things don't work out—and I still hope they do—at least he'll know the situation." She quickly made two sandwiches as she talked and put them on little white plates. She set one in front of Carol and said, "Go ahead and get started on the sandwich. We can have the soup when it's warm."

"Thanks, this looks delicious," Carol said, picking up the sandwich. "Sure, I'll talk to him. He's so easygoing that I probably don't even need to, but I know you want me to, so I will. Are you still up for having dinner over at his house with us tonight?"

"Yeah, I can't wait. He's making my favorite: lasagna. I wouldn't miss that for the world and besides it's my first real outing. I'm so excited."

"Wait until you see his place, it's beautiful," Carol said between bites.

Amber got up and poured the soup into bowls. The two women finished their sandwiches in comfortable silence. When the soup had cooled, they slurped it exaggeratedly and giggled at each other. "Thank you for lunch," Carol said with a big smile when they were done.

"You're welcome," Amber said, getting up to gather the plates.

"How's your neck been feeling?"

"Sore, but better now." She put the dishes in the sink and turned to face her friend. "Carol, I hate to do this, but would you mind if I went and soaked in the tub so I can start getting ready for tonight?"

"Sure, I'll go watch the news. When you're done, we can go to my house to get Chuck and then head over to Tim's."

"I'll be out in a little bit."

Amber grabbed her towel, washcloth, and clothes and went into the bathroom. While she ran the bath water, she got undressed and took off her bandage. It was healing, but still looked horrible. At least it wasn't gaping open anymore. She climbed into the tub and lay back to relax. She kept the water level low so that it wouldn't touch her neck. *After tomorrow, when I get my stitches out,* she thought happily, *I'll be able to soak all the way in the tub.*

Anna came home from work while Amber was still in the tub.

"Carol, what are *you* doing here?" she asked rudely, loud enough that Amber could hear her.

"Waiting for Amber to get ready."

"Amber, I need to use the bathroom," she said, knocking impatiently at the door.

"I'll be right out."

"Hurry up." Anna tapped her foot impetuously, her arms crossed.

"I will." Amber got out of the tub and dried off as quickly as she could, then wrapped herself with a towel.

"Are you almost done in there?"

"Two more seconds. Sorry."

Amber opened the door and smiled at Anna sheepishly. "Sorry about that."

"Well, aren't you going to drain the water? I want to take a bath. I'm going out tonight," Anna said, her face filled with disbelief.

"Oh, I thought you had to go to the bathroom. I wasn't done."

"Well, you are now."

"This isn't working out too well, is it?" Amber said softly.

"This is my house. What do you mean this isn't working out?"

Carol intervened. "What I think she's trying to say is, when you get home tonight, she won't be here. Come on Amber, let's get your stuff."

"Does this mean I don't have a job anymore?" Anna asked, turning her icy glare to Carol.

"If I could fire you for this I would, but legally I can't. What you just did was *unforgivably* rude, Anna. Especially considering everything that Amber has been through."

"You know what, Carol? I'm giving you my two weeks' notice," Anna spat out, her hands planted firmly on her hips. "If I find a job sooner than that, then I'll quit sooner."

"Sounds good to me," Carol said, her eyebrows raised. "I had a few customers complain about you, and now I know why. You're just plain rude." She put her hands on Amber's shoulders and led her down the hallway to her room.

"I can't believe the gall of that woman," Carol said through clenched teeth, grabbing Amber's belongings angrily and shoving them into a cardboard box. They quickly gathered up the rest of her things and headed out the door.

"Amber, I hope you don't mind me stepping in like that, but I couldn't stand by and let her treat my best friend like that. And I figured you were in no condition to argue this one out with her. I hope you're not upset with me," Carol said, her face still filled with disgust as they pulled away from Anna's house.

"No, not at all. I'm glad you did what you did. Can you believe how she acts? That's what I've been trying to tell you. That's how she's been acting pretty much since I got there. I don't understand why she treated me that way. Did I do something wrong?" Amber asked, looking confused.

"If she didn't want you to stay there, she should have said so. You know, Amber, sometimes people are just that way. It wasn't anything you did. I always sensed she was jealous of you."

"She has no reason to be, but I appreciate you sticking up for me." Amber turned to Carol. "You're right. I wasn't ready for that kind of confrontation. I should have just stayed at Tim's in the first place and none of this would have happened."

"I understand you not wanting to stay with a man, but one thing is for sure. Tim would never treat you that way. Don't worry about it, sweetie. Things will be fine. You can finish getting ready at my house."

"Can we make one stop at the store?"

"Sure. What do you need?" she asked, putting her hand on top of Amber's.

"A new toothbrush, things like that. I also need some make-up and a curling iron and blow dryer."

"We can do that. We have plenty of time," Carol said, her eyes on the road.

Amber watched the oncoming traffic thoughtfully. "I guess you won't have time to talk to Tim about me moving in, huh?"

"I'll call him up and explain what happened while you get ready. That way you won't feel uncomfortable just showing up tonight with your stuff in hand."

"Thanks again," Amber said sincerely. She could tell Carol was trying to make her feel better.

Chapter Sixteen

After they finished shopping and went back to Carol's, Amber fixed herself up in the bathroom. She put on a cute black miniskirt with a small trinket chain belt and a peach-colored shirt, cut to show a little cleavage. She also wore black flats and an anklet. She curled her hair, then put it up. She put on some earrings, but couldn't wear a necklace. She thought it would make her feel better to do something with herself, but after looking in the mirror, she decided to put her hair down instead, so she put her long, wavy hair to the front, hoping it would at least cover part of her wound.

She finished just as Chuck walked in the door.

"Hi Amber," he said, hugging her tightly. "It's nice to see you out and about. You look better than the last time I saw you. I hope that means you're feeling better?"

"It's nice to be able to move around again," Amber said, smiling. "And thanks, I am feeling better."

"I'll be ready to go to Tim's house shortly. I just need to change my clothes," Chuck said, already halfway up the staircase.

Carol and Amber sat back and watched a little television. Carol put her arm around Amber. "Amber, this is the last time I'll say this, but I can't believe that woman. I suppose I need to hire two more people. I better put an ad in the paper. Once Mary Jo finds out Anna is leaving, she'll surely quit too, since they're such good friends. Maybe that's why I've had customers complain about them. They're both very selfish people. Treating you like that, after everything you've been through. And you, you would never hurt anyone. Sorry I went off, but that just irritates me."

"It's okay," Amber said as she grabbed Carol's hand.

"I'm ready to go," Chuck said, walking into the room in jeans and a sweater. "Is there something you need to talk about?" he asked inquisitively, sensing something in the looks on their faces.

"No, I'll tell you when we get to Tim's," Carol said, standing and gently pulling Amber up with her.

"Okay honey. Amber, let's go." He put his hand out to let them walk ahead.

When they pulled into Tim's, Amber couldn't believe her eyes. "He has a beautiful home. Look at all the flowers. They're so pretty." *How do I tell him I'm moving in?* she thought, her mind racing.

"I knew you would fall in love with the flowers. Now you have something to keep you busy," Carol whispered, squeezing Amber's hand.

They went up to the door and rang the bell. A moment later, Tim opened the door with a big smile on his face. *He has so much confidence,* Amber thought.

"Hi! Come on in," he said, stepping back exaggeratedly and bowing. Everyone laughed and walked into the foyer. Amber couldn't believe her eyes. There was a huge chandelier and a marble floor. Off to the side was a hallway table made of cherry wood. Everything was more than she could have ever imagined. "Amber, would you like me to show you around?"

"Yes, that would be wonderful. Your home is beautiful."

"Thank you."

"Tim," Amber started, inhaling audibly, "first, I need to say something." *There, I said it,* she thought.

"Is it about what Carol called me about?"

"Oh, she did end up calling you?" *What a relief,* Amber thought, taking another deep breath in and then exhaling. *I feel so much better already.*

"She did. Don't worry about a thing," he said, stepping forward and lightly touching her forearm. "You can stay as long as you like."

"I knew she was going to call you, but I didn't see her do it, so I wasn't sure." Amber smiled, suddenly relaxed. "Are you sure it's okay? I won't get in your way."

"Like I said before, wipe your sweat off, treat my home as if it were yours."

"Oh, I feel relieved," Amber said, tending to her brow. "Thank you so much."

"Don't mention it."

"Does somebody want to tell me what's going on?" Chuck said, holding his hands out in front of him.

"Yeah," Carol said, smiling and taking his hands. "While Tim shows Amber around, I'll fill you in. Honey, let's go sit in the living room," she said, leading Chuck away.

"We'll meet you there," Tim said, then turned his attention back to Amber.

"How long have you lived here?" she asked.

"Seven years. I'll never move. I love it here too much."

"I can see why, and you couldn't live in a better neighborhood if you tried. You might have a hard time getting rid of me." They both laughed.

"Let's go and get your stuff."

"Okay," Amber said as Tim gently touched her lower back, leading her toward the car.

"You travel light," Tim commented, eyebrows raised, as he picked up her box.

"I know. I need to do more shopping," Amber said, following Tim back into the house. "Thanks for carrying in my stuff for me."

"My pleasure."

"Tim, if you wouldn't mind, I would like a tour first. This is just so beautiful; I can't wait to see the rest," Amber said with excitement.

"Sure, follow me. As you know, this is the foyer. Do you want to start to the left or to the right?"

"Hmm," Amber said, thinking for a moment as she looked both ways. "Left. Is that your dining room?"

"You would be correct. The only time I eat in here is when I'm entertaining," he said, walking into the spacious room. "It's too big to eat in here by myself."

"I can see that." There was a huge oak dining table and a beautiful china hutch. The furniture in the entertainment area was made of gorgeous white leather. There was a crackling fire in the fireplace in front of the sofa. Everything was matched perfectly, and Amber couldn't help but wonder if he had an interior decorator. The wall hangings, the hutches, the shelves, and the books, everything was perfect.

"Shall we go on?"

"Yes, what's next?" Amber asked, her eyes quickly drinking in every detail of the room.

"The kitchen."

The kitchen was to die for. It had an island in the middle with copper pans and silver utensils hanging above it. The floor was tiled, and all the appliances looked state of the art. There was a large wine rack and crystal wineglasses.

"It's like a home from a magazine," Amber said, still unable to comprehend that this was her new home, at least for a while.

"That's because I had an interior designer do it. I just told her what I wanted and she made it happen," Tim said, fidgeting absentmindedly with a pair of brass candlesticks.

"I thought you must have had an interior designer, or instead of being a police officer, you should have *been* an interior designer."

Tim laughed, taking her arm to continue the tour. He led her over to the sliding glass doors and motioned for her to peek through. Off the kitchen was a three-season porch, and off of that was a gazebo with a jacuzzi in it.

"Wow," Amber whispered.

Tim turned her around and walked her to the other side of the kitchen. "If you go straight down that short hallway, you will find the bathroom. You don't want a tour of that, do you?"

"No, thank you."

"To the right here is the living room, just small and cozy. This is where I spend most of my time."

"It looks very comfortable," Amber said dreamily, smiling and waving briefly to Carol and Chuck, who sat on the couch. There was another fireplace, more books, a television, and a stereo system.

"If we keep going, you will find we're back at the foyer. I'll grab your stuff and we can go upstairs. And that is where we will find your bedroom."

At the top of the steps, there was a bedroom to the left and another to the right.

"Mine is to the left and yours is to the right. They both have full bathrooms attached, so you can have some privacy. I will lay your things on the bed. You can organize them later," he said, setting her box down just outside the door to her room. "Well, that's the grand tour."

"You have a beautiful home. Thanks for showing me around. Thanks for everything," Amber said sincerely, looking into Tim's eyes.

"My pleasure. Shall we go downstairs?"

"Yeah. I'll be right down. I have to use the restroom." Amber felt like a princess. She walked through her beautiful new bedroom, looking around in wonder. She walked into the bathroom, which seemed enormous, freshened up her make-up and hair, and then headed downstairs.

"Something sure smells delicious," she said, joining everyone in the kitchen.

Tim looked up and smiled at her. "That's my lasagna."

"That's my favorite food."

"Mine too," replied Tim, pushing the casserole dish back into the oven.

Chuck stared at Amber compassionately. "Amber, I'm really sorry about how Anna treated you today. I can't believe she behaved that way. That's horrible. You don't deserve that. I can assure you that you'll be treated wonderfully here."

"I already know that. I feel blessed to have met someone like Tim." The way Chuck stared at her let her know how blessed she really was. She smiled broadly at him. *Chuck is such a good man*, she thought. *I've always secretly wished I could meet someone as sweet as he is.* Chuck was wide-shouldered, tall, and blond with sparkling brown eyes. He had a small scar above his right eye. Looking at him and the way he spoke in a deep, matter-of-fact tone, people might think that he was a rough rogue, but in reality, he was soft at heart. Amber had always admired his relationship with Carol.

"Thank you, Amber. You've been through a lot, and you certainly don't need people like that in your life. You're better off without her."

Amber nodded thoughtfully. "I guess when I come back to work there will be new employees to work with. That will be nice. Maybe we can find some people who are easier to work with."

Carol grimaced in agreement. "Next time I'll do better. I promise. Last time I needed help quickly. I just got lucky I got you."

"You're much too kind, Carol."

"Well, it's time to eat," Tim interrupted. "I hope you brought your appetites."

They all headed into the big dining room. Tim carried the food from the kitchen.

"Tim, do you need help with anything?" Amber said, heading toward the kitchen.

"No, you go sit down. You just got out of the hospital, and besides, I enjoy doing this," he said, edging her out of the kitchen with his elbow.

Amber sat down at the table. "Mmm, looks delicious," she stated, her eyes fixed on the steaming lasagna.

They all dug in. "This is wonderful, Tim. You can cook for me anytime you'd like," Amber said between mouthfuls.

"Good. I love to cook," Tim said, looking up and smiling at Amber.

"Yes, this is delicious," agreed Chuck and Carol.

After dinner, they retired to the living room, where they lazed by the fire and talked contentedly. After about an hour, Chuck and Carol had to leave, as it was getting late. Amber and Tim walked them to the door.

Amber made her way back to the living room and sat down with thoughts of Tim on her mind. *He's so sweet. I've never met anyone like him before. It seems like he'd do anything for anyone. Thank God there are people like him in the world.*

"I'm done cleaning up in the kitchen," he said, drawing her out of her thoughts. "You know, I was thinking. I have a bunch of vacation they've been hounding me to take or I'll lose it. What if I take it now? That way you don't have to be alone. Would that be okay with you?"

"You don't have to do that for me," she said, shifting in her chair, feeling somewhat embarrassed, "if you don't want to. Maybe you would rather go somewhere. I don't want to stop you from making any plans."

"No, you're not stopping me from anything. I want to do this," he said, sitting down on the couch.

"Well, I wouldn't mind at all. You know I don't like being home alone. So you'll get no argument from me."

"It's settled then. I'll go call work right now. I'll be right back." He got up from the couch and headed to the phone in the kitchen.

Amber sat in the chair in disbelief. *He's going to take vacation so I won't have to be alone*, she thought. *How nice.*

Tim came back into the living room and sat down. "Well, it's a go. I'm on vacation. They were surprised. I haven't taken a vacation in I don't know how long."

"Thanks so much for doing that for me," Amber said, relief making her feel less embarrassed. "Nobody has ever done anything like this for me before. I really appreciate it."

"Don't mention another word of it."

Amber talked to Tim as he busied himself straightening the magazines on the coffee table. "Tim, you know when we were talking before about our parents?"

"Yes. What about it?"

She moved from the chair to the couch. "Well, I have all these problems that stem from childhood. Like always picking the wrong kind of man. I've only dated four men, and then I married the fifth man I dated. I pick men like my father, really abusive. What I'm really looking for is love. But I just seem to look in all the wrong places. I guess that's one of the things I carry from childhood. But you don't seem to have any problems. You seem to have your life together. How did you do that?"

"Amber . . . I'm not as perfect as you may think I am. I have my hang-ups too. Like, I have a terrible rage for child abusers. So, working as a police officer, I really have to step back and keep myself in control, because when we arrest child abusers, I feel an anger I can't explain. I want to hurt people who abuse their children." Tim paused and stared into the fire for a moment. "I remember being abused like it was yesterday. All the pain, and I'm not talking about physical pain, but emotional pain. It's still right there on the surface. I have to tell you, I was suspended once."

"You were?"

"Yeah, something I'm very ashamed of," Tim said, his gaze locked on his hands. "I punched a man who had abused his son. Now, when any child abuse case comes in, I stay away from it. I can't handle it. The captain knows why I can't handle it."

Amber put her hand on Tim's hands, which were clenched in his lap. "I would never have thought in a million years that it would affect you like that. You seem so calm, so together. I could never imagine you even getting mad."

"Well, it's pretty hard to get me mad. I'm usually pretty easygoing, but child abusers don't have a place in my heart." He looked up at Amber, breathing deeply. "I guess we both have our hang-ups. We just have different ones and handle things differently. You know, Amber, it's none of my business, but you said you've always been looking for love. Haven't you ever found it?"

"No, I haven't. I've never been loved by anyone besides Chuck and Carol, not really. Not in any healthy sense of the word." She smiled at him. "And now I have your friendship."

He smiled back at her for a moment, then turned serious again. "That's so sad. I don't understand it; you are one of the nicest, sweetest people I have ever met. I'm sorry to hear that." They sat in comfortable silence until Tim spoke again. "You know, I'm glad we had this talk. I've never told anyone about my rage before. It feels good getting it off my chest."

"I'm glad we had this talk too. I'm really going to enjoy staying here with you. I can't believe what a beautiful place this is," she said, shaking her head and looking around.

"I bet you're wondering how a police officer can afford to live in a place like this."

"Well, actually, I was. But I didn't want to be impolite."

"When my parents died, I got my dad's life insurance when I turned twenty-five, so that was part of it. Also, my grandparents on my mom's side raised me. They were wonderful people. They were so good to me," Tim said. He stood and walked around the room, straightening cushions, folding blankets.

"What happened to your grandparents?"

"My grandpa died when I was twenty-two, and then my grandma died a few years back, which leads me to the rest of the reason I can afford this house. They dabbled in stocks, hit it big, and left it all to me, their soul beneficiary. I actually don't *have* to work, but I love what I do." Tim stopped, a chenille blanket half-folded in his hands. "I really feel I'm helping people, and that I make a difference. And that's important to me."

"Being a police officer is a very important job. I really admire you for what you do. I didn't know your grandparents raised you. But I'm happy that they were wonderful to you, and you got out of the living situation you were in with your parents."

He finished folding the blanket, sat down, and leaned back on the couch, putting his feet up on a stool. "Now that I'm older and I can look back on it, I really feel sadness for the way they lived. If only things could have been different. If they had been better equipped to deal with things, I could have had my parents in my life. That would have made me so happy." Tim paused and chewed on his lower lip thoughtfully, looking at the fire. "But I'm so thankful for my grandparents. I have to say I really lived a great life with them. My life changed when I turned eight, for the better." He looked up from the fire. "Now you have a chance to make your life good too. Take the chance and go with it. Do what you've always wanted to do, and be what you've always wanted to be, Amber. You've had it hard, but now is the time when things could really change for you." He leaned forward, put his elbows on his knees and his hands under his chin, and stared directly into her eyes. "And you are just the type of person who can do it."

"That's my plan. For the first time ever I feel free, and plan to take advantage of it." By the light of the fire, Amber's fair skin seemed to glow.

Tim nodded solemnly. "By the by, how did your counseling appointment go?"

"Really well. They did put me on some medication, though. But the talking helps," she answered, bouncing her leg a little.

"I think it might be a good idea to have you on medication. You've been through a lot. And I know, for me at least, talking always helps. I was in counseling for so long. It really helped me to understand people and the things they do more. And as a police officer, that's a very valuable tool. I have found that if you respect the people you arrest, for the most part, they respect you also. I spend a lot of time listening, and they seem to appreciate that."

"How long have you been a police officer?" Amber was grateful that the conversation had not lingered on her medication. She suddenly felt a panic shoot through her. *I don't know why talking about being on medication bothers me so much*, she thought. *Maybe because there is a certain stigma that goes along with being on an anti-depressant, like I'm crazy or something.* Her breathing quickened.

"Ten years. Are you okay, Amber?"

"Yeah, I'm fine. So you must be around thirty-two years old," Amber said, trying to act normal despite the fact that her heart was pounding.

"Yes, I am. You're good. Let me guess your age." He leaned back and examined her quizzically. "I would say you are twenty-seven."

"Thank you, you flatter me," Amber said with a smile. "I am also thirty-two."

"Wow, you look great. You look a lot younger than thirty-two."

Amber blushed. "Well, thanks. Chuck and Carol were right; you are very easy to talk to, Tim."

"They were right about you as well. You are very charming."

Amber's face turned even more pink. *He thinks I'm charming. He's the one who's charming*, she thought.

"You're looking tired. I should let you get some sleep," Tim said.

"I *am* tired," Amber said, standing. "I should get to bed."

"I've enjoyed our conversation," he said. "Next time I won't bring up your medication. I saw how nervous it made you, but I do want you to know it's not a big deal."

"Was it really that noticeable?" Amber asked, her eyes wide.

"Plain as day. Amber, it's nothing to be ashamed of."

"You have a way of making me feel so comfortable," she said, leaning down to put her hand on his. "But for now, I think I need to go to bed. I know it's early but I'm exhausted."

They both went to bed with peaceful thoughts on their minds.

Chapter Seventeen

A few weeks had gone by, and Tim and Amber were getting along better than ever. Amber had her stitches removed, and her pain was lessening every day. Her counseling was going well. She was sharing things she had never shared with anyone before. Tim still had plenty of vacation left. He had vacation carried over from the previous year as well. Amber mainly stayed at the house all the time, but also got to spend a lot of time with Chuck and Carol.

Tim walked into the living room. Amber was reading on the couch. "Chuck and Carol called and canceled. Something came up, so they won't be able to come over."

"That's too bad," Amber said sadly, closing her book.

Tim thought for a moment. "Well, why don't we just barbecue some steaks on the grill instead?"

"Sounds wonderful. You must like to cook, huh?"

"Yes, I love to. I get it from my grandmother. I really miss her a lot. She taught me to cook. Do you like to cook?"

"Yes, but I'm only a fair cook compared to you. Not that it's any of my business, but how come you're not married? Surely a man that cooks, cleans, and is as nice as you would be a good catch. How did you manage to stay single?" Amber blurted out, then began to turn red. *What am I saying?*

"It's not that I managed to stay single, it's that I haven't found the right woman yet."

"Well, some day—" She was interrupted by the phone. "Hold that thought, Amber. Let me grab the phone."

As he stepped away, Amber started thinking. *I can't believe the questions I'm asking him. I must have lost my mind; I don't ever act like this. I need to quit asking so many personal questions.*

When Tim came back, he seemed different, more serious.

Amber picked up on it right away. "I'm sorry if I offended you. I don't know what's gotten into me, asking all these personal questions. I'm usually not like that."

"Oh, that. That's okay," he said distractedly, moving toward the kitchen to prepare for dinner.

Amber followed him. "Are you okay? You look ill."

"No, I'll be fine. It was just a phone call from work about a man I arrested. Really, I'm okay. Say, do you like movies?"

"I sure do."

"I have a bunch over there. Go ahead and pick one out."

Amber walked over and examined the titles. When she walked back into the kitchen with a movie in her hand, she could see how pale he'd grown, but decided not to say anything about it.

"How's this movie?" she asked.

"Do you like mysteries?"

"Yeah."

"Then you'll love that one." Tim put his arm around her and led her back into the living room. He popped the movie in and sat down next to her on the couch.

Halfway through the movie, Amber fell asleep.

Tim went to the kitchen and called Chuck back. "Yeah, she's asleep right now. How should we handle this? I don't think we should say anything to her. She's gone through enough."

"But the guy said he knows Amber is staying there, and that he will be coming to get her." Chuck's voice wavered.

"Chuck, you need to start with getting Carol out of there."

"I know. We already called her sister, and she's going to stay with her until we can catch this guy. By the sound of his voice, he seemed pretty convinced that he will be coming after her. She'll leave tomorrow after we come over to your house. We figured we better come over so Amber doesn't think anything is wrong."

"Good idea," Tim said quietly, careful not to wake Amber.

"They've already put an extra patrolman around our neighborhood, our alarm system is on, and I'm not going to bed tonight. I need to make sure we're covered."

"Sounds like you've got it under control. How's Carol doing?"

"She's a little shook up but doing alright. She's more worried about Amber than anything."

"Sounds like Carol," Tim said, wrapping the phone cord around his index finger. "Always more worried about someone else, instead of herself." He paused. "I know Amber wants to go back to work soon, but I can't let her do that until this guy is caught."

"Yeah, she definitely can't go back yet."

"What is Carol going to do about the café?"

"She's putting one of the new girls in charge. Apparently she's just great, and Carol said she had managerial experience."

"I'll have to keep Amber close to home, just in case. I might have to take even more vacation time."

"Not a bad idea."

"I thought I heard you in here," Amber said, startling Tim. "Oh, sorry, I didn't know you were on the phone."

"That's alright. I was just getting off anyway," he said to Amber, then turned back to his conversation with Chuck. "Well, I'll let you go and see you tomorrow. Bye." He hung up the phone and smiled sheepishly at Amber. "That was Chuck. We were setting up the plans for tomorrow."

Chapter Eighteen

The next day, when Chuck and Carol arrived, it was bright and warm.

"What a perfect day for a barbecue," Amber said when she opened the front door.

"It sure is," Carol replied.

"Chuck and I are going to go get things started," Tim said, walking toward the kitchen. "You girls just get some fresh air. Would you like anything to drink?"

Carol thought for a moment. "Sure," she said finally, "I'll have a glass of wine."

"What would you like, Amber?"

"I guess I could have one glass of wine also, but that's it. Any more than that on these pain pills probably wouldn't be such a good idea."

"Sure, I'll be right back with it."

Carol and Amber made their way out onto the porch. "I'm so glad you came over today," Amber said as she dropped into a lounge chair.

"Me too. I can't stop thinking about Jim doing this to you. How horrible it must have been for you." She looked at Amber empathetically.

"It was horrible, but don't worry. I'll be fine now that he's in jail. I just can't wait until he's behind bars for good." Amber looked up at Carol, squinting slightly in the sun. "Why don't you have a seat?"

"Good idea," Carol said, taking the lounge chair next to Amber. "I can't wait until justice is served either. But you know the legal system. It takes a while to get the wheels turning, but don't worry, before long it will be over. Then you can really move on with your life."

Amber looked over at Carol with a confident smile. "The weird thing is, I have moved on in a lot of ways."

"Well, good. I'm glad to hear that."

"Hello, you bathing beauties," Tim said from behind them. A wineglass appeared in front of each of them. "Here you go. I hope you like it."

"I'm sure it will be fine. Thanks," Amber said, shading her eyes to look up at him.

Tim went back into the kitchen. Amber sipped her wine and looked at her friend. She scrutinized her face closely. "What's wrong, Carol?"

"Amber, you know I love you and would do anything for you, don't you?" Amber nodded. "Well, it's just that I got a phone call from my sister last night, and she's having a lot of problems with her husband right now, and she wants me to come stay with her for a couple of weeks, maybe less, maybe more."

"So, what's the problem? Go ahead and stay with her, she needs you," Amber said, frowning slightly. *She almost looks guilty or something*, she thought. *I can't quite put my finger on it.*

"Yeah, but I feel like I really need to be here with you. Especially with everything you've just gone through."

"I will be just fine. I have Tim here and he's been very helpful. I feel very comfortable and safe. Don't worry about me."

"But I feel so bad," Carol said, tears in her eyes.

Amber sat up, put down her wineglass, looked directly into Carol's eyes, and placed her hands on top of Carol's. "Don't. Your sister needs you more than I do right now. Go help her out."

"Amber, you're such a sweetie. I knew you would understand," she said, rubbing Amber's hands.

Amber scanned Carol's face closely. "You still look like you're bothered by something. What is it? You know you can always tell me anything."

"It's nothing, really. I'm okay. I just feel a little blue about leaving you, that's all."

"There's nothing to worry about anymore," Amber said reassuringly.

The blood appeared to drain from Carol's face as Amber spoke. "I've just been real tired lately, that's all," she managed.

"Maybe you should go to the doctor to make sure everything is okay."

"No, I just haven't been sleeping very well."

"Would you like to lie down before we eat dinner?" Amber asked.

"No, I'll be just fine. By the way, my sister Bethany sends her love and hopes you're doing well." Carol took a long sip of her wine.

"Tell her I said hello and I hope everything works out for her."

"Amber, I will call you when I'm there just to check up on you." A look of sadness overcame Carol, and she dabbed quickly at the corners of her eyes.

"Sounds good. Don't be so sad . . . everything will be fine," Amber said, stroking her friend's arm gently.

"How is the wine?" Tim said, walking with Chuck out onto the porch.

"Excellent," they both chimed in.

"I hope you girls are hungry. We just threw the steaks on the grill, so we'll be eating a lot earlier than we expected. I hope that's okay with you." Chuck and Tim took seats next to the girls.

"That's fine. Carol wasn't feeling well, maybe she will feel better if she eats," Amber said.

There was an eerie kind of silence. *Everyone seems out of character,* Amber thought. *I wonder what's going on, but there's no sense in asking. I know they will just tell me that everything is fine.*

Tim broke the silence. "Oh, Amber, I meant to tell you. I took more vacation time from work. I hope you don't mind, but I thought you could probably use the company, and maybe that would make you feel safer."

Amber thought to herself, *Something is going on that they're not telling me about.* "You don't have to do that, Tim. I'll be fine."

"I have a lot of vacation time," he said. He took a sip of his wine. "They've actually been telling me to take my vacation or lose it, so I figured, why not now? You don't mind, do you?"

"No, that's fine. Anyway, it's your house; you can do whatever you want. And besides, I like your company." Amber stared directly into his eyes and held his gaze. He didn't turn away as they smiled at each other.

"Good, then it's settled," he said, standing. "Well, the steaks should be done. Let's go eat."

Dinner was quiet and uneventful, except for the glances Tim kept giving Amber. She couldn't help but look into his beautiful green eyes. *I can't believe it. I feel like a little girl with a crush, except I feel something much stronger than that. He makes me tingle everywhere, a deep, tingling sensation I have never felt before. He must know. I can feel the blood rush to my head. He has to know what I'm thinking. The way he keeps staring at me! He has never looked at me like this before today. Could he be feeling the same way? Not possible. He couldn't possibly think of me like that.* As Amber sat quietly thinking, she realized that she hadn't taken her eyes off of him, and he had held her gaze. He didn't seem to mind; in fact, he seemed to be quite flattered by it. When dinner was over, they cleaned up and had a cup of coffee before Chuck and Carol had to leave.

"I'll make sure I call you from Bethany's, to see how you're doing."

"I look forward to hearing from you. Take care. I love you," Amber said, reaching out to hug her friend.

Carol squeezed her tightly. "I love you too, and I'll be fine."

As she stepped back from their hug, Amber noticed that Carol looked like she might cry. She waved as they drove off, but neither Carol nor Chuck could manage a smile as they waved back.

"You must be getting tired," Tim said as he shut the door.

"I am. I think I'll go to bed."

"I think that sounds like a good idea. I'm pretty tired too." Tim gently put his hand under her elbow and led her upstairs.

Amber stretched out in her bed and wondered what was going on. *Everyone sure was acting peculiar. All these mixed emotions. Carol leaving. I need to get out and go somewhere. What are all these feelings about Tim? Isn't it too soon to be having these kinds of feelings? But he is so different from anyone I've ever met. So handsome, so nice. Even on Jim's best day, he couldn't surpass Tim.* With her head spinning with thoughts, Amber soon fell asleep.

Chapter Nineteen

Amber woke to bright, warm sunlight shining through her window. *What a beautiful day. Maybe I should go for a walk today*, she thought, *or go see the new employees at Carol's Café. What's that wonderful smell? French toast with cinnamon? Mmm.* She went to the bathroom, freshened up, and went downstairs.

"Good morning, Tim."

Tim turned from the stove. "Good morning. I hope you're hungry."

"I sure am. It smells wonderful."

"Go ahead and have a seat."

"If you insist," Amber said, plopping into one of the kitchen chairs.

"How did you sleep last night?"

"I had bad dreams, so not too well."

"What about?" he asked, furrowing his brow.

"Are you sure you want to hear this? It's a true dream, about something that happened to me and something I have been thinking about a lot."

"I definitely want to hear it then."

"I don't know how much Chuck and Carol told you," she began, "but the night that Jim cut my throat . . . he also drugged me . . . and then he raped me."

"I didn't know that," he said sadly, his elbows on the island and his chin in his hands.

"Well, when I was with him, he would give me a couple drinks and make me drink them. He wouldn't let me refuse. Then I would wake up . . . feeling different. And have the worst hangover." Amber began to fight back the tears.

Tim walked over and sat beside her at the table. He wrapped his arm around her and placed his other hand on hers.

"The doctors found evidence of rape. And they found the drug roofies in my system. They also found Jim's semen in me. And I hadn't had consensual sex with him in over a month. I'm sorry to unload all this on you . . . I know this is all very personal. It's really been bothering me a lot. For some reason I felt like I needed to tell you."

"I didn't know. I am so sorry he did that to you. He will be going to prison for a long time." Tim's eyes filled with tears. He hugged her tightly. "Let it out . . . let it out. It's okay. He can't hurt you anymore. Things are going to get better for you."

"I'm sorry, I didn't mean to make you cry too," Amber sniffled into his shirt.

"That's okay. I just feel so bad for you. Your life shouldn't have turned out like this. How could such horrible things happen to such a wonderful person?"

"Sometimes I think it's partly my fault because I choose the wrong people, but I don't know why I do."

"Amber, it is not your fault. The men that you've been with tell you that, but it's not true." Tim kissed her forehead. "You're not a bad person."

Amber started to feel better. "Thank you, Tim. You're right. Sometimes, when I get down in the dumps, I feel that way about myself."

"I understand. But do me a favor; don't think that way about yourself. *Ever.* You need to remember always that you're a good person." He gave her another big hug.

Amber closed her eyes and absorbed how good the hug made her feel. "Thank you, Tim. I needed a hug."

"There's plenty more where that come from. You're welcome to a hug whenever you want one. You don't even have to ask, just walk up and give me one and I'll hug you back."

"Well, enough with this crying stuff," she said, wiping her cheeks. "I hope that wasn't too much information?"

"No, I've heard a lot of crazy things as a police officer. And besides, we're friends, right? And that's what friends are for."

"Yeah, we're friends. Thanks for your shoulder. I may need it again sometime."

Tim walked over to the stove. "Are you ready to eat?" he asked, stacking thick slices of French toast on plates.

"Yeah, I'm starved."

He handed her a plate and sat down next to her.

"Tim, I think I would like to go shopping or something today so I can get out of the house," Amber said, drizzling syrup on her breakfast. "I'm feeling much better now."

"Well, you look sort of pale," Tim said a little nervously. "Why don't we see how you look tomorrow? Maybe one more day of rest will do it."

"But really, I'm fine."

"Amber, I don't think it's such a good idea."

I don't know why he doesn't want me to leave the house. I don't get it.

Chuck calls all the time since the other day and he gets up and goes into the other room, like it's private. Something is going on around here, something they're not telling me.

Amber put down her fork, suddenly too upset to eat. "Tim, I'm going to lie down for awhile."

"Aren't you hungry?"

"To be honest with you . . . a little. I just need to get out, but you're probably right, I should wait until I'm feeling better."

"I just don't want you to end up feeling worse. When I'm done eating, I'm going to run to the store real quick. I'll be back soon. The doors will be locked, and I'll turn on the alarm system. Do you want me to get you anything?"

"No thanks," she said, making her way upstairs. "See you later."

"Bye."

Amber went upstairs and sat quietly on her bed. It wasn't two seconds after he left that Amber grabbed her purse and headed for the door. She knew the code on the alarm system because Tim had walked her through the safety measures, and she also knew where the extra house key was. She even knew where he kept his gun.

She decided she'd better leave him a note and let him know she was going down to the café. She had missed working and wanted to go visit the new girls. After she locked the door, she walked down to the bus stop. About five minutes later, the bus arrived. *It feels so good to be out and on my way somewhere.* Within ten minutes, she was there.

When she walked in, the café was almost empty.

"Hi, I'm Amber," she said to the tall brunette behind the counter.

"Hi Amber," the woman said, smiling broadly. "I've heard so much about you. It's nice to finally meet you."

"Nice to meet you too."

"I'm Sue and this is Joan." Sue pointed to a cherub-faced redhead. They all shook hands.

"Hi," Joan replied, flashing a smile that lit up her whole face.

"How are you girls holding up here?" Amber asked, taking a seat at the counter.

Sue tucked a long, curly piece of dark hair behind her ear. "Great. We love working here."

"Good," Amber said, nodding. "I can't wait to be back to work."

"How are you feeling?" asked Joan.

"I'm doing pretty well. But they don't want me back to work yet. Hopefully pretty soon. I miss working so much, and seeing all the regulars."

"Carol told us about what happened to you, and even though we don't know you, we were sorry to hear about it, and hope you get better soon," Sue said.

"I have some customers," Joan said, smoothing her apron. "You stay here and keep Amber company, Sue."

Amber turned to Sue. "I'm hoping to come back to work in a few weeks or so. My psychiatrist said that whenever I'm comfortable coming back to work, that was fine with her. In a couple more weeks, I think my scar will look better, and then I'll come back."

"We can't wait. Carol has said so many great things about you. Besides, I'm not used to working full-time, I can't wait to go back to part-time."

Amber stood. "I would love to stay and chat, but I really should get back home."

"I'm glad you stopped by," Sue said, walking her to the door.

"Me too. I'll come back soon. See you later." Amber made eye contact with Joan and waved. "Bye, Joan. Nice to meet you."

"Hope to see you back real soon," Joan responded, returning the wave.

Chapter Twenty

As Amber waited for the bus, she noticed a strange man in a blue sedan staring at her. She didn't recall ever seeing him before. He had long stringy hair, pockmarked cheeks, a large nose, and bulging eyes. *Maybe that's why I'm feeling afraid, because of the way he looks. I'm just being paranoid*, she thought. *Where's that bus? It should have been here a few minutes ago.*

The car moved a little closer, and Amber's stomach felt like it was in knots. Her face grew pale. Her eyes widened in alarm, darting everywhere for a safe haven. The car pulled up to the stoplight and waited for it to turn green.

The driver looked forward. Amber began to feel more at ease. *He's just waiting for the light*, she thought, when all of the sudden he got out of the car, raced after Amber, grabbed her, threw her in the car, and sped off.

A man on the corner witnessed this and called 911. He gave the license plate number and a description of the car and told them what had happened.

They put out an alert to all police officers to respond.

Tim was on his way home from the store when he heard the alert. Instantly, he felt sick to his stomach; he knew it was Amber. He was driving as fast as he could when he heard an officer come over the radio and say they were on Broadway and Seventh. Tim was two blocks away when he saw another officer in pursuit. There were no other vehicles coming. Tim sped around the officer and the car Amber was in and slowed down so both officers blocked him and he couldn't go anywhere. The car stopped.

Both police officers got out with their guns pulled, giving him orders to get out with his hands up. He tried grabbing Amber and bringing her out with him, but she began to fight him off. Tim ordered him to drop his weapon.

The man had his gun pointed right at Tim. He yelled again, "Drop your weapon or I'll shoot." The man pulled the trigger and both officers fired on him. He went down.

Amber ran to Tim. "Are you okay? You've been hit! Sit down."

"Amber, did he hurt you in any way? Do you need to go to the hospital?"

he said, groaning his words.

"No, I'm fine. It's you I'm worried about. We need an ambulance for you." Amber began to cry. "Tim, I'm sorry I didn't listen to you."

"Amber, it's not your fault, it's mine. I'll explain when we get to the hospital."

"Did he shoot you anywhere else besides your arm?" Amber said as she applied pressure to it to try to stop the bleeding. She slowly helped him sit down.

"No, just the arm."

The other policeman called for two ambulances. They arrived within minutes.

Amber rode to the hospital in the ambulance with Tim. When they got there, the doctor came right in. Amber sat right next to his bed with her hand on his leg. Tim's blood was all over her hands.

"Tim, I'm Dr. Knowles. I need to examine your arm." As the doctor lifted his arm, Tim began to moan with pain. "Sorry about that. We'll get you something for your pain. You're going to need surgery to get that bullet out. Then we'll take a look around to make sure nothing else was damaged." Dr. Knowles made some notes on his clipboard. "The good news is, if everything goes well, you'll be home later tonight."

"Well, that is good news," Tim replied weakly.

"We'll be back in to get you shortly. Who wrapped you up?"

Tim tilted his head in Amber's direction. "She did."

"Well, you did a good job getting his bleeding under control," the doctor said approvingly.

"Thank you. Doctor, he should be fine, shouldn't he?" she said, her voice filled with fear.

"He'll be just fine. Thanks to you, he didn't lose too much blood." The doctor smiled at both of them and left.

"Oh Tim, I'm glad you're going to be okay," Amber said, her voice still shaking. "You had me so scared. I wonder if the man who kidnapped me is going to make it."

"It's hard to say. I hope he does, so we can figure out who he is and get to the bottom of it." Tim spoke slowly and with difficulty.

"Do you know what's going on?" Amber asked, tuning in to her earlier intuition.

"Yes, I do. I need to tell you something that might make you very angry with me, Chuck, and Carol. But before I tell you, you have to know that we did it to protect you."

As he spoke, he hugged her tightly with his good arm, like he was afraid of losing her. Tim told her everything. "Aren't you going to say anything?" he asked when he was finished. He looked afraid of what she might say.

"I don't know what to say. You guys *knew* there was someone after me the whole time, but said nothing. You thought I might get mad, well, you're right. I can't believe you knew the whole time, but you chose not to tell me. Don't you think this is something I should have known?" By this time, Amber had reached her boiling point. "How could you keep something like this from me? All this time with me asking you guys what's wrong? All this time with you guys acting strange around me, and you going in the other room whenever you talked to Chuck, you knew?" she asked furiously.

"Yes, but Amber, please listen." Tim fumbled for her hand and squeezed it. "We thought we were protecting you. We thought if we could keep you in the house and away from the café, you would be fine. You see, Amber, they thought you were at Chuck and Carol's, so they were calling over there."

"So that's why Carol went to her sister's? Not because of her sister having problems but because of me? I put her in danger," Amber cried, losing some of her anger.

"No, it's not like that, Amber. She's fine, and now you're safe."

"Am I? I'm not so sure anymore." Amber turned her head from Tim.

Tim put a finger under her chin and gently brought her eyes level with his own. "You're safe," he said slowly, looking right into her eyes. "We have him in custody. I'm sure there's a link between Jim and this man. We just felt that you had been through enough and didn't want to add extra stress to your life. But now, after everything that has happened, you're right. We should have told you. All of this could have been prevented." He sighed forlornly. "I feel like this is my fault. If anything had happened to you, I don't know what I would have done. I am so sorry. I hope you can forgive us. We just didn't want to put you through anything else. We thought we were doing the right thing, but we were wrong." He closed his eyes.

Amber sat quietly for a few minutes before she began to speak. "I understand what you were trying to do, and I do forgive you, but in the future, no more secrets. I am a strong woman, and I can handle what you have to tell me. It's the not knowing that I can't handle. And now, because of me, you were almost killed. I am so sorry."

"It's not your fault. Everything will be fine. If we had told you what was going on, none of this would have happened. Here I thought I was protecting you, and I put you in harm's way." He paused. "Thank you for forgiving me. I just don't know if I can forgive myself."

"Don't be so hard on yourself; you thought you were doing what was best for me. I can live with that, so you should too." She smiled at him, her anger completely dissipated.

The doctor entered. "Tim, we're ready for you in surgery."

Amber bent down to kiss his forehead, and he reached up and kissed her right on her soft lips. Amber couldn't believe it. *Oh my God*, she thought, *he kissed me*! They gave each other a hug. Amber watched as they took him away to surgery, her heart pounding. She walked lightly down to the waiting area.

Chuck arrived a few minutes later. He ran up to Amber and hugged her.

He was frantic. "Are you okay? Is Tim okay?"

"Yes, I'm fine. And Tim is in surgery. They have to take the bullet out and make sure that everything is okay. The doctor said he should be able to come home tonight," Amber said, holding Chuck's arm.

"Thank God. I was so worried." He exhaled loudly in relief, collapsing into one of the plastic chairs. "I'm sorry we didn't tell you."

Amber took the seat next to him. "It's okay, Tim explained everything to me. I know you guys were trying to protect me."

"Yeah, well, that backfired." He ran his fingers through his hair, collecting his thoughts. "Amber, instead of you having to go down to the police station later, would you mind if I asked you some questions, so I can file a report?"

"No, not at all. Go ahead."

He pulled out a pad of paper. "Basically, you just need to tell me what happened."

When Amber finished, Chuck was very quiet.

"It's okay, Chuck. I know you didn't mean for this to happen," she said soothingly, her hand on his.

"I stopped at the front desk. They said the man who kidnapped you is named Dan Deliano. And that he would be out of surgery shortly. I'm going to go check. When he wakes up, I need to question him. I'll see if Tim's done too. Are you okay sitting here by yourself?"

"Yes, I'm fine."

After a few moments, Chuck came back. "Amber, Tim is in recovery. Everything went fine. He'll have full use of that arm again, but he will need physical therapy after he heals. So he will need to be off work for awhile longer. Follow me. You can come see him now."

Amber followed Chuck down the hallway. "He's right in there," Chuck said, pointing. "I'm going to go question Dan now. I'll see you in a few minutes."

Amber squeezed his hand and walked toward Tim's room. When she saw him, she ran up and hugged him. "How are you feeling?"

"Sore," Tim said, gingerly touching his arm, which was wrapped in bandages. "But other than that, I'm doing well. I'm just happy you're safe."

"And I'm happy he didn't kill you. Chuck is here. He's questioning the guy who kidnapped me. I guess his name is Dan Deliano. That's all I know so far."

"Does that name ring a bell to you?"

"No, I've never heard of him. The doctor says you'll need to be off work and will need physical therapy. Now *I* get to take care of *you*. You have taken care of me long enough. Oh Tim, you had me worried." Amber took his hand. They sat in silence for some time, pondering the many events of the day.

Twenty minutes later, Chuck walked in. "Hey, Chuck," Tim said brightly, happy to see his friend. "Did you question that guy?"

"Yeah. He's Jim's cousin, and he has a list of priors, just like Jim. He was hired by Jim to kidnap Amber, then kill her. Once he found out he would get a lesser sentence if he gave it up, he did, and rather quickly. Now we need to send someone down to speak with Jim and tell him what we know. With his list of priors, and attempted murder, rape, domestic abuse . . ." Chuck ticked the list off on his fingers. "Let's just say he's going away forever."

"Chuck, do you want to go down there and question him?" Tim asked.

"Sure. I'm going to call Carol and tell her what happened and let her know she can come home. Then I'll head down there. I'll call you later to fill you in," Chuck said, putting his coat on.

"Sounds good. We'll talk to you later. We should be home sometime tonight."

"I'll talk to you then. I'm glad to see you're okay." The two men shook hands and then Chuck left.

Tim turned his attention back to Amber. "Are you okay? You look so upset. Would you like to talk?"

"It's just that I don't know how much more I can take of this. And I'm upset with myself at how I yelled at you; I didn't understand what you were trying to do. I'm sorry, Tim. You have done nothing but extend a pleasant, warm welcome, and you have helped me out so much. You have made me feel so wonderful, and what do I do? I repay you by yelling at you. I know you guys had my best interest at heart. And I'm upset because you could've been killed." Amber sat down on the bed next to him.

"Amber, there is no reason for you to apologize. I understand where you were coming from. I would have probably felt the same way. And as far as me almost getting killed, I was shot in the arm. It's really not that big of a deal."

"Thank you for always being so understanding. I've never met anyone like you, Tim. I enjoy being around you so much." She laid her hand on his.

"Amber . . . I have my own confession to make." His eyes sparkled with pleasure.

What is he going to say? Amber wondered excitedly. *He looks so happy.*

Tim took a deep breath, then began. "I've never enjoyed the company of a woman like I do with you. You are so strong. And the most pleasant, cheerful, and beautiful woman I've ever met. Even after all you've been through, you manage to stay positive. You are definitely one of a kind."

Amber couldn't believe her ears. Could he feel the same way about her as she did about him? Maybe it didn't mean anything. *He's just being nice*, she thought. *But it's hard to tell when he stares at me so adoringly.* "Thank you. I feel the same about you."

"Oh, you think I'm a beautiful woman too? I've never had a compliment like that before."

Amber began to laugh. "No, what I meant to say was that you . . . are very pleasing to the eyes also." She blushed. "I can't believe I just said that. I never just come out and say what I am feeling. Then again, I have never met anyone like you before."

"The feeling is mutual."

Amber smiled shyly, her eyes lowered. She was not used to being complimented, in any way, by a man.

Chapter Twenty-One

"Amber," Tim said as Amber helped him into the house, "with the kind of day you've had, I think we should get you something to eat. Then you can relax, and if you want, we can talk about what happened today or about Jim or anything else that's on your mind."

Amber situated Tim comfortably on the couch, then went into the kitchen and made sandwiches. She brought him his food and sat down on the chair. They were so exhausted from the day's events that they could barely keep their eyes open. They both fell asleep downstairs, Amber on the chair, Tim on the couch.

When Tim got up to go to bed, he woke Amber. She was so startled, she began to cry. Tim hugged her with all his might until the tears stopped flowing down her face.

"I am so sorry; I didn't mean to scare you. I was just waking you up to go to bed. Are you going to be able to sleep tonight?"

"Yes, I'm totally beat. You just startled me when you woke me," she said meekly.

"Well, after today, and what happened, who could blame you." Tim kissed her forehead and hugged her tightly, trying to make her feel more secure and calm. He spoke quietly and said, "I can't believe anybody would want to hurt you. This must be so difficult for you. I know I'm having a hard time taking all this in." He took her hands. "But Amber, I *promise* to protect you. You have to promise you won't leave like that again. If you want to go anywhere, I will take you with no argument."

"You mentioned this must be tough for me." Amber paused and studied Tim's face for a moment. "It is, but I guess being here with you has made me feel more secure, like everything is going to be fine."

"It will be fine. No more worries. You just need to take care of yourself, and for the first time in your life, think about you. From now on, you come first, and you need to remember that."

"With reminders from you, I will." She smiled.

He whispered, "Let's bring you up to bed."

Amber stood and they headed upstairs. She helped Tim into bed and tucked him in tightly.

He smiled at her and said, "I'm right across the hall. If you need anything, just yell."

Amber walked into her room and crawled into bed. She snuggled into the warmth of the blankets. *I'm so glad today is over*, she thought. *It feels so good to finally be in bed.* Two seconds later, Tim came in and used his good arm to tuck her in.

"Hey, you weren't supposed to get out of bed," she said, hitting him playfully.

"I know, but I couldn't help it," Tim said, giving her a huge hug with one arm. "Now get some rest."

"I will. Tim, can you leave the door open, please?"

"Sure."

Amber felt a sense of security knowing Tim was right across the hall. It would be a long time before she would leave the house by herself. Amber couldn't believe the lengths that Jim would go to, even from behind bars, to hurt her. She knew he was crazy, but had ignorantly thought that when he went to jail, it was all done with, and the only thing she had to worry about was court.

She *was* worried about court, because she knew every detail would have to be brought out into the open, things she didn't ever want to tell anyone, not even Carol. All the things he used to make her do rushed back into her mind, flooding her brain. She began to shake and cry; her breathing became labored. No matter how much she tried to think about other things, she couldn't. It was like Jim was right there. She panicked and yelled out for Tim. He ran into the bedroom.

"What's wrong?" he asked, his face concerned.

"I'm afraid."

He kneeled next to her bed. "Did you see something?"

"No. Court . . . I can't go through with it."

"You're hyperventilating. Take in a big, slow breath, now blow it out slowly. Do that again." He held Amber's hand as she took several more deep breaths. "There, that's better. Don't try to talk until your breathing is back to normal. Shh, it's going to be okay, Amber. Just keep breathing slowly. There, that's much better. What about court? Why can't you go through with it?"

Amber rolled onto her side and forced herself to look Tim in the eyes. "Tim, you don't understand. There are things that happened—things he did to me, things he made me do—that I've never told anyone. I can't do it. It would be too humiliating."

He put his hand on her cheek. "But Amber, you don't need to feel that way. I don't know what happened, but you couldn't help it. You did what you had to do to survive. Amber, no one will hold that against you."

"They may not. But they will look at me differently. Even you will. I am so ashamed and embarrassed. How can I go through with it?" she asked, closing her eyes tightly.

"Amber, we have to get you in to see Dr. Dahl tomorrow. Maybe she can help. And it wouldn't hurt to have something around here, in case you experience another panic attack, that I can give you to help calm you down."

"Yeah, I think that's a good idea. I'll call her tomorrow for an appointment. Tim, I know this is asking a lot, but could you please just lay here with me until I fall asleep?"

"Of course." He climbed into bed next to her. "Amber, I'm glad I have extra time off, so you don't have to be alone." He put his arm around her and she snuggled into him. "Thanks for helping me today. You did a good job. You made me feel very calm."

"I wish you hadn't gotten hurt, but I'm glad you have extra time off too. You'll need the extra time to heal."

They talked and talked until they both fell asleep.

A couple of hours later, Tim woke up to Amber tossing and turning. Suddenly she let out a loud scream, startling Tim so much that he nearly jumped out of bed.

"Amber, Amber! It's okay, you're just having a nightmare." When Amber came to, Tim had his arm around her. "You're okay," he said into her hair. "It's just a nightmare." Amber couldn't stop crying. "What was your nightmare about?"

"Jim. He came back for me."

"It's only a bad dream. You're safe here with me."

Tim held her until she fell asleep, and then he too fell asleep.

Chapter Twenty-Two

The next morning when Amber awoke, she found Tim's arms around her and her arms around him. She felt so secure, so wonderful, and so aroused all at the same time. She never remembered a point in her life where she had felt so warm and tingly and . . . *complete*. She didn't want to move because she didn't want to wake him; she didn't want this feeling to end. She lay there for half an hour with her eyes closed and thoughts flowing through her mind.

When he woke up, she opened her eyes as if she had been sleeping. Tim gazed into her eyes so lovingly, so passionately, that her heart melted. She returned his gaze. For the first time, she knew there was a mutual attraction, but she also knew that it wasn't going to be that easy. There were so many things happening, she didn't know where to begin.

Knowing what he knew about her, and what he was about to find out, could he love her the way she wanted to be loved? Would it all be too much for him? She didn't know, but the thought scared her.

In just the short time she had known Tim, she knew he was the one for her. Surely he wasn't perfect, but his imperfections didn't bother her one bit. She had her own imperfections, not to mention a past that was far worse.

Amber realized that she was still gazing into his eyes, and for that brief moment, she forgot herself and her problems. It was all about Tim.

Tim spoke first. "Good morning, sunshine."

"Good morning to you too."

"Did you sleep a little better the rest of the night?"

"Yes, I did. Thank you for staying here with me. I know that was a lot to ask of you."

"No, it wasn't. I'm glad I could help."

She yawned. "And you did help, you made me feel so secure, not frightened at all. In fact, tonight I think I can go to sleep on my own."

"Ooh, does that mean I don't get to sleep with the most beautiful woman I have ever met?" he asked disappointedly.

"Yeah, I guess so." They both began to chuckle.

"Would you like some breakfast?" Amber asked.

"Sure. I'll help you make it."

"No, no, you don't, you're having breakfast in bed this morning."

"I am? You don't have to do that. I'm totally capable of helping you."

"I know. But with you just being shot yesterday, I don't think so," she said, propping herself up on her elbow and looking down at Tim.

"Yeah, but you're still not healed either. By the way, how is your neck?"

"I wish it was all the way healed," she said, touching it self-consciously. "Now I will have to spend the rest of my life covering it up."

"Once it heals, it will look just fine. You worry too much. A gorgeous woman like you doesn't need to worry about a scar. When people look at you, believe me, they won't be staring at your neck. You know what else I noticed? Your voice has come back. It's not all raspy sounding anymore. You have a very beautiful voice."

"You are much too nice," she said as she lowered her eyes, a big smile on her face.

"Nice isn't the word. *Honest* is."

"You rest while I go make breakfast," she said, climbing out of bed.

Amber went downstairs, took out the eggs and bread, and started making French toast. She could barely concentrate with all the thoughts of Tim running through her mind. *I can't believe I got to sleep with Tim last night . . . that was so nice. He makes me feel so safe and secure. I can't believe I'm having these feelings for him already.* Amber put a glass of orange juice and French toast on a tray and headed upstairs.

"Here you go," she said as she set the tray on his lap.

"Looks delicious." He looked down at his food and then up at Amber flirtatiously.

Amber came up a little while later and sat next to Tim in bed with her own breakfast.

Amber finished eating and decided to go freshen up a bit. She had an appearance to keep up. Since she had met Tim, she had to admit she always wanted to look her best for him. She felt like a teenager again, but with mature feelings. She finally felt like she had a new chance at life and at love, but this time, the right way. *Happily ever after?* she thought. *I hope so, but I'm getting way ahead of myself. He still doesn't know everything about my past.* Amber went back into the bedroom to check on Tim.

"This is the first time I have ever had breakfast in bed."

"You've got to be kidding me."

"I'm not."

"Well, I'll make sure to do it again."

"You don't have to do that," he said, taking another bite.

"Yes, I do. Not because I have to, but because I want to."

"I meant to tell you," he said between bites, "Carol will be coming over today."

"Great!" Amber said, happiness flooding her veins. "She's finally back. I've missed her so much."

"She misses you too."

"I'm going to make a bed for you on the couch so you can be nice and comfortable," she said as she headed for the door.

"Thanks, but you don't have to do that."

"I know. But I'm going to anyway. What time is Carol coming over?"

"She should be here anytime now."

Amber went downstairs and put some blankets and pillows on the couch. She helped Tim into his new bed, then sat down in the chair to read her book. It wasn't ten minutes later that the doorbell rang. Amber jumped up to get it.

"Carol!" she exclaimed, throwing her arms around her friend. "I have missed you so much. It seems like forever since I last saw you."

"I have missed you too; I've been so worried about you." Carol began to cry as she hugged Amber tightly. "I'm sorry, I am *so* sorry I didn't tell you about what was going on. I wanted you to feel secure, to be protected." The words flooded from her mouth. "I never fathomed what would happen. Amber, I didn't want to keep anything from you, I never have until then, and knowing what I know now, I will never ever keep anything from you again. We almost got you killed. We didn't know. I'm so very sorry." She went over and hugged Tim. "I'm so sorry, Tim. Are you okay?"

"Yeah, I'm fine. Amber won't let me do anything, though," he said playfully.

"Carol, don't cry. I know, I know, now shh . . . it's okay. I understand. Tim explained it to me. Please don't cry. I'm okay, really," Amber said comfortingly, her arms around Carol. "It's going to be fine; things are going to work out. You'll see. Carol, you're not the only one who has kept secrets. I have too."

"About what?"

Amber grabbed Carol's hand and brought her over to sit in the living room. "I'm not ready to talk about it yet. I have told you everything I thought you could handle about what Jim did to me, or had me do, but the things I kept from you were things I was too ashamed to tell you. I just wanted to let you know because, besides you being my best friend, things will come out in court. I don't want you to be too shocked, but please understand, I had no choice." Amber began to cry uncontrollably. "I did these things to save my life."

"Amber, you have nothing to be ashamed of. You were in a bad situation; you did what you needed to do in order to survive. We all do things we're not proud of. The only difference is, most of us have a choice. You didn't. Amber, it's okay, honey, settle down. Nothing you have done is going to change how I feel about you. *Nothing*. Do you understand?" Carol stroked Amber's hair, looking into her eyes.

"I can't stop thinking about it. I don't want to go to court, because I never want these things to come out."

"I understand, but I will not judge you, nor will anyone else. Amber, you need to get in and see Dr. Dahl. I'm going to call her right now. Is that alright with you?" She asked as she headed to the kitchen.

"Yes. The number is over on the counter. Tim and I were just talking about that. I just haven't done it yet. I guess I'm ready now. I can't keep feeling like this." She stood and followed Carol apprehensively.

Carol picked up the phone and dialed. There was a moment of silence, and she looked sympathetically over at Amber wiping her tears away with the backs of her hands. "Yes, may I talk to Dr. Dahl please?" She paused. "This is Carol calling for Amber Labell. She is having an anxiety attack, and she needs to come in and see Dr. Dahl as soon as possible." She paused again, smiling sadly at Amber. "Yes. Yes, two o'clock sounds fine. Okay. Thank you. See you at two."

Chapter Twenty-Three

It didn't take long for Amber's appointment time to arrive. Tim and Carol sat quietly in the waiting room as Amber went in with the doctor. About an hour and a half later, Amber came out looking much calmer, though her eyes were bloodshot and puffy.

Tim and Carol immediately went to her and hugged her.

Dr. Dahl smiled. "You're so lucky to have such wonderful friends."

It didn't take long for Amber to respond with a smile. "Yes, don't I know it."

"Amber, stop at the front desk and set up the next couple of appointments. We'll go from there. I'll see you next time." She squeezed Amber's arm gently and disappeared through the door.

"Thank you for everything, Dr. Dahl." Amber turned her attention to Tim. "Tim, you look tired. You should have stayed home and rested."

"I know, but I felt like I needed to be here for you."

They walked silently out to the car. It was quiet for a while until about half way home.

"How did things go?" Carol asked.

"They went very well. I got a lot out, but we still have a lot more to discuss and work on. Dr. Dahl was very helpful. She gave me a different perspective on things." Amber paused, sighing deeply to clear her head a little. "By the way, Carol, can we stop at the pharmacy? I have a couple of prescriptions I need to get."

"Sure, not a problem," Carol said, turning to look at her briefly. "What did she prescribe?"

"She gave me something for anxiety, something for depression, and something to help me sleep if I'm having trouble. She said that'll help, but we need to keep up with therapy. She wants me to see her two times a week. She said, as time goes by, we will go down to one time a week, then slowly I'll go less and less as things get better. Which brings me to you, Tim," she said, turning around to look at him. "Do you think you would be able to bring me to the appointments?"

"Of course I can," he said, reaching forward to squeeze her shoulder.

Amber leaned her head back on the headrest and smiled. "I want to thank both of you for everything you have done for me."

Carol replied, "That's what friends are for."

As the car ride grew silent again, Amber thought about the long road she had ahead of her. *Think positive*, she scolded herself. The thought of her friends, and the spark between her and Tim, just made it that much easier to want to get better as quickly as possible. *I know I can do this. I know I will make the right choices. As Dr. Dahl said in session, one day at a time. I can live like that. Things are going to be good.*

By the time they stopped at the pharmacy and made their way back home, Amber needed to rest. Carol saw her off to bed and went down to talk to Tim.

"I think we should have Chuck come over after work, and we can all sit down and have a talk about what was said at the prison."

"I think that's a good idea," he said tensely. "Why don't you give Chuck a call now. Tell him to bring his appetite."

Chapter Twenty-Four

A few hours later, Amber woke up and went downstairs.

"Hey Chuck! I didn't know you were coming over," she said, giving him a hug. "How nice it is to see you."

Tim walked over and put his arm around Amber. "Honey, the lasagna you made is in the oven. Carol got it started. You have to be starving by now."

"Now that you mention it, I am."

"Well, if everyone else is hungry we can go eat," Tim said, leading her gently toward the dining room.

Everyone nodded enthusiastically. The conversation was light, which was fine with Amber since she was still waking up. After dinner, Carol and Amber cleaned up while Tim and Chuck went off to work out some details. When they were done, they joined Tim and Chuck in the living room.

"Dinner was excellent, Amber. Thank you," Tim said. Chuck and Carol chimed in their agreement.

"I'm glad you all liked it."

There was an odd silence, and Amber was suddenly aware that something was up. "What's going on, guys? Don't tell me nothing."

"Well, Amber," Tim said, sitting next to her on the couch and taking her hand, "the real reason for tonight is to talk to you about Chuck's conversation at the prison with Jim."

"Yes, go on," she said nervously.

"Well, at first he denied it over and over, even when I told him that his own cousin, Dan, said that he was hired to kidnap and kill you. Then I began to make him angry, talking about how tough he was to be able to beat up a woman, and I brought up other things."

"Like what?" Amber asked.

Chuck paused, glanced at Amber timidly, and then looked down at his hands. "That he must be sexually inadequate to have to put a woman out using drugs and then rape her." He cleared his throat and looked up. "That's all it took to get him to confess. Believe me, he didn't mean to, but his anger problem made him do it. He became enraged, his face turned blood red, and he began to sweat. Then he started shaking and breathing heavy, and that was his breaking point. He started yelling and spilled his guts."

"What did he say?"

"Are you sure you really want to know?"

"Yes, I do," she said, shifting forward in her seat.

Chuck pulled out his notepad and studied his notes for a moment. "He started yelling, 'That fucking bitch deserved it! If I can't have her, no one can. I want her dead in the ground, do you understand? No matter what it takes. I will find someone. Until the day I die, I will stop at nothing until she is in the ground where that whore deserves to be.'" He stopped, looking at Amber. "Are you okay?"

Amber stood and began pacing the room. "Yes, go on."

"Well at that point, I grabbed him by the throat and slammed him into the wall. I told him that I would see to it that every day he is in jail, he will suffer if he dares to hurt you. I told him he would pay, and pay dearly. I told him I could have him killed, and believe me I'd do it. Amber, he signed a confession; he was on tape spilling his guts."

Amber stopped pacing and looked right at Chuck. "Are you going to get into trouble?"

"No. I turned off the tape recorder before I said what I had to say."

"Good. I don't want you getting into trouble over me." She resumed pacing.

"Amber, you are my friend and I want you protected. That's what we all want. And that's what we're going to do. We'll do what we need to in order to protect you. After this confession, he's going away forever. You won't have to worry anymore."

Amber chewed thoughtfully on her lower lip. "I'm glad you told me everything. I appreciate your honesty. I'd rather know. So I guess it didn't take you long to figure out how to get him angry."

"He's like a time bomb, ready to go off at any minute. I'm just glad the worst of it is behind you," Chuck said.

"Do you think he'll hire anyone else?"

"No. He is being monitored at all times."

"Good, that makes me feel more at ease." Amber stopped pacing and sat down on the couch near where Tim was lying.

Carol stood, her hands clasped in front of her. "We hate to eat and run, but I have to get up early to open the café."

"That's okay, we understand," Amber said, standing to see them out. "When do you think I can come back to work?"

"Let's give it a few more weeks."

"Do you think you can last that long?" Amber asked.

"I think so."

Chuck put his coat on. "We'll see you guys later. Have a good night." Hugs were exchanged.

Amber and Tim waved from the door as Chuck and Carol drove away.

"Tim, I'm going to go soak in a nice, hot bath for a while, just so I can calm my nerves."

"I think that's a good idea. Maybe that will help you sleep a little better tonight."

"I sure hope so."

Amber headed upstairs and started the water. She added some lavender-scented bath soak, lit some aromatherapy candles, and climbed in. She tried not to think about what Jim said to Chuck, but the thought wouldn't stay away. She couldn't believe he wanted her dead so badly. *To think, I could have left my friends, the people who mean the most to me, and he would have found me and killed me.* The thought sickened her. She was glad she had stayed, even though he didn't leave much of a choice that horrible night. Just then there was a knock on the bathroom door.

"Are you okay in there?"

"Yeah."

"Do you need anything?"

"No."

"I just wanted to make sure everything was okay because you've been in there for over an hour."

Amber hadn't realized how much time had gone by. "Have I really?"

"Yes."

"I'm fine. I was just thinking about what Chuck said to me about Jim. I must have lost track of the time."

"Amber, are you glad you were told, or would you rather we hadn't given so many details?" Tim asked.

"No, I'm glad I was told everything. I just can't believe how much he wants me dead. In my worst nightmares I never imagined he had so much hate for me."

Tim's voice was slightly muffled through the door. "Amber, I've seen guys like him. What's really getting to him is the fact that he has no control over you anymore. That's where his hatred is coming from. It's very common for men like him to think that if they can't have her, nobody will."

"When I was with him, I knew how dangerous he was, but I wasn't expecting what I came home to that night. I thought I would be out of there before anything else happened to me. Oh, how wrong I was. I've made mistakes in my life, but never like the mistake I made when I married him."

"If you don't mind me asking, what was he like when you first met and married him?" he asked as he sat down outside the door.

"He was so charming and sweet. He used to say the sweetest things to me. He would buy me flowers and small gifts, take me out. I never expected him to be this way. I missed the signs, I guess." Amber paused to collect her thoughts. "Except for one day, about a month before we got married. That was the first time I noticed him acting really different. Not at all like the man I had grown to love. I had him over for dinner, and let's just say, at that point in my life, my cooking left a little to be desired."

"Had he tried your cooking before then?"

"Oh yes, many times. He never complained, in fact he complimented me. I knew he was just being sweet, though." She breathed deeply, then went on. "He became very angry about how the food tasted. He went on and on about how if we were going to be married, I needed cooking lessons. I just took his behavior as a bad day. It was as if he was having a tantrum, like a little child. That was the worst he had ever behaved.

"I took cooking lessons. My cooking did become better in time. But you know, in retrospect, there were other things he used to do too. After that tantrum, I noticed he became angrier more easily. I thought it was wedding jitters, so I sat down and talked with him, to make sure everything was okay. He became very charming for a few days.

"It wasn't just his anger that bothered me. Everything he was in the beginning slowly started to slip away. He would slam things down, and he was very crabby. He told me it was due to problems at work. I believed him. So you see, I had some signs, but at the time I didn't understand what any of it meant."

"Before you were married was he ever violent with you?"

"No, not ever."

"What happened?"

"We got married. Jim and I had talked about having two children and the happy family life that we had both always longed for. I was very excited about what life would bring me.

"A few months after marrying Jim, things got bad real fast; there was nothing that I could do right. After two months, he hit me for the first time, slapped me across the face. I was in awe. I couldn't believe it. He cried and begged me not to leave, told me it wouldn't happen again. 'I just don't know what got into me, baby; you know I would never hurt you.' He blamed it on the pressure he was dealing with at work. He bought me flowers and a necklace to make up for it. I was naïve and fell for it. I should have left then, but I believed in him.

"Things were fine for a few months, and I ended up getting pregnant. I was extremely happy about it, and he seemed to be too. But about two months into my pregnancy, he began ranting about how he had never wanted children, and how I was trying to trap him. He said we couldn't afford an extra mouth to feed. He wanted me to get an abortion. I refused. He became so enraged. I had never seen him that angry before. That night was my first encounter with his demon-like side."

"Amber, what happened?"

Amber was silent for a moment. "Just a minute. Let me collect myself and come out."

"Do you want something to drink?"

"Sure."

"How does hot cocoa sound?"

"Sounds good."

"I'll be right back."

Amber was sitting on the bed when he returned. He handed her a steaming cup and sat next to her. They both sat in silence, sipping their hot cocoa, until Amber was ready to begin again. She took a deep breath and was just about to speak when Tim interjected. "Amber, if this is too painful for you, you don't have to go on if you don't want to."

"No, that's okay. I need to talk about it." She looked into her cup and collected her thoughts. "Jim went ballistic. Everything changed about him. The way he looked at me, the way he talked to me, everything. He became so enraged he was sputtering out his words, spit flying all over my face. His voice was as cold as death. I felt the hairs on the back of my neck rise; it felt as if my heart was going to pound out of my chest. I couldn't breathe, and that's when I felt my first punch, right in the stomach. Once wasn't good enough for him; he hit me over and over again. I let out a scream and he grabbed me around the neck and ran my head right into the wall, knocking me out. When I woke up on the floor, he was gone. I could barely move. That night I became violently ill, and all my dreams of a happy family life vanished. I went to the bathroom and that's when I saw all the . . . all the blood. I knew right then I had lost my baby." Amber began to cry. "And I knew I was doomed. I vowed that night to never become pregnant again. He came home the next morning with flowers, promised to never do it again. But I knew, deep down, this was just the beginning. I didn't know where to go or what to do; I had no one. From that point on, I did whatever it took to make him happy." Tim put his arm around her and she buried her head in his shoulder and sobbed for a few moments. "What happened when Jim found out you lost the baby?

"His voice became very distant. He began to weep and apologized over and over. Do you know what I did? I consoled him and told him everything was going to be fine. I consoled him until he quit crying. After that day, he acted as if nothing had happened. A part of me died that day, along with my baby. And you know, as time went by and things got worse, I was thankful that my baby was in heaven with God. I wanted to be there with my baby." She looked up at Tim, her face wet with tears. "I've never shared this with anyone, not even Carol. I have felt so ashamed for feeling that way. But I knew my baby was in a better place. Someday we will be together, but for now, God is taking care of him."

Tim had tears in his eyes. "I'm so sorry, Amber. I'm sorry that this happened to you. I can't believe such a sweet, intelligent, wonderful person . . . I mean, why would anyone do that to you? He didn't know what he had in you, and he was too sick to even care. Amber, you have lived such a hard life. I look at you and I want so much more for you."

"Thank you, Tim. I think that's the sweetest thing anyone has ever said to me."

"I'm glad you shared this with me. You have nothing to be ashamed of. I understand why you feel the way you do. I agree that your baby is in a better place. Who knows what he would have done to your child if he had been born. I want you to know that, no matter how ashamed you feel, you can always come to me and talk. Believe me, I will understand."

"Thanks for listening to me and being so supportive. That means a lot," Amber said, smiling.

Chapter Twenty-Five

Days turned into weeks. The more time Amber spent talking with Tim, the better she felt and the happier she became. Chuck and Carol visited often, and Carol and Amber talked on the phone every day. Her life was changing for the better; life felt suddenly good, safe, and secure.

Tim went back to work, and Amber decided it was time to step foot into the café and start working part-time. She still went to counseling two times a week. Dr. Dahl and Amber were making good progress. Amber felt so rich, with the friends and love she finally had in her life. She was learning how to live all over again.

During one of her sessions with Dr. Dahl, she brought up something she had been thinking about for some time. "I need to do something before court arrives," she began.

"What's that?"

"I need to confront Jim, so that when I'm in court I have no fears, and I will be able to face him confidently."

Dr. Dahl peered at Amber over the rims of her glasses. "I don't think that's such a good idea."

Amber stood and walked to the window. She watched the people rushing about below, each one with problems and joys she would never know. "I've been thinking about it for a long time, and I'm going to do it. You can't change my mind, no matter what you say."

"Well, as your psychiatrist, I need to let you know that seeing him at this point may set you back on your progress. It may also make your nightmares come back in full force."

Amber kept looking out of the window, her back turned to Dr. Dahl. "I have to face him in court. I might as well face him now so I can begin to move on and maybe get over the fear I'm having."

"Yes, but this may also instill more fear in you, and I don't want to see that happen." She walked over and stood next to Amber.

"I appreciate your opinion, as my doctor, but I have to do it."

"I guess your mind is made up."

"It is."

On the way home, Amber told Tim what she wanted to do.

"Amber, are you sure this is what you want?" He looked into her eyes, his own filled with concern.

"Yes, I have to do this," she said adamantly.

"Well, first things first. That lawyer we got you, Brenda Johnson, I think we need to talk to her."

"I never thought about that. I'll call her when I get home, but my mind is made up. I'm still going to see him. I have to in order to move forward."

"So that takes care of the second thing I was about to ask. You sound pretty sure that this is what you want."

"Yes, I'm *very* sure," Amber said, crossing her arms stubbornly. "I've been thinking about this for a long time."

"Since your mind is made up, could I come in with you to make sure you're okay? It would set my mind at ease to be there for back up."

"You can come, but there will be the glass between us, and I really need to do this on my own to prove to him that I am no longer afraid of him."

"I understand. I will wait outside, but if you need anything, you just yell for me or tell the guard to call. Amber, I understand why you have to do this, I really do. I just worry about you. But I guess if I were you, I'd feel the same way. You know, we're a lot alike," he said, looking over at her.

"I know, we are. It's almost scary." They both began to laugh.

When she got home, Amber immediately went to the phone and dialed. "Hi Brenda, this is Amber."

"Hi Amber, how are you?"

"Good. How are you?"

"Great. I've looked through everything. Amber, your case is very clear, cut and dry. He will remain in prison for the rest of his natural life."

Amber collapsed into a kitchen chair with a sigh. "You have no idea how happy that makes me. But I'm actually calling to consult with you about something."

"What can I do for you, Amber?"

"I've been thinking about it for a long time, and I want to go confront Jim."

The line was silent for a moment before Brenda spoke. "From a legal standpoint, I'm not certain that's such a good idea."

"Why not?"

"If that's brought into court, they may feel you're not afraid of him. Since you were abused by him, they may think that you wanting to see him is not normal. It could draw the jury to conclude that it wasn't as bad as we say it is."

"Brenda," Amber said, leaning forward in her chair, "you have his confessions, his prison record, his arrest records for domestic abuse. You have the hospital records, and you have everything we need to prove what he's done."

"That's true. I guess you have your mind made up."

"Yes, I do. I just wanted to let you know what I was planning."

"Thank you for that. When are you going?"

"I don't know. I have to set up an appointment."

"Please call me and tell me what happened."

"I will. Any word on how long it will be before we go to court?"

"No not yet. I will call you when I get the date."

"Sounds good. I'll call you. Talk to you later. Bye."

Amber stood holding the phone in her hand for a few moments, a far-off look in her eyes. Tim walked over, took the receiver from her hand, and gently placed it in the cradle.

"Well," he said, "I will call Chuck and set up an appointment for you. Do you want the appointment as soon as possible, or do you need time to prepare?"

"The sooner the better. As much as I've been thinking about it, I'm prepared."

"Okay, I'll take care of it."

Amber left the kitchen and sat down on the couch while Tim made the phone call. "Amber, how does Wednesday at nine o'clock work for you?" he called from the other room.

"Excellent, I'll be ready," Amber replied.

Chapter Twenty-Six

Time couldn't go by fast enough for Amber. Two days seemed to take forever. Finally Wednesday arrived.

"Amber, how are you feeling about today?" Tim asked when she walked into the kitchen that morning.

"Nervous and anxious," she said, sitting at the table, "but don't worry, I took my medication. I'm ready to face him. I need to do this. I hope you understand."

"I can't put myself in your shoes, but I think I understand. I made you a big breakfast, so I hope you're hungry."

"I'm starved."

"Good. Let's eat," he said, setting dishes on the table.

Amber examined the spread: bacon, eggs, toast, grapefruit. "This looks delicious, Tim."

"Amber, you look very nice today; you have a glow about you. What's that all about?"

"I feel like another part of me is almost free. I haven't faced him yet, so I don't know the consequences of this, but I feel a sense of freedom. Once I do this, he will know that I am no longer afraid of him and that he has no control over me. In the end, I will have won, not him. I don't know how he's going to be able to live with that."

"Hopefully, he can't live with that. I want nothing more than for him to suffer for the rest of his natural life."

Amber nodded in agreement as she chewed.

"You do know that when he goes to prison, they don't like men like him there, men who abuse women. He will not fare well in prison. Right now he's safe because he's in jail, and no one can get to him, but prison is another story."

"I know this sounds horrible, but it makes me happy to know that he will live in the same hell he put me through every day."

"Amber, I think anyone can understand that."

After breakfast, Amber went upstairs and took a few minutes to get her thoughts together. When she came down, she felt more collected. She was ready to go face the man whom she had started out loving and later grew to hate.

"Are you ready to go?"

"I couldn't be any more ready than I am right now."

As she walked into the county jail, Amber began to feel very anxious and stopped to take a few breaths.

"Are you okay?" Tim asked as he put his hands on her shoulders.

"Yes, I'm fine. My stomach is tied in knots." She chewed nervously on her bottom lip.

"Amber, you're going to be okay. He can't do anything to you anymore. He can't hurt you, Amber." Tim gave her a supportive hug. "I am going to be right outside that door. If you need me, I'll be there."

With that, Amber started to feel a sense of security again and they headed in. She walked in with the guard on duty and took one last look at Tim as the door shut behind them. He smiled weakly at her, took a big gulp of air, and paced the floor. She could tell his thoughts were running rapidly as she turned to Jim.

As Amber walked into the room, her thoughts immediately went to that last night they were together, and the fear and pain she endured. She felt a wickedness about her, and that was her strength. She took a seat before him.

She could tell by the look on his face that he thought she was there to save him. He looked at her like he had when they were in love. He smiled at her and a cold shiver went up her back. Amber smiled back, not because she was happy to see him, but because she knew she had him. She knew he thought she was going to be his savior.

"I wasn't expecting you to come visit me. I thought you would hate me forever."

"You thought I would hate you?" she asked, sitting straight up, staring at him with an unwavering, penetrating gaze.

Jim fidgeted in his chair. "Well, yeah."

"It runs deeper than that."

"What do you mean?"

Amber stood up and leaned toward the glass, staring directly into his eyes. "Did you really think that I was here because I love you? You stupid, pathetic fool." All the nerves she had felt were replaced with anger, an anger that she had never known. Her nostrils flared, her teeth clenched, and her hands turned to fists. It took all she had to maintain control when she spoke. She bellowed out, "For every time you hit me, drugged me, and raped me, and you think I'm here because I *love* you? All this time I thought you were too big, and too strong, and you're only an insecure, pathetic little man who can't control his own life, let alone anyone else's. And to *think* I was once afraid of you! Now I look at you and see nothing but a scared little man. To think I was ever with you sickens me. You hired someone to kill me, and you think I'm here to help you? You must be the most ignorant son-of-a-bitch I've ever met. You are going to rot in prison until the day you die! You think it's bad here, just wait until you go to prison. I know what they do to guys like you. You'll be somebody's toy to use, and you can spend the rest of your life the way I spent the first part of mine, being beaten and raped. You're going to get to see what it's like to live the way you made me live, in fear and pain. You will be looking over your shoulder all the time, like I had to. So live large now because you have it easy here. Just wait and see. They're going to get you in prison. I only hope you live long enough to endure what I have!" She was yelling so loud that Tim could hear every word.

Jim's mouth hung open. He had never seen her like this before. He couldn't speak, he just stared.

"How does it feel to be treated like this? Guess what? This time you can't do a thing about it. I pity you. You are nothing but a worthless piece of shit. I spit on you. You took a part of me, but now I have it back and there's nothing you can do about it. When you killed my baby, I wanted my life to end. It took years to want to live again, but guess what? I *do* want to live and now I know my baby is in a better place. You will never see that baby, because when you die, you're going to hell. But when I die, I will be able to see and hold and touch my baby.

"You better do a lot of praying, because where you're going isn't a pretty place. Jim, you no longer control me or my life. You are a nobody. I live for *me* now, not you. See you in court."

Amber got up and walked toward the door. Jim sat there unable to speak or move. She turned around when she reached the door. "Oh yeah, Jim. I won, not you." Then she opened the door and walked out. She met Tim's eyes and they both smiled and hugged each other.

"You're a very courageous woman," he said, pulling back from the hug to look at her. "I heard everything, and I am very proud of you. I think tonight we should celebrate. Where would you like to go?"

"How about to an Italian restaurant?" Amber asked, a smile lighting her face.

"Sounds great. I know the perfect place."

Chapter Twenty-Seven

Amber came down for dinner in an elegant, form-fitting dress with a slit up one side. The bottom of the dress flowed behind her.

"You look absolutely beautiful," Tim said as soon as he saw her. "Never before have I seen such a beautiful woman."

Amber blushed. "Oh, stop it."

"No. You are the most gorgeous woman I have ever had the pleasure of laying eyes upon."

She could feel the heat rising up her neck. "Thank you. You look dashingly handsome yourself."

Tim reached for her hand at the bottom of the steps. "Actually, we make a very handsome couple, don't you think?"

Amber grabbed his hand tightly and took the last step down, following his lead. "Yes, I do," Amber replied. She had never seen his romantic side before, but she liked it.

"Would you like to have a glass of wine before we go?"

There were butterflies in her stomach. "Sure. That sounds wonderful."

He went to the kitchen and poured two glasses of wine. She could hardly take her eyes off of him. He handed her a glass and held his aloft. "Let's toast to your newfound freedom."

She raised her glass by its delicate stem. "To newfound freedom."

They each took a long sip of their wine. "I can't believe how well you did today with Jim. He couldn't say a word." He led her gently by the elbow over to the fireplace. Orange and blue flames danced up the sides of the logs.

"I know. He just looked at me, in shock at the way I was talking to him. I've never talked to him like that before. It felt great to get all that off my chest. It was very liberating."

"You even shocked me. I couldn't believe what I was hearing. I was so afraid you might back down, but you didn't. You didn't even give him a chance to respond. Would you like to have a seat?"

"Sure." She took his hand and he led her over to the couch. He guided her gently down. "Well, I bet you right about now he's so angry that he wishes he could get his hands on me."

He sat next to her, his thigh pressed against hers. "I'm sure he is pissed off, excuse my French."

"That's okay. You heard me talking to him today the way I did, and I don't ever talk like that, or at least hardly ever. Can you believe he thought I was coming to help him in some way?"

"No, I can't," Tim said, shaking his head solemnly. "What an idiot. You know he is definitely mentally ill. A normal person wouldn't think that way."

"I know."

Tim stared into her eyes. She could tell he was about to say something to her, but then he looked away for a moment, and when he looked back, he said, "Well, what do you think? Should we get going?"

"Yes. I'm starving."

The hostess seated them at a secluded corner booth. It was perfect.

"Have you ever been to this restaurant before?" Tim asked.

"No. I really haven't been anywhere. Jim wouldn't allow it."

"Well, that's all about to change," Tim said as they both scooted into the booth and he slid around next to Amber.

"How's that?"

"Well, I'm going to bring you around to places you've never been. You've really missed out on a lot."

"I know I have." *I can tell he wants to tell me something important*, she thought. *What does this mean, that he wants to take me places? I hope it means what I think it does.* "I'm very excited for what life has to offer me." She could feel herself melt a little more each time she looked into his eyes.

"You should be. There's a lot out there for you to see and experience."

Amber handed one of the tall, burgundy menus to Tim. "Look at this menu! It's going to be hard to choose what I want."

Tim set the gilded menu down without even looking at it. "Well, I'm going to get the stuffed manicotti; I've had it before. It's delicious."

"I trust your opinion, but I think I'll get something different so we can share." She scanned the menu's elegant script. "Have you ever had the veal parmesan?"

"No, but I'm sure it's delicious."

"Then that's what I'll get."

"Do you want red wine?" Tim asked as he leafed through the black leather wine menu.

"Yes, I do."

"I'll order a nice bottle of cabernet sauvignon."

"Sounds wonderful to me."

"Oh, believe me, it is."

The waiter came, took their order, and brought back the wine.

Amber tried it and was very pleased. “So far so good.”

“If that impresses you, wait until you get the food.”

The restaurant was dim except for the candles lighting the tables. Amber and Tim both scooted close to each other. The restaurant was very romantic, and they were dressed perfectly to match the atmosphere. Amber flirted coquettishly with Tim and he reciprocated. He touched her hand as often as he could, appearing smitten.

“Amber, when we’re done here, how about if I take you out to a club for a couple drinks, and we can dance the rest of the night away?”

“I’d love it, but I have to be honest with you. I haven’t danced in years, so I don’t know how good I’ll do.”

“That’s okay,” Tim said, smiling at her reassuringly. “I’m sure you’ll do fine.”

“This is so exciting! I can’t wait.”

Tim and Amber made small talk until their food got there.

“This looks delicious,” Amber exclaimed when the waiter set her plate down in front of her.

“You think it looks good, wait until you try it,” Tim said, winking at her.

She held up her wineglass. “Let’s toast to a wonderful night.”

“Here, here,” replied Tim, threading his arm through hers as they both took a drink.

When Amber took her first bite, she couldn’t believe the flavor. “You definitely have good taste in restaurants, Tim. This is wonderful, delicious! Without question the best veal parmesan I have ever had.”

“Want to try mine?” asked Tim.

“Sure. It looks great.”

Tim reached over and ever so gently placed the fork on her tongue. “Mmm, tastes delicious. Would you like to try mine?”

“Sure.”

Amber cut a big bite, and carefully fed it to him. She couldn’t help but stare at his mouth; she wanted to touch her lips to his.

“I’m definitely getting that next time,” he said. “It’s delicious.”

“We lucked out, both ordering such good entrees. I’m glad we can share.”

By the time they finished, over two hours had passed.

Tim smiled at her broadly. “I enjoyed having dinner with you. I don’t know if I’ve ever enjoyed myself so much.”

“This is the best time I’ve ever had, too. Thank you, Tim,” replied Amber.

“Just you wait until we go out dancing. Now, that’s going to be fun.”

“Tim, thanks for tonight, and for everything. You have been very good to me."

He laid his hand on hers and looked into her eyes. "You're easy to be good to. I really enjoy being with you. You know, you don't have to thank me so much. Whether or not you know it, you have done a lot for me also. The way you took care of me when I was injured, and just having you around has made me so happy. Since you've been around, I never feel down. You have really changed my life."

"I enjoy being with you too. You have made my life full of happiness." *This feels so good,* she thought, *the way he touches me. I can't believe he's still holding my hand. I know he has something on his mind. I wish he would tell me.*

The check came. Tim paid it and left a very nice tip, and then they were on their way. "You're really going to have fun at this club."

"What's it called?"

"Club Marquette."

"I've never heard of it before."

He opened the car door for her. "Well, considering how you never got to go anywhere, that's not surprising."

When they pulled into the parking lot, Amber was amazed at the size of the club. "It's huge," she said incredulously, her eyes wide as she tried to take it all in.

"They have different bars with different kinds of music playing in each one. What type of music do you like?"

"Well, what are my choices?"

"Everything."

Amber thought for a moment. "Let's start off fast and finish slow."

"So we'll start off with some rock and roll and make our way to light music," he said as he put his arm around her. "Then we can slow dance."

"Sounds like the perfect ending to a perfect evening." She looked up at him, her eyes filled with stars. "Tim, are you a good dancer?"

"I manage not to look like an idiot, but that's about it. I guess I'm okay. You're not still worried, are you?"

"I'm a little nervous," Amber admitted. "I used to be a pretty good dancer, but I don't know anymore."

"You'll be fine. You know the old saying. It's like riding a bicycle; you never forget how to do it. Come on, let's go enjoy ourselves. We can start off with a drink and then work our way into dancing."

They headed into the club. After their first drink, they decided it was time to dance. The first song they danced to, they were both a little stiff. They decided to loosen up a little by having a few more drinks and talking. They found a table away from the dance floor where they could hear each other talk but see all the action. When they both started tapping their toes and snapping their fingers, they decided they were ready.

Tim led her onto the dance floor. Colorful lights twisted and turned everywhere they looked. There were people of all different ages. The atmosphere was very happy and energetic. Tim led the way to the middle of the dance floor. When they began to dance, it was like magic. They fit perfectly.

"Tim, you are a very good dancer. Better than most," Amber said.

"Thank you."

"Here all this time I thought you couldn't dance, but you are the best dancer out here."

People near them started to notice this handsome couple, dancing up a storm. It didn't take long for Tim and Amber to realize that everyone had circled around them, clapping to the music and cheering them on. When the song ended, everyone applauded. Amber and Tim smiled, bowed quickly, and left the dance floor.

Amber was out of breath when she sat down at their table. "Oh my God, I can't believe how they surrounded us! Nothing like that has ever happened to me."

"Me neither," replied Tim.

Amber turned to him, still catching her breath. "Tim, this has been the best day of my life. I never knew how much fun I'd been missing out on."

"Amber, don't worry. I'll show you everything." He took her hand. "Would you like to go to one of the other bars for some slow dancing?"

"Sure, that sounds great."

As they left the crowded bar, Tim tightly gripped Amber's hand and led her out. When they got to the entryway, Tim didn't let go of her hand. He held onto her as if it was the last time he would ever be able to hold her hand. They talked as they walked to the next bar, but Amber's mind was filled with thoughts of Tim. She wished this night would never end. She felt like a princess.

When they reached the next place, they looked at each other admiringly, and then entered. Amber felt butterflies in her stomach and that same tingling feeling she had felt before. They found a table in a dimly lit area, ordered a drink, and waited for the next song.

When the next song began, Amber jumped up. "This song is my favorite! Let's go dance."

Tim agreed and they headed out onto the dance floor. At first, it was a little awkward. They looked at each other, then moved slowly together, staring into each other's eyes. Once they began to dance, there was no more awkwardness. Amber laid her head on Tim's shoulder, and Tim held onto her snuggly. She had never been held like that before. She knew she wanted to be held like that again, but only by Tim.

When the song ended, she looked up at Tim with her beautiful, glowing eyes and thanked him. She noticed that Tim seemed to be enjoying himself also. As the next song began, they stayed out there. In fact, they danced to several songs without leaving the floor once. Then the song "Unchained Melody" started to play and something felt different. As they beamed into each other's eyes, there was a mutual feeling. They both knew it.

It was then that Tim asked, "May I kiss you?"

Amber moaned softly, "Please do."

He bent down and looked in her eyes. He took her beautiful face in his own strong hands, and ever so softly and gently, their lips became one. Their lips begged for each other. When his tongue met hers, Amber's tongue gladly accepted, and she let out a little moan of satisfaction.

Amber opened her eyes. She saw that his were dark and smoldering. She felt a deep tingling that she could not explain, for she had never felt anything like that before.

Tim whispered, "Would you like to go home now?"

"Yes, I would," she said suggestively.

When they got into the car, Amber scooted all the way over next to Tim. "Do you mind if I sit here?"

"Not at all. In fact, I want you to." They smiled at each other.

On the way home, they talked about what a wonderful, perfect night it had been. By the time they pulled into the driveway, they both agreed it had been a very long day, and that it was almost time for bed. Amber made some coffee and brought each of them out a steaming mug.

"Tim, thank you so much for everything," she said for what seemed like the hundredth time. "This evening was perfect."

"You're welcome. But I also would like to thank you for the best night of my life," he said, snuggling closer to her on the couch. "You make things new and exciting for me."

"Surely you've had many fun times, even more exciting than tonight. A handsome, warm, friendly man like you should have no problems meeting women."

"It's not that I have problems, it's just that I've been waiting for the right woman to come along. Someone . . ." He paused, gathering his courage. "Someone . . . like you."

"Like *me*?" Amber asked in disbelief. "Compared to you, I'm just damaged goods."

He took her face in his hands, staring intensely into her eyes. "Don't ever say that again. You're not damaged goods. You are perfect. A beautiful, loving, caring, and strong woman. That's what you are," he said, biting his lower lip, "and that's what I want."

"You . . . want me?" Amber could hardly believe her ears.

"That's an understatement." He was silent for a moment, gathering his thoughts. "I'm not yet able to put into words the way I feel about you. Do you feel the same about me?"

"Yes," Amber sighed, relieved to be able to say finally what had been on her mind for so long. "I can't stop thinking about you. Ever since I met you, I knew there was something different; you're like no one I have ever met before. With you, everything is exciting and new."

He took her hands and kissed them impulsively. "Nor can I get you off my mind. But I think we should take things slow. You've been through a lot, and I don't want to move too fast. I think you need time to heal."

"I understand your concern. I agree that we should move slow." She breathed deeply and put her head on his shoulder. "Right now, I'm more concerned about what you'll think about me after the trial is over."

"Amber, please don't worry about that," he said, stroking her hair gently. "It's going to be alright."

"Okay, I won't." Amber thought again about the evening, and how wonderful it had been. She knew that, despite the fact that she had said she wouldn't, she couldn't help but worry. *He will not be able to look at me the same after he's done hearing what is said in court. I guess only time will tell. As Dr. Dahl would say, one day at a time.*

Tim got up and poured them each another cup of coffee. "Amber, are you okay?"

"Yes, I'm fine. I was just daydreaming, that's all."

"You must be drained from today's events."

She took a long drink from her mug. "I am."

"You want to call it a night?"

Amber looked into his eyes. "I think I'll have to, or pretty soon I won't be able to keep my eyes open."

Tim and Amber gazed into each other's eyes. Tim leaned toward Amber, and as he began to touch her, she felt that same tingling feeling, but this time she wanted more. The look in his eyes was a look of sheer lust. She knew he wanted her and wanted her right now. Their mouths met and their tongues began to dance in delight. She couldn't tell whose heart was pounding the hardest, his or hers. Their breathing became heavier as his tongue darted in and out of her mouth ever so seductively. She thought that she might lose control. She probed his hard, masculine body with both hands.

He began kissing and gently sucking her neck, and then he whispered,

"You are so beautiful and sexy."

Amber noticed his manhood protruding, and she let out a moan. She had a warm, tingling sensation in all the right places. As he stroked and kissed her, she felt herself losing control, and she moaned, "Take me, take me, I'm yours."

"Amber," he managed to breathe out, "we should . . . slow down." He was breathing heavily. "I want you too, but maybe it's too soon. I don't know. It just feels so right, so perfect."

"That's because it is right, and so perfect."

She leaned forward and he took her in his arms. He looked into her eyes as if searching for the right answer and found it. She was right there in front of him. They both knew the answer.

He succumbed to the question that was troubling him and again kissed her ragingly. They moved upstairs toward the bedroom. He led her with his body, and she had no problems following. Their bodies tangled deliciously as they slowly undressed each other. They left a trail of clothing all the way to Amber's bedroom.

Tim gently laid Amber down on the bed, and again his tongue found hers. He ran his hands up and down her naked body. She could not keep her hands off of him; his muscles protruded from his body. Oh, how she ached for him.

He began to gently suck on her neck, then slowly moved downward. He breathed harder and harder as he kissed and licked her breasts and stomach. Amber moaned soft, quiet moans of delight. There was sheer lust in the air.

He reached the small of her abdomen, then stopped. He looked up at Amber, his eyes smoldering lustfully. Amber tingled everywhere. He slowly went between her thighs. Amber let out a loud moan. "Oh Tim," she cried. The way he touched her was like nothing she had ever felt before. Amber's hips began to thrust with passion as she gasped wildly. She let out one last moan, and she was in ecstasy. Her back arched, her hips bucked, and then she shuddered everywhere.

Tim slowly made his way up and laid next to her, continuing to stroke her gently. Amber rolled onto her side, Tim onto his back. She looked at him excitedly. Wildness was in the air. She touched his hard body, running her fingertips up and down his torso. With every touch, she could feel his body respond. She moved her lips and tongue about his body, passionately licking and nibbling. His breathing grew more intense, more rapid the lower she went. She reached his abdomen, her breasts rubbing against his manhood, her hands still up by his face. He began to suck each of her fingers. She moved just a little lower, took him into her mouth, and he let out a loud moan. His body at first tensed, then gave into the deep, sensuous feeling.

Amber rubbed his thighs as she worked her mouth over his manhood, her back arched. Before long, his phallus pulsated with an explosion. He moaned for Amber as his hips bucked uncontrollably.

He pulled her to him. She lay her head on his chest. He stroked her hair. They lay there silently for a few luxurious moments. Then he rolled over on top of Amber, and began to kiss her.

He slowly began to penetrate her, his phallus as hard as the first time. "Oh Amber," he moaned out. He hadn't yet entered her all the way, just moved the tip slowly in and out at first, holding her tightly. He buried his face in her neck and let out a cry as he entered her all the way in one big thrust. "Tim," she moaned. Their hips thrust back and forth, as they gasped and cried out for each other until finally, with one last thrust, they both moaned loudly and shook together.

They lay there holding each other. He gazed into Amber's eyes lovingly. "Amber, I've been trying to tell you for a while now, but I love you with all my heart. You are the woman I have been waiting for my whole life. You asked me why I haven't gotten married yet; well, you're the reason why. I've been waiting for you."

"Oh Tim, how I longed to hear those words!" she exclaimed, laying her leg over his. "I too have been holding back my feelings for you. I love you; you fulfill my life and give it reason. You have made me the happiest woman alive. I only regret that I didn't meet you years ago."

"And you have made me the happiest man alive." They kissed tenderly, and before too long, they were both sleeping peacefully in each other's arms.

By the next morning, things had cooled down. They ate breakfast and talked about the night before and how wonderful it had been. Their eyes locked many times, but they knew they must get ready for work, so they could have no repeats of the night before, at least not right then. They were both all smiles, each glowing in their own right.

Tim dropped Amber off at the café on his way to work.

Chapter Twenty-Eight

"Good morning, Carol. How are you this morning?" Amber asked brightly as she walked into the café.

"Great, thank you," Carol said, looking up to study Amber's face for a moment. "You look pretty happy this morning, so I guess I don't need to ask how you're doing. Why so happy? You're positively glowing!"

Amber gave Carol a knowing glance. Then she related to Carol her visit to see Jim in jail and everything that was said.

Carol pushed the button on the coffee machine; it spurted and bubbled brown brew. "Amber, that's a big step for you. I can't believe he didn't say anything. That's hard to believe."

"I know it is," Amber said as she tied on her apron. "But, like I was telling Tim, I bet you he's pretty mad by now."

Carol squinted at Amber, examining her expression. "Amber, I can tell there's something you haven't told me. What is it? There's another reason why you're so happy," she said, sitting at the counter, propping her chin up with her hand. "Spill the beans."

"Well . . . Tim and I decided to go out and celebrate, and—" Amber began.

"And . . . and what? Tell me."

"Let's just say we hit it off."

"No, you and Tim?"

"Yes."

"Details, give me the details." Carol demanded, leaning forward intently.

"We went out to eat and went dancing. He's a great dancer. Can you believe we cleared the floor? I had the time of my life." She sat next to Carol.

"Tell me the rest."

"He kissed me. Believe me, he knows how to kiss."

"Tell me more," Carol said, her eyes wide.

"Let's just say it was a very romantic evening. He told me he loves me; I told him I love him. I'm so happy! He's the man of my dreams. Carol, I'm so happy you and Chuck introduced us. Thank you," Amber said, her words tumbling out in a rush.

"Oh my God! He professed his love for you? And you for him?"

"Yep. I'm in heaven."

She hugged Amber, squeezing her tightly. "I'm so happy for you two. I won't ask what else happened," she said with a knowing glance. "I can't wait to tell Chuck."

"Do me a favor and thank him for me."

"I definitely will. Amber, you have chosen the right kind of man, just like you said you would. I'm so proud of you."

"For the first time in my life . . ." Amber began, looking out of the window dreamily, "I know everything is going to be okay."

"Oh honey, I'm just so happy for you," Carol said, wiping the counter. "Now I understand the glow. By the way, Sue said she could come in at noon today to cover the rest of your shift so you can go see Dr. Dahl."

"Great. By the way, I love the new girls. You did a great job hiring them."

Carol smiled in agreement as the door opened. "First customer," she said. "We better get to work."

Time flew by, and before Amber knew it, it was noon and Sue was there. "Hello, Sue. Thanks for coming in for me; I appreciate it. I owe you for this one."

"Okay, I'll remember that," Sue said with a smile.

"I bet you will. See you guys later," Amber said as she opened the café door and stepped into the bright sunlight outside.

As she stood on the corner in front of the café, memories of that day came back, more vivid than ever. It was as if it were just yesterday that Dan had kidnapped her. She started to panic. She looked around frantically to make sure she was safe. Carol, watching from the window, saw Amber's face and came out to check on her.

"Amber, what's wrong?"

Amber's hands instinctively went to her neck. "Oh Carol, thank God it's you. I was afraid something was going to happen to me."

Carol put her arm around her protectively. "Amber, you're okay. I was watching you from the window the whole time. Why don't I call Tim? Maybe he can come pick you up and bring you to your appointment."

"The bus will be here any minute."

"Amber, I don't think you should take the bus. I'm calling Tim. Come in and wait for him."

"Okay, maybe you're right," she said, her voice still sounding unsure. "I just don't want to bother him at work."

Carol took her hand and led her back into the café. "He'd be more upset if we didn't call. Here, have a seat. I'll get you a cup of coffee and go call Tim."

"Carol, you're the best friend ever."

"I know." They both started to laugh.

Tim arrived within fifteen minutes. He came in, went up to Amber, and hugged her tightly. "Are you alright?"

"Yes, just a little embarrassed."

"You have no reason to be embarrassed," he said, pulling back to look into her eyes. "Come on, let's go. I'll bring you to your appointment, then I'll wait until you're finished, and we can head home. I got the rest of the day off."

"I don't want you going and getting in trouble over me."

He grabbed her hands and squeezed them. "I'm not in trouble. They know everything you've been through, and they understand. In fact, they're the ones who told me to take the rest of the day off."

"Are you sure?" she asked uncertainly.

"Yes," he said, opening the door for her.

Chapter Twenty-Nine

When Amber arrived at Dr. Dahl's office, her palms were clammy and her hands shook. Her face was drained of all color.

"Amber," Dr. Dahl said when she saw her, "you look shaken up. Are you okay?"

"Yes, I'm fine. I just got a little scared waiting for the bus. I thought maybe Jim might have hired someone else to kill me," Amber said, sitting down in the recliner in Dr. Dahl's office.

"Amber, I think, for the time being, you shouldn't be by yourself until you feel secure enough," Dr. Dahl said, tapping her pen on her notebook.

Amber fidgeted with her hands. "I think that's a good idea."

"How are you getting home when you leave here?"

"Tim came and picked me up, and he's going to take me home. He took the rest of the day off to be with me."

"Good. He's such a nice man. So tell me, how did it go with Jim?"

Amber smiled and pulled her thick hair back, off her face. "Excellent. You should have been there. You would have been proud of me. For the first time in my life with Jim, he didn't say a word. I did all the talking. You know, he actually thought I was there to help him."

"I don't doubt that," Dr. Dahl said, shaking her head. "He's a sick man. He thinks you depend on him. He has no idea how strong you have become."

"Going to talk to him made me feel free again."

"Well, good. I'm glad to hear that. What about the nightmares?"

"They're gone. So far so good."

Dr. Dahl made a note on her pad. "I'm glad to hear that."

"I also wanted to tell you about Tim."

"What about him?"

"I really care about him. A lot. He's so charming, handsome, kind, and caring. He's really a wonderful man. In fact, I'm crazy about him. I've never met anyone like him before. We are so compatible. We're in love. But don't worry, we're taking things slow." Amber's voice became dreamy and she had stars in her eyes as she talked.

Dr. Dahl made a few quick notes on her pad. "Good," she said, looking up at Amber. "I'm happy to hear you're choosing the right kind of man. You're breaking the cycle." She paused contemplatively. "I do worry, because it is so soon, but you have come a long way in your therapy."

"I know, and I feel great about it. For the first time in my life, I know things are going to be good. My thoughts are very clear; I now know I can make the right decisions."

"I believe you're right, and I have a lot of faith in you. Amber, I'm glad you shared that with me. Thank you."

"No, thank *you* for everything. You have helped me out tremendously. You taught me how to think things through, and I appreciate that. You're a wonderful psychiatrist," Amber said, smiling genuinely at Dr. Dahl.

"Thank you, Amber. You're very lucky. Most women search their whole lives for a man like Tim, never to find him. You got him. You've been through the worst, and you deserve the best. And remember, as lucky as you are to have him, he's even luckier to be with you."

"You think so?"

"I *know* so," Dr. Dahl said, leaning forward on her desk with her elbows. "Amber, he sees what a wonderful woman you are. He knows what's inside of you. Between me and you, I don't think he'll ever let you go."

Amber's bright smile turned quickly to a frown. "I hope you're right, especially after he hears everything in court."

"Amber, he knows the real you. He also knows you were fighting to survive, so relax, it will all turn out."

When Amber and Tim got home, the phone was ringing. Tim ran to answer it. Amber followed behind. As Tim listened to whomever was on the line, Amber started to feel very concerned. It looked as though something was terribly wrong. Tim's face had turned pale. His eyes filled with redness. The color slowly started to creep back into his face and he turned red with rage, his jaw clenched.

When he got off the phone, he stood there for a brief moment. "Amber, we need to talk. Let's go into the other room." He led her quickly to the couch.

"What's wrong, Tim? What's going on?"

Tim grabbed her hand. "When you left work today, Sue answered the phone. It was Jim."

"Oh my God, what did he say?" Amber asked, fear flooding her brain.

"He said to tell you that you haven't won yet, and that no matter what it takes, somehow, he's going to kill you. He said, 'She thinks she can come here and talk to me however she wants? Well, she's wrong. And, for as long as I am alive, she better look over her shoulder, because I will find a way to get her. In the end, I will have won. Tell her she's a goner. I will make sure she is tortured. It will be a slow, painful death, you tell her that. You tell her everything.' Then Sue hung up on him."

"Oh no! What have I done? You guys were right. I shouldn't have talked to him. He will find a way to make sure I'm dead." Amber nervously fidgeted in her seat, her face pale. Her thoughts raced through her head rapidly; she couldn't slow them down.

"No, Amber," Tim said, wrapping his arms around her. "Whether or not you went there, he was going to try to find a way to kill you. At least you got to say what you wanted to say to him for years. Amber, I'm going take another leave of absence at work."

"You can't do that, Tim. I don't want you to get into trouble, or worse, get fired."

"Amber, that won't ever happen, and if it did, it doesn't matter. I . . . I just want to protect you, and that's what I'm going to do."

"Oh Tim." Amber began to cry, and she dropped her head onto Tim's chest as he held her tighter.

"Amber, you're not going to die," Tim said, kissing the top of her head. "I'm going to see to it that you are safe. Amber, I would risk my life to save yours. I love you."

"I love you too," she said, her voice muffled in his shirt. "But I don't want you to risk your life for me."

"I know you don't, but I can't live without you in my life. I *need* to protect you, Amber. Can't you understand that?"

"I understand exactly what you're saying."

"Nothing is going to happen to you." He held her tightly in silence for a few minutes. "Amber, I know you don't like guns, but you at least have to know how to use one, just in case."

"Alright. If you think it's necessary, I will do it."

"I think it's absolutely necessary. Honey, instead of you going to Dr. Dahl's office for your appointments, we need to see if she will come here."

"You're right. I'll call her right now and tell her what's going on." Amber got up and made her phone call while Tim stood behind her. When Amber got off the phone, she exhaled in relief. "She said she could make me her last appointment of the day and swing by on her way home."

He put his arms around her. "That's so nice of her to do that for you. Amber, I'll also ask Chuck and Carol if one of them would come over when I have an appointment or need to go grocery shopping. I'm sure it won't be a problem."

Amber sat down and sighed deeply. She stared at her hands for a moment, then looked up and her eyes met Tim's. They looked quietly into each other's eyes for a moment, and then Amber spoke. "All you guys are so wonderful to me; you are truly the best friends I have ever had."

"Amber, you would do the same for any of us."

"I would, but I don't want to put any of you in danger."

"It's okay, Amber." He knelt in front of her and put his hands on her thighs. "Everything will be fine. It will all work out in the end." He exhaled audibly, smiled at Amber, and leaned his head onto her chest.

She placed both hands on his head and raked her fingers through his thick hair. "I hope you're right."

"I am, don't worry. By the way, Chuck and Carol are coming over later for dinner. We're having baked salmon. I hope you like salmon."

"I do. That sounds delicious. I love any kind of seafood."

Tim reached up and in one fluid motion took both her hands in his as he leaned back onto his heels and stood. "Amber, why don't you go lie down for awhile and get some rest? I can start to prepare for dinner." He pulled her to her feet and wrapped his arms around her.

"I can stay up and help," she said into his shoulder.

"Amber, you've got to be emotionally drained. The best thing you can do is get some rest."

"I'll be okay. Besides, you can give me a couple of tips in the kitchen, since my cooking is a bit lackluster."

"Honey," he said, putting a hand on either side of her face and softly stroking her creamy skin, "I really think you should get some rest. We're having company over tonight."

"If you insist," she murmured, hypnotized by the golden flecks in his green eyes.

"I will be right up to tuck you in." He kissed her gently on the forehead.

Tim entered the bedroom as Amber was just climbing into bed. "Amber, I'm sorry things keep happening to you, but I do know you will be okay." He sat on the edge of the bed and straightened the blankets around her.

"With you protecting me I know I will be fine," she said, settling back into the pillow.

"I'm glad you let Carol call me when you started to panic at the bus stop today. I'm always happy to help you. I hope you know all you have to do is call and I will be there for you, no matter what."

"I know. I was embarrassed about panicking, though."

He stroked her hair lovingly. "Amber, after what happened at that bus stop, you weren't behaving ridiculously at all. Anyone in your situation would have acted the same way."

"Thank you, Tim, for making me feel so normal about my thoughts and feelings." She paused, looking up at him, her eyes becoming droopy with sleep. "Tim, are you sure your work is okay with you taking a leave of absence?"

"Don't worry about it. I've been there long enough that I can get away with stuff like that. Before I met you, I almost never took any time off, so they're very understanding."

"Good. That makes me feel better."

"Well, I better let you get some rest." He pulled up the blankets, kissed Amber's forehead, and gave her a hug. They looked into each other's eyes, remembering the night before. Tim bent down and gave Amber a long, slow kiss.

After Tim left, Amber couldn't help but smile. *He makes my heart flutter*, she thought. All her troubles seemed to fade away when he kissed her. *Amber Lundquist. Doesn't that sound nice? Yes, his last name fits well,* she thought. *But I shouldn't let my imagination run away with me. He gives me a kiss like that and expects me to fall asleep.* About thirty minutes later, Amber finally drifted off to sleep.

Chapter Thirty

Two hours later, Tim woke Amber. He shook her gently and she sat up with a gasp, startled from a nightmare.

"Amber," he said, concern creasing his forehead, "you're all sweaty. Did you have a nightmare?"

"Yes," she panted, her eyes still filled with fear.

"About Jim?"

"Yes."

He rubbed her back in a soft, circular motion. "Are you okay?"

"Now that I'm awake." She pressed the heels of her hands into her eyes. "How long have I been sleeping?"

"Two hours. Chuck and Carol are here now," he said gently.

"Okay. Let me freshen up and I'll be down."

"Are you sure you're okay?"

Amber got out of bed and stretched. "I'm just fine," she said, moving toward her bathroom. "Really, it's okay, Tim." She paused at the door and looked at Tim with a smile. "You can go downstairs."

"There's our girl," said Carol, smiling broadly as Amber descended the staircase a few minutes later. "Are you feeling better?" she asked, walking over to give her friend a hug.

"Yes, I am. And thanks for earlier."

"It's time to eat," Tim said, holding up a hand donning an oven mitt as if for proof.

They all headed to the dining room. Chuck and Carol sat on one side of the table, Amber and Tim on the other.

"Amber," Tim began, "we've all been talking about Jim's phone call today. We want to know if you are comfortable with the plans we made. We realized that we never even asked you what you wanted. Is there something else you want, or do you want things set up differently?"

"No, everything is fine," Amber said, putting her hand on top of Tim's. "The only question I have is, what if I want to get out of the house?"

"If you really want to get out, we can, but Chuck and Carol will have to come along. We need the extra backup," he said as he gave her hand a firm squeeze.

"That's alright with me. Otherwise, I understand why you set things up like this, and I appreciate it. It just shows me how much you love and care about me," she said with a smile. They all smiled brightly back at her.

They made small talk for the rest of the meal. When everyone was finished, Tim stood and gathered up the plates. "Amber and I can clean up," he said, walking into the kitchen. "It's getting late." Everyone nodded in agreement.

"Tim, dinner was wonderful," Carol said, putting on her coat. "You guys make sure you lock up after we leave."

"Thanks for coming," Amber said as they saw their guests to the door.

Tim shut the door and turned to his beloved. "Amber, I'm exhausted. It's been a long day."

"Yeah, I know. I had a long nap but I'm pretty tired myself."

"We can clean up in the morning. Why don't we get ourselves to bed?" Tim asked, leading her toward the staircase. As they walked upstairs, Tim took Amber's hand and walked her to her room to tuck her in.

"Just a minute," Amber said, going into the bathroom. "I need to get ready for bed. I'll be right out."

A few minutes later, Amber came out in a cute little nightgown.

"You look too beautiful for bed," he said, his eyes gleaming.

"Thank you." Amber climbed into bed, and Tim covered her up. He could not take his eyes off of her.

"Amber, do you mind if I lie with you for a minute?"

"Not at all."

He got under the covers and lay on his side. Amber turned to face him. They wrapped their arms around each other and stared into each other's eyes.

"Are you going to be able to sleep by yourself tonight?"

"I don't know, we'll see. It depends on if I have a nightmare or not."

"Well, I'll make sure to listen for you," he said, stroking her hair.

"Okay. If I have a bad dream, will you come in and lie with me?"

"Of course. Amber, I worry about you all the time. How much can one person go through?"

"I don't know. I just want this to end." She paused to collect her thoughts. "I knew Jim was a dangerous person, but I never thought he would be so vindictive. You know what I keep thinking?"

"What's that?"

"When he said, 'If I can't have you, nobody will.' That just keeps going through my mind. He can't stand the thought of me being happy. He's always made sure that I was unhappy, and now that he's lost control, he's gone even crazier."

"Yeah," Tim agreed, nodding solemnly. "He thinks that the way he feels about you is love. It's not, though. It's an obsession. When he lost control of you, that just put him over the edge."

"I think you're right. Tim, I'm so appreciative of everything you have done for me. I feel so lucky. You took me from a very bad situation and treated me better than I've ever been treated before. I feel like a princess when I'm with you. I feel as if I'm in a dream, and if someone were to pinch me, I'd wake up," Amber said. Tim pinched her playfully. "Ouch, you pinched me."

"I know. I was just showing you that you weren't dreaming."

They both began to laugh. Then they began tickling each other. They laughed so hard they finally had to stop. "I feel much better now," Amber said, gasping for air.

"Good. So do I." He slid out of bed. "I should let you go to sleep."

"I suppose. Goodnight."

"Goodnight, my princess." Tim gave her a kiss and went off to bed.

Chapter Thirty-One

It was three o'clock in the morning when Tim woke up to Amber screaming. He ran to her room, turned on the lights, and hugged her tightly.

"Shh . . . shh. It's okay," he said, rocking her gently. "It was just a bad dream. Damn him, he even invades your dreams." Amber's cry turned into a soft whimper.

"Tim . . . he killed me . . . he found me and killed me," she sobbed.

"Honey, that was just a bad dream." He held her more tightly. "He's not going to hurt you. I'm here to protect you. Besides, he's in jail; he can't hurt you anymore."

"What if he hires someone like he said he would do?" Amber asked, her hands covering her face.

"He won't find anyone to do it."

"You're right," she said, taking a deep breath and looking up at Tim. "I'm thinking irrationally."

"No, you're not. You've been through a lot, that's all."

"Could you please sleep with me tonight?"

"Of course. Let me get you a cool washcloth. You're really sweating," he said, disappearing into the bathroom for a moment. "Here you go." He gently swabbed her face.

"Thank you. That feels good," Amber said, calming down.

"Amber," he said, putting his arm around her, "this may not be the best time to tell you this, but Jim put the house on the market."

"Can he sell it while he's in jail?"

"He sure can. Are you going to try to get some of the money after it sells?"

"No. I want nothing to do with it. Besides, I would have to fight him for it. The house is in his name."

"Well, that doesn't matter. You could get half of everything."

"He made sure everything was in his name, so that I would never benefit from anything."

"Sounds like him," Tim said, shaking his head. "What a jerk."

"You got that right. Tim, let me think about it. I'm not sure I want to go through any more trouble than I already have. Do you understand?"

He kissed her on the forehead. "Yes, I sure do. It's up to you, but I do have plenty of money, so if money is an issue for you, don't worry about it."

"I know, but I wouldn't feel comfortable spending your money. It just doesn't seem right."

"It may not be okay with you, but it is with me. I was going to talk to you later about this, but I guess now is as good a time as any. Amber, I've been thinking about you a lot—all the time, actually—and I really enjoy having you here with me. I enjoy every minute we're together. You never bore me. I know in the beginning we talked about you living here temporarily, but I have to say that I would really like it if you would stay here longer than that."

"How long were you thinking? After court is done?"

He bit his bottom lip and smiled shyly. "I'm thinking however long you would like, and if that's permanently, well, that's just fine with me."

"But won't I be intruding on your privacy?"

"Privacy? I don't want privacy from you. In fact, I want you to know everything there is to know about me. I want to share my life with you. I know that's a lot to take in, so I will give you time to think about it. You can let me know what you come up with. Of course, you'll have to put up with my obsessive cleaning habits." They both started to laugh.

"How much time do I have?"

"As much time as you need."

"Good, because I'm ready to give you my answer now." She paused and looked into his eyes for a moment. "Tim, you shocked me. I wasn't expecting that. I figured you were too good to be true."

He took her face into his hands. "That's how I feel about you."

"Well, I'm glad the feeling is mutual."

"So what's your answer?"

"Tim, I would love to stay and share my life with you. I'd love to learn all I can about you, and I'd like to share my thoughts and feelings with you as well. The answer is yes. I will stay with you." She pressed her forehead to his and closed her eyes.

"Great! That's settled then." He kissed her softly on the lips. "Whew, that was a lot to get off my chest."

"Were you worried I would say no?"

"I wasn't sure."

She snuggled closer to him. "I would be nuts if I said no. I've been thinking lately about having to find my own place. I didn't know what I was going to do not being with you every day. It made me feel horribly sad."

"I was thinking the same things. Oh Amber, I love you so much."

"I love you too. And from now on, if either of us have something to say, we just need to come out and say it," she said, nuzzling his neck.

"You've got yourself a deal. Amber, I was thinking about what you said about being with Jim. I can't believe you were with him for that long. And you even dated him a year before marrying him. It just makes you think. You can be with someone for that long and not even know that he's like that."

"I know. Carol was shocked about that too. She couldn't believe he changed that much after I married him," she said, rolling onto her back and looking up at the ceiling. "You know, he let me keep my friends at first. He seemed to like them as much as my friends liked him."

"Is that where you learned how to dance?"

"Well, not from Jim, but we used to go dancing all the time, and before I met him I used to go out dancing with my friends a lot. One guy in particular that I dated, we used to dance pretty often."

"What happened to him?"

"He became very obsessive and controlling. I've never had a normal, healthy relationship, besides ours." She pursed her lips and thought for a moment. "I think I know why Jim was the way he was. He grew up in a family that was also very dysfunctional. His dad used to treat his mother the same way he treated me. He watched his mother get beaten all the time. In the beginning, I think Jim tried to fight his rage, but he couldn't. He was too angry." She shook her head. "His father used to tell him that the man is to run the house and the woman is to do what she is told. He watched this his whole life." She turned to Tim. "But even though he grew up that way, I don't feel sorry for him. He didn't have to follow in his father's footsteps. He could have gotten help, like he promised he would so many times. He just insisted on always doing things his way."

"You think that's why he was like that?"

Amber shrugged her shoulders. "I don't know. It was all he knew. It became a way of life for him. But then you have other people who grew up in the same kind of household and would never think of being like that."

"Yeah, it's hard to say what the real reason is. But one thing is for sure, he had an anger he couldn't control." Tim was quiet for a moment, mulling over his thoughts. "Maybe it was because of the way he grew up. No matter the reason, I'm just glad he didn't kill you."

"Me too," she said, giving him an Eskimo kiss. "I'm glad we had this talk. But now I think we should go to bed. The sun is coming up already."

Tim and Amber wrapped their arms around each other and kissed goodnight. They were so tired that it didn't take long for the both of them to fall asleep.

♠ Chapter Thirty-Two ♠

The next morning, Amber and Tim awoke to the sound of the phone ringing. Tim fumbled for the receiver and managed a hello.

"Did I wake you?" It was Chuck.

"Yes, but that's alright," Tim responded, yawning. "What's wrong? You sound shook up."

"It's Carol. She's leaving me."

"What?" Tim blurted out, sitting up on one elbow, a look of disbelief on his face.

"She's leaving me," Chuck said, his voice shaking.

"I know what you said, but why?"

"We've been having problems for some time now, but I didn't think she would leave me."

Tim sat on the edge of the bed. "Do you want me to come over there?"

"No. How about if I come over there?"

"That's fine, come on over." He thought for a moment. "Maybe Carol can come along so she can talk to Amber."

"I'll see if she will, but I can't guarantee anything."

"Are you okay to drive?"

"Yes, I'll be fine."

"I'll see you in a bit."

Tim set down the phone and turned to Amber. "You'll never believe it."

Amber's eyes were wide with shock. "I heard. Why is she leaving him?"

"He said they have been having problems for some time now. Has Carol ever said anything to you?"

"No, nothing," Amber said, shaking her head incredulously.

"Neither has Chuck. Those two can't split up. They're perfect for each other."

"Maybe I should call Carol and see if I can talk her into coming over."

"Yeah, why don't you do that?" Tim leaned over and kissed her forehead.

Amber picked up the phone and dialed quickly. Carol answered on the third ring. "Carol, are you okay?"

There was silence for a moment. "No, not really."

"What's going on?"

"I'm leaving Chuck."

"Why?"

"We just don't get along anymore. All we ever do is fight. He works all the time. Whenever he gets an opportunity to work overtime, he takes it. I don't know why. It's like he doesn't want to be here with me anymore. He doesn't work because we need the money." Carol took in a long, shaky breath. "Amber, I think he's having an affair. We don't make love anymore. He barely notices I'm around. He used to be so sweet to me, but now he never has a nice thing to say. I can't live like this anymore."

"Carol, why don't you come over with Chuck? You and I can go to another room and talk."

"No. It's not that I don't want to see you, but this is on him. If he wants this to work out, he needs to start treating me better."

Amber frowned. "What about tomorrow? Can you come over tomorrow?"

"I don't know. I might be the one leaving. I haven't decided yet. Amber, I know this isn't all Chuck's fault. I know I'm not perfect, but I'm also not the one having an affair."

"Carol, just let me know what you're going to do, and remember," she said, cradling the phone with both hands, "I'm here for you if you need me."

"I know that. I'll call you."

"Carol, have you two tried talking about this at all?"

"No. All we ever do is fight."

"Well, maybe you should make an appointment with Dr. Dahl."

"Let me think about it, okay?"

"Okay."

"I'll talk to you later, Amber."

"Okay. I love you, you know?"

"Yeah, I know. I love you too. Bye."

"Bye." Amber hung up the phone and laid back in bed with a sigh.

"What did she say?"

"She said they haven't been getting along, and she thinks Chuck is having an affair."

"What? No way."

"She sounded pretty convinced."

Tim's brow furrowed. "I can't see Chuck doing that," he said, shaking his head.

"Neither can I." She sighed again. "They haven't even talked about this. She said she'll think about going to see Dr. Dahl."

"I hope they do," Tim said as the doorbell rang.

"Should I stay up here?"

Tim got out of bed. "Yeah, I suppose so. He may not feel comfortable talking in front of you. I'll let you know when he's gone."

"Okay. Good luck."

"I need it." He bent down and gave her a soft kiss, then headed down the stairs to talk to Chuck.

"Hi. Come on in," he said, opening the door.

"I'm sorry to bother you like this."

"You're not bothering me at all. That's what friends are for. Come in and sit down. Do you want some coffee?"

"Sure."

Tim walked into the kitchen and started brewing a pot.

"Where's Amber?" Chuck called from the living room.

Tim yelled back, "She's upstairs. We weren't sure if you wanted to talk privately or not." He walked back into the room and handed Chuck a steaming cup. "Here's your coffee."

Chuck took the mug with both hands and inhaled deeply. "Thank you. You know, I would really like it if Amber came down here and joined our conversation."

"I'll go get her." Tim climbed the stairs two at a time to retrieve Amber. When he returned, Amber followed hesitantly behind him.

"Hi Chuck."

"Hello Amber. I hope you don't mind coming down. I just wanted your opinion and maybe some advice on what to do."

"Not a problem. You're both very good friends to me."

Chuck stared morosely into his mug. "Carol told me she might move out."

"Do you know why she doesn't want to be with you anymore?" Amber asked, sitting on a chair near the couch.

"She said it was because we weren't getting along."

"Chuck, you need to be honest with me if you want my opinion."

"I have nothing to hide."

"Okay, well," Amber began slowly, "Carol said that you don't treat her very well anymore, and that . . . sorry to be personal, but you don't make love to her anymore, and that you're having an affair. Is that true?"

"An affair? No way would I have an affair! I love Carol with all my heart."

Amber studied Chuck's face for a moment before continuing. "She said that you work all the time, but you don't really need to because you don't need the money. She thinks you're working just so you can be away from her."

Chuck looked from Amber to Tim and sighed. "I've been planning a second honeymoon because we didn't really get a first honeymoon. She had just started her business at the café and couldn't take time off work. I've been saving money so I could take her away. She's always wanted to go to Jamaica."

"How sweet. You two really need to talk." Amber stood up from the chair and sat next to Chuck on the couch.

"I know. She won't talk to me, though. I've also been saving up for a new wedding ring for her. I know I've been crabby. I've been working way too much, and I haven't been very pleasant to be around. I know I shouldn't take it out on her; it's not her fault. The reason we haven't made love is because I have been so tired. I just don't seem to have energy anymore. I never thought of what this might look like to her, but now that you've told me everything, it makes sense."

Tim frowned pensively. "Chuck, how much more money do you need?"

"Four hundred dollars. I already bought the tickets. I just need four hundred more for the ring."

"How about I loan you four hundred dollars, and you go buy the ring. Amber will call and have Carol come over tomorrow. We'll make a nice romantic dinner for the two of you, and you can give her the tickets and ring and explain everything."

"Do you think she'll come over?" Chuck said, searching their eyes as if they held all the answers.

"Yeah, we can get her to come over," Amber replied sympathetically.

"You guys would do that for me?" Chuck asked, almost in tears.

"Of course," Tim said. "You guys are our best friends. We would do anything for you."

Chuck closed his eyes and took a deep breath. "Thank you for everything."

"You're welcome. Let me go get the money." Tim turned and headed upstairs. He returned looking relieved and handed Chuck an envelope.

"What time should I be here tomorrow?"

"Six o'clock sharp."

"Thanks for everything. You saved my marriage," Chuck said, wiping away a single tear that rolled down his cheek.

"No, we didn't. You did it all on your own."

"See you tomorrow."

Amber and Tim sat silently together on the couch for a few moments. "Now here's the hard part," Amber said finally. "Getting Carol to come over. I better call her back and make sure she comes over tomorrow.

Amber got up and headed into the kitchen. She dialed the number and then stood staring out of the window. "Hello Carol," she said when her friend answered.

"Hi," Carol responded, sadness in her voice.

"Carol, I'm calling to beg you to come over tomorrow. Before you make any decisions, I'd like you to talk to me. Could you please do that for me?" Amber asked urgently.

Carol let out a deep sigh, giving in. "Yes, I will come over. What time?"

"How about five-thirty?"

"That will be fine," Carol responded, her voice monotone.

"Oh yeah, don't eat. We'll have dinner here."

When Amber got off the phone, she went back into the living room and sat down next to Tim. "How did it go?" he asked, taking her hand.

"She sounds so distant and withdrawn. I feel horrible for her. She agreed to come over, so everything is on for tomorrow."

"Good. Don't worry, honey, everything will be fine."

Chapter Thirty-Three

The next day couldn't go by fast enough. Tim and Amber spent a good part of it getting things ready. They wanted everything to look perfect. For the menu, they decided on steak, baked potatoes, fresh asparagus, garlic bread, and salad.

"Amber, when they come in, we'll have them sit down in the dining room in front of the fire," Tim said, his eyes sparkling with excitement.

Amber's face glowed. "I already put the flowers in there, and the wine is chilling."

"We'll give them a little time to talk, serve dinner, and the rest is up to them."

Amber leaned against Tim and said playfully, "Then we can shut the doors and enjoy our *own* meal and wine."

Tim wrapped his arms around her. They stared into each other's eyes. Her lips parted and she began to suck ever so softly on his lower lip, then slowly moved up and kissed both lips. She could feel him breathing heavier as their tongues became one.

He moved his hands up and down her spine and to the nape of her neck while she gently touched his chest; she then slid her hands down and rubbed his engorged phallus. She could feel his heart race even faster as he let out a moan of sheer delight. He moved his hands to her bosom and gently began to touch her erect nipples. Amber let out a little moan and kissed him even more feverishly.

Their bodies begged for more until they both gave in to their heated desires. Tim went to his knees, still kissing and undressing her. He slowly pulled Amber down with him. They voraciously kissed and touched each other. Amber assertively pushed him onto his back as she kneeled over him, their hearts pounding rapidly, their breathing heavy with passion. Amber leaned forward and gently sucked his neck. He let out a lustful moan.

Tim took hold of her voluptuous body and gently set her upon him. As he slowly entered her, they both let out a loud moan. Amber threw back her head and closed her eyes in total rapture. Tim firmly caressed her breasts, then brought down one hand and placed it between her thighs. Amber lost all control; she moved about wildly. It didn't take long before Amber shuttered with ecstasy.

Tim took Amber in his arms and rolled her to her back. He whispered in her ear, "I love you."

"I love you too, Tim."

They intertwined as he slowly and passionately made love to her. Their bodies moved as one. They looked into each other's eyes, one more sultry kiss, and they were both in heaven.

They lay there for what seemed like a lifetime, silently staring into each other's eyes, their bodies still intertwined. It was as if no words could say what they were both feeling, a complete and utter love that neither had ever felt before.

"Honey," Tim whispered softly, "you're truly amazing. I'm so glad our paths crossed. How else could I have gotten the chance to spend my life with you? I love you."

"That's the sweetest thing anyone has ever said to me." Amber rolled onto her side and kissed him. "I love you too." Out of the corner of her eye, she caught a glimpse of the clock. "Oh no! It's five fifteen. We need to get ready."

"Why don't you go do what you need to do, and I'll get the door if you're not ready when Carol gets here."

"Okay." They gave each other one more kiss. Amber grabbed her clothes and hurried upstairs. While Amber freshened up, she heard the doorbell ring.

Amber yelled out, "I'll be right down."

Tim answered the door. "Hi Carol, come in." He gave her a big hug. "Amber will be right down. Go ahead and have a seat."

Carol walked over to the couch and sat down. She looked around nervously.

"Carol," Tim said reassuringly, "everything is going to be fine. I know it may not seem like it right now, but it will be."

"I hope you're right." Carol looked up just as Amber made her way down the staircase.

Amber ran up to Carol and hugged her. "I'm glad you came over! I figured you could use someone to talk to."

"I'm glad you made me come over. I really do need to talk to you," Carol said, her eyes already brimming with tears.

"I'll go get you something to drink. What would you like?" asked Tim.

Amber looked up at Tim, her arm still around Carol. "How about a martini?" she asked as they sank down onto the couch.

"Sure, I'll be right back."

When he came back into the room, Carol was crying. He set the martinis on the coffee table and quietly walked back into the kitchen to finish dinner.

"Carol, everything is going to work out. You'll see," Amber said, still hugging her friend.

"I don't know if it will, Amber," Carol sobbed into her hands. "I love Chuck, but if he had an affair, I could never forgive him."

"You need to talk to Chuck. He loves you so much that I don't think he could do that. I'm sure there's a simple explanation for his behavior, but you need to talk to him. If you don't talk to him, you will never know, and you will regret that for the rest of your life."

"You're right. I do need to see what he has to say."

Just then, there was a knock at the door. Amber got up to get it. It was Chuck.

Carol stood quickly when she saw who was at the door, a look of surprise on her face. "What's going on here? What's he doing here?"

"Carol, sit down for a second and I will explain everything. Tim and I set this up. You two need to talk, you just said so yourself. So we want you to go to the dining room. We'll give you your privacy," Amber said, trying to keep her voice even despite the excitement rising deep within her stomach.

Carol agreed.

"Chuck, what would you like to drink?"

He noticed Carol had a martini, and said, "I'll have what she's having."

Amber and Tim followed them into the dining area. When they walked in, Carol looked around at the beautiful way the table was set, and asked, "What's going on here?"

"You'll see, Carol. Go ahead and have a seat. Chuck will explain everything. For now, we'll leave you alone," Amber said as she closed the dining room door behind her.

Tim made Chuck's drink quickly and knocked on the door. There was silence. He opened the door slowly.

"Here's your drink, Chuck."

"Thank you."

"You guys really need to talk, so you can work things out. Chuck, why don't you start?" Tim asked, then left the room.

"Amber," he said quietly, shutting the door behind him, "they weren't even talking yet."

"Oh no! They need to talk," Amber said, shaking her head.

"Well, I told Chuck to start, so hopefully he will, and then everything will be straightened out. I suppose we better get things ready for dinner."

"Good idea."

"Say, I was hoping we could pick up where we left off a little bit ago, with you in my arms," Tim said with a wide grin.

Amber blushed. "I think that's very possible. I've never felt as excited before as I do with you."

"I feel the same way about you. There is no comparison." He kissed her softly on her forehead. "We'd better quit talking about this before we get ourselves in trouble again."

"Yeah, you're right," Amber said, wrapping her arms around his waist and giving him a squeeze. "Do you think we should bring them a glass of wine?"

"Why don't we bring the glasses and the whole bottle of wine so we don't disturb them?" Tim asked as he walked over to the wine rack to pick out a bottle.

"Yeah, I think we better."

Tim knocked on the door. "I'm just going to bring in some wine," he said as he slowly pushed the door open. He set down the wine and the glasses. "Won't be disturbing you again, sorry," he said, backing out of the room.

He motioned for Amber to come over to the door. They leaned toward it, barely able to pick up on the conversation.

"Carol, honey," Chuck began, "I know that I haven't been real easy to be around, and I've been working a lot, but it has nothing to do with you. And I'm *not* having an affair. I would never do that; I love you too much. You are all I want and all I have ever wanted."

Carol's eyes brimmed with tears. "Then what's going on?"

"It's true I've been working a lot, and I've been very crabby, and I'm sorry for that. But the reason I've been working so much is," he said, looking down and taking both her hands in his, "I've been saving up money to get you something special, something you deserve. The reason why we haven't made love is because I am so exhausted from working so much."

Carol sniffled, "So there is no one else?"

"No, honey, only you. Here, let me do this the right way." He handed her the envelope with the tickets in it. "Open it up."

Carol opened the envelope and looked inside. Her jaw dropped. "Oh my God! That's why you've been working so much."

"Yes. We never got a real honeymoon, and I know you've always wanted to go to Jamaica. I figured we could have a real honeymoon, just you and I." A huge smile lit up Chuck's whole face.

Carol began to cry. "I'm so sorry I thought all those things."

"No, honey, I understand why you would think that. It's just too bad I couldn't figure it out before it got to this point." He gently wiped the tears from her cheeks and then kissed her. "Honey," he said, pulling away, "that's not all I have for you."

"It's not?"

"No. Here you go," he said, placing a maroon velvet box in front of her. "Honey, before you open it I just want to say that I love you, and you're all I really need in my life to be happy. I want to spend the rest of my life with you. When we go to Jamaica, will you marry me again?"

Carol smiled. "Yes, I will."

"Open it up."

She opened the box slowly. Her eyes widened in disbelief. "Oh Chuck, it's beautiful! A wedding ring. I'm so sorry I ever doubted you. You mean the world to me. I love you with all my heart."

"I love you too."

"Thank you for this," she said, slipping the ring on her finger. "this is the best present I have ever gotten."

"You're welcome."

Carol kissed Chuck, then pulled back. "Let's go get Tim and Amber and tell them the news."

"I think that's an excellent idea."

"Tim, Amber!" Carol called out. They opened the door with huge smiles on their faces. "We're getting remarried in Jamaica!"

"Congratulations! We're both so happy for you!" Amber said, rushing into the room to give hugs to Carol and Chuck. "We knew you would work it out."

"Instead of us eating alone tonight, we would really appreciate if you would eat with us," Chuck said.

"Are you sure don't you want to be alone?"

Chuck and Carol smiled at each other. "We'll be alone when we go to Jamaica."

Amber plopped down on a chair and propped her chin with her hand. "When are you going?"

"Next week," Chuck replied.

Carol turned to him, her brow furrowed. "Honey, how can we go next week?"

"I made arrangements with Sue and Joan to work and take care of everything while you're gone," he said, smiling coyly.

She punched him playfully on the arm. "You little devil! I guess you have been up to a lot lately."

Chuck looked up at Tim. "Please come in and eat with us?"

By the time the evening ended, it was very late. Amber and Tim walked Chuck and Carol to the door and headed to bed themselves.

Chapter Thirty-Four

The days passed. Before they knew it, Chuck and Carol had gone to Jamaica, renewed their vows, and come back. Amber and Tim were going a little stir crazy from having to stay inside all the time.

One morning, Amber came downstairs and announced that they had to get out of the house, and today was the day.

"Where would you like to go, Amber? Dinner and a movie?" He walked up and gave her a good morning hug.

"How about if we go to the park for a picnic?" she asked as she gazed into his beautiful, sparkling eyes.

"That's a good idea. We can stop at the deli and get what we need. I'll bring a picnic basket. Should we bring Chuck and Carol for backup?" He turned and headed toward the kitchen.

"I'd rather just have it be the two of us."

"Are you sure, Amber?" He turned back to her, a concerned look on his face.

"Yes, everything will be fine," she said, waving her hand dismissively. "Besides, I have my big, strong, handsome man to protect me." Amber began to laugh as Tim flexed for her.

"Even though we're going to go alone, I want to call them and tell them exactly where we're going and approximately when we'll be back." He turned back toward the kitchen and went to call Chuck and Carol.

"I'll get our things together," Amber called after him.

Tim picked up the phone and began to dial. "Okay, sweetheart."

At that, Amber got the picnic basket, a blanket, and a few other odds and ends. By the time she finished, Tim returned from his phone call with Chuck. "You ready?" Amber asked.

"Yep. I told Chuck we would be home around six o'clock. Does that sound okay with you?"

"Yeah, that will give us a nice, long day in the sun together," Amber said excitedly.

Tim walked toward the mailbox. "Let me get the mail real quick, and then we'll go." He grabbed the mail, leafing quickly through the letters. "Amber, you got a letter from the courthouse. You should come open it."

"Do you think it's about the court date?" Amber asked, swallowing nervously.

"Wouldn't Brenda have called you and told you about that?"

"She's on vacation, so she wouldn't know. She'll be back tomorrow," Amber said vacantly, reaching out slowly for the letter.

Tim put his arm around her. "Maybe we shouldn't look at it right now, at least not before our picnic. I'm sorry, Amber. I didn't know."

"It's okay," she said, smiling at him genuinely. "I knew it was coming up anyway." Amber opened it: August 4, 2004. "That's only a month and a half away."

"Amber, it will be okay, because that's the date he's going away forever."

"I know." She took a deep breath. "It's just all the things that will be revealed that I don't like."

"Amber, no matter what you did in the past, I know you did it to survive, not because you wanted to. It won't change the way I feel about you." He pulled her into his arms to comfort her.

"You know, I still want to go on that picnic," she said defiantly, her chin set. "I'm not going to let him ruin my life anymore."

"That's my girl."

After they stopped at the deli, they headed off to the park. Once there, they found the perfect spot, under a big oak tree. They laid their blanket down, set out the basket, and sat down. They were ready for a long, relaxing day.

They spent the whole day talking and learning everything they could about each other. They watched all the people around them play frisbee and walk their dogs.

"Tim," Amber said, laying back and stretching luxuriously, "we have talked so much about everything today, but the one thing we haven't talked about was family. What are your dreams? Do you ever want to have a family?"

"Actually, I thought I would never end up with one. Sure, I've dated, but they were never right for me. Do you know what I mean?" he asked, twirling a blade of grass between his fingertips.

"Yeah, I guess I do."

"I was waiting for someone special, so I never thought about having a family. I never thought that special person would come along. Then you showed up, and now I have been thinking about having a family. I would love to settle down and have children. What about you, what do you want?"

"I always dreamed about having a family, but as you know, I never chose the right type of man to have a family *with*. But now I feel excited that it could happen for me." Amber dropped back her head to take in the day's sunlight. "So, who's the right person you've been thinking about?"

Tim started to laugh. "Of course I'm still waiting."

Amber glared at him playfully. "Oh, thanks a lot."

"No, seriously, you are my dream woman," he said, leaning back on one elbow and playing with her hair. "Whenever I think about you, I think about having children. I think about having something I thought I would never have, and that's you and a couple of little ones running around the house."

Amber started to cry with happiness. "That's exactly how I feel about you." Amber laid down next to Tim, and he wrapped his muscular arms around her.

Tim wiped her tears away, and when she looked up, a man was running at them. Amber screamed. Tim looked up and got to his feet as fast as he could. In the next second, he realized the man was just going to catch a football.

Tim sat back down. "Amber, relax. They're just playing football. He's not here to harm you." Amber took in a deep breath and they hugged each other until Amber felt safe again. "Would you like to call it a day?"

"I think that's a good idea," Amber said, her heart still racing.

"I've had an excellent day with you, let's end it at that. Let's get our things together." They packed their things up and headed toward the car.

On the way home, Amber said, "That was honestly the best time I've ever had with anyone. We shared so much. It felt wonderful to be able to talk to someone the way we talked today. But that last part scared me to death."

"Yeah, me too. I wasn't expecting that."

"Neither was I."

When they pulled into the driveway, Amber was happy to be home. She felt such a sense of security in Tim's house. They held hands as they walked into the house together.

Tim said, "I have to call Chuck to let him know we're home and okay."

"Yeah. And tomorrow I need to call Brenda and talk to her about the trial. I'm sure there is some preparation we have to go through."

"That's a good idea," Tim said as he closed the door behind them.

Chapter Thirty-Five

The next day, the sun shone through the curtains. It was another beautiful day. Amber got up and headed downstairs to grab some coffee and read the paper.

"Good morning, Amber." Tim stood up and greeted her with a big kiss. "How did you sleep?"

"Actually, I slept very well. How about you?"

"I slept well," he said, pulling out a chair for her.

She sat at the table. "I think it was from all that fresh air we got yesterday."

"You're probably right. Would you like a cup of coffee?"

"How did you know?" Amber asked. "That's exactly what I want."

"You get the coffee, and I'll get the paper," Tim said, walking toward the front door.

When Tim returned, he looked flabbergasted.

"What's wrong?" Amber asked as she handed him his mug of coffee.

"I can't believe this! What happened to you is in the paper. They even have your trial date in here," Tim said, collapsing into a chair.

"Oh no! Does that mean anyone can come in and watch the trial?" Amber could feel the color leaving her face.

"I'm afraid so." He looked at Amber sympathetically.

"Why did they do that? I don't want everyone knowing what happened to me. It's humiliating," she said in a very quiet voice.

"You have nothing to be ashamed of. If anything, as embarrassing as it is to you, women can learn from your experience." He reached for her hand. "It might help to save another woman's life."

"I never thought of it that way. Tim, like I told you before, there are things that are going to come out at the trial that I'd never want anyone to know, let alone the whole world," Amber said, starting to feel angry.

"Why don't you talk to Brenda and see if it can be a closed courtroom?"

"I'll do that. In fact, I'm going to go call her right now." Amber went to the phone and dialed her office, but no one answered. She left a message, then sat back down at the table with Tim. "She's not in yet. I hope she calls me right away when she gets in."

"I'm sure she will, honey. Don't worry."

"It's been an hour and she still hasn't called."

"She'll call," Tim said as he closed the paper. "You need to quit pacing the floor. Come sit down and try to relax. Let's talk about something else."

"I can't think of anything else."

He studied her face for a moment. "Why don't you go soak in the tub? Or better yet, sit in the jacuzzi for a while."

"Yeah, maybe that will help relax me." Amber headed upstairs and grabbed her bathrobe and a towel.

When she went to the jacuzzi, Tim was lighting candles. He had even added bubbles. "Would you like a nice glass of wine? Maybe that will help you to relax," he said gently.

"Yeah, that's a good idea. Thank you. You are so good to me."

"Only as good as you are to me. Would you mind if I joined you?"

"No, not at all. In fact, I'd love it."

Amber got undressed and climbed in. She closed her eyes and took several deep breaths to calm herself down.

A few moments later, she heard Tim's voice. "Here's your wine, honey."

"Oh thank you. This is so relaxing."

"I'd like to make a toast," he said as sat on the side of the jacuzzi. "Here's to us, and the beginning of our new life together."

"To us." They both drank. There was romance in the air. They looked into each other's eyes with desire.

"Amber, would you like a massage?"

"That would be nice."

He massaged her back ever so gently, and she started to loosen up a little. He took his time; Amber was enjoying it every bit as much as he was. He leaned down and kissed her neck, and she gave into him.

"Why don't you come in with me?"

He started to slowly undress as he stared passionately into her eyes. She lustfully watched as he took off every last piece of clothing. Her body ached for him. He was so sexy, so beautiful. Never before had she seen a man like this, and never before had she felt like this. His chest was thick with hair, his stomach ribbed with muscles. Everything was built just perfect.

She let out a deep breath. She could tell he was as excited as she was when she looked at his enlarged, stiff phallus. He climbed in behind her and continued to massage her neck and shoulders. He worked his way down her back, touching her not too hard, yet not too soft. He sucked gently on her neck, and she arched her back a little, leaning into his manhood.

He whispered in her ear, "I want you."

She let out a moan and whispered back, "Oh, I need you."

He moved his hands around to the front of her, gently running his fingers over her abdomen and up to her breasts. He massaged her breasts passionately, then took his fingers and firmly rolled her erect nipples back and forth until she let out a gasp. He kept one hand on her breast and moved the other hand down between her legs; he could feel how excited she was by how slippery she felt and the warmth that was generated.

He stroked her until she was gasping and moaning. Then he gently turned her around and placed her on him, entering her. He continued stroking her while they thrust their hips wildly against each other. She arched her body and her head fell back. He thrust even deeper until they both let out a moan and shook with delight. He grabbed her around her back and pulled her toward him and kissed her.

He whispered, "Amber, I love you."

"I love you too."

"Why don't we dry off and go take a nap together? We can cuddle."

"I'm exhausted. Let's do that."

As they lay in bed naked together, Tim couldn't help but run his hands up and down her back; her skin was so silky smooth. Amber laid her head on his chest and ran her fingers through his chest hairs, and they both fell fast asleep.

The ring of the phone awakened them.

Tim reached over and answered it.

"Is Amber there?"

"Yes she is," he said, and handed the phone to Amber.

Amber put the phone to her ear. "Hello?"

It was Brenda. "Hi Amber, I got your message, and I got a notice in the mail with the trial date."

"Did you look at the paper yet today?" Amber nervously wrapped the phone cord around her finger.

"No, why?"

"My story is in there, along with the court date. I don't want people coming to court to hear my case."

"I'm afraid that may be unavoidable. But I can ask the judge if it could be a closed court, due to the extra stress it puts on you."

"Would you please do that?" Amber asked, her voice sounding more hopeful.

"Sure. All we can do is try."

"I wish it wasn't in the paper," Amber said morosely.

"Well, you know reporters. Once they get wind of a story, they take it and run."

"Does that mean reporters are going to want to ask me questions?"

"Probably, but you don't have to answer. In fact, you can tell them that your lawyer won't allow you to discuss the case at this time. You don't have to say anything at all, just ignore them. It's up to you how you want to handle it." Brenda paused. "Amber, let me see what I can do about the closed court and I'll get back to you. But, just so you know, we may have to wait until the day of the hearing to find out."

"Okay, thanks for calling me back. I was feeling a little anxious about the whole thing."

"I can understand that. Amber, we'll have to get together a few times before court just to go over a couple more things."

"Okay," Amber said, sighing. "Just let me know when and I'll be there."

Chapter Thirty-Six

"Carol, I'm glad you came over," Amber said, relief washing over her at the sight of her best friend's face.

"Amber, I can't believe this!" Carol exclaimed. "How long have the reporters been out there?"

"Since the article came out a week ago," Amber said, leading Carol over to the couch.

"That must be driving you crazy."

"In the beginning it did, but now I've gotten used to it, and since we don't go anywhere, they can't question me. When they first showed up, they were knocking at the door, but Tim put a stop to that. Now they just sit out there waiting for us to go somewhere." Amber took a deep breath and crossed her eyes in comic exasperation. "Today will be a little different because Tim needs to go grocery shopping. That is, if Chuck can come over today so he can leave."

"Chuck can come over or, if you would like, you can make out a grocery list and I can go shopping for you." Carol sat down on the couch and grabbed Amber's hand, pulling her down next to her.

"That's a good idea too. Let me go talk to Tim and see what he wants to do. I'll be right back."

Amber stood and walked into the kitchen. "Tim, Carol had a good idea. If you don't want to deal with the reporters, we can make a grocery list and she'll go shopping for us."

Tim thought for a moment. "That's very nice of her, but Chuck's already on his way. Maybe I can end this if I let them know you won't be leaving the house and your attorney told you not to comment. Maybe they'll take the hint."

"That might work. Okay, I'll go tell Carol."

"Tell her thank you anyway." He patted her bottom as she turned and left the room.

Amber turned and smiled. She walked into the living room, sat down next to Carol, and explained Tim's plan.

"That Tim is a smart man," Carol said. "That just might work."

"You know, Carol, having the reporters out there almost makes me feel a little safer. Who in their right mind would try to do anything with a bunch of reporters out there?"

"I can understand how you feel," Carol said, flipping absentmindedly through a magazine. They both looked up when the doorbell rang.

"Oh good," Amber said, "Chuck is here. Would you get the door, Carol?"

"Sure." She set the magazine down, went to open the door, and kissed her husband.

"Hi Chuck. Thanks for coming over," said Amber.

"Not a problem."

"Tim is in the kitchen."

Chuck headed toward the kitchen. "Hey, how's it going?"

"It would be better if I could go out in the yard and do things without the reporters being here," he said as he jotted down a few more things on his grocery list.

"Well, maybe after you give your statement they will leave."

"I hope so, but you know how reporters are."

"Tell me about it," Chuck said, putting his hand reassuringly on Tim's shoulder.

"Chuck, I should only be gone for about an hour or so."

"Take your time. Do whatever else you need to do while you're out."

"Thanks again for everything," Tim said as he stood and put the list in his pocket.

"Don't worry about it." Chuck patted Tim on the back. "You would do the same for me."

"Okay, I'll see you later." He walked into the living room. "Amber, I'm leaving now."

"Okay," Amber said, looking up at him from the couch. "Good luck getting through the mob out there."

"Thanks. I'll need it."

"Tim, I'm sorry about all this."

"It's not your fault." He bent down to kiss Amber goodbye. "I love you," he said softly. "See you in an hour or so."

"I love you too. Bye."

When he stepped outside, the reporters fired all sorts of questions at him. "How's Amber?" "Will she come out and make a statement?" They all talked at the same time until Tim spoke.

"Amber's attorney, Brenda Johnson, has informed us not to talk to the press while the case is pending."

The reporters ignored him, continuing to ask questions, so Tim got in the car and drove off.

Amber sighed pessimistically. "Well, considering they didn't shut up, I don't think that's going to make them leave."

Chuck joined Amber and Carol on the couch. "Amber, I think after a while the crowd out there will get smaller and smaller when they realize that they're not going to get any information."

"You really think so Chuck?"

"Yeah, I'm pretty sure. But you can bet that on August 4, they will be out there again." He shook his head before changing the subject. "So Amber, I see you and Tim are really hitting it off," he said with a huge smile on his face.

"Yes, we are." She returned the smile.

"Did I hear him right when he said he loves you?"

"You sure did."

"That's so romantic," he said, poking her in a teasing way.

"He is so wonderful. I never got a chance to say thank you to you two, but thank you so much for everything you have done," she said, grabbing their hands and shaking them excitedly. "Particularly for finding the man of my dreams."

"You're welcome," they both chimed in.

Amber slapped her thighs with both hands and stood. "Would you guys like some sandwiches for lunch?"

"Sure, that sounds great," Carol said.

They all went into the kitchen, made their own sandwiches, and sat down at the table.

"Amber," Chuck said between bites, "I don't know if this is a good time to bring this up, but Jim's house sold."

"Already?" Amber said, setting down her sandwich and looking shocked.

"Yes, and he made good money off of it. Are you sure you don't want to fight for some of that money?"

"You know it's not worth the stress that I would have to go through."

Chuck nodded. "I can understand that. Anyway, you have nothing to worry about when it comes to money. Tim can take care of you."

"Yeah, I know, but I would like to pay my way a little too."

Chuck took the last bite of his sandwich. "I understand, and in time you will be able to help when things settle down." He paused. "Sounds like Tim is home already."

They came out of the kitchen, and sure enough, it was Tim.

"Let me help you bring in the groceries," Chuck said.

"Okay." Chuck and Tim brought the rest of the groceries in.

"It only took you an hour to get all these groceries?" Chuck asked. "You must be a fast shopper."

"I am when I need to be. I don't want Amber going through all this stress on her own, so I shopped as fast as I could," Tim said as he set to work taking things out of the bags and putting them away.

"You are so sweet," Carol replied. "Amber," she said, looking out of the window, "I don't think the reporters are ready to leave yet."

"It would seem that way," Amber said sadly. "Oh well. Like I was telling Carol, it's like extra security. I don't think anyone would be dumb enough to try anything while they're out there."

"That's the spirit. I never thought of it that way," replied Tim.

"I have to get back to work," Chuck said, heading toward the front door. "Carol, I'll be home around six."

"Okay." Carol crossed the room to kiss him good-bye. "I'll meet you at home then. I'm going to stay here until then and visit with Amber and Tim."

"See you at home," he said as he walked out of the door.

"Tim," Amber said, "I have to call Brenda to see how we're doing on the divorce. I don't know if she got Jim to sign papers yet."

"Good idea. The sooner you're officially divorced, the better it will be for you."

"I agree," Amber said, picking up the phone and dialing Brenda's number. "Hi Brenda. I just wanted to call and see how you were doing on the divorce papers."

"Well, you know I was having trouble getting him to sign the papers, but when I went to see him yesterday, he finally signed them."

Amber smiled at Tim and Carol. "What made him sign them all of a sudden?"

"I'm not sure. Do you want to hear what he had to say about you?"

"It doesn't really matter what he said," Amber said, rolling her eyes for the benefit of her friends. "You can go ahead and tell me, it's okay."

"He said he had been thinking about it for a while, and he doesn't want to be married to a whore. And I told him you are not a whore. I told him I didn't want to hear any more of it and to just sign the papers. So he signed, but he also said a lot more that I don't want to discuss over the phone."

Amber sighed. "Brenda, I need to explain to you about things he used to make me do."

"Well," Brenda said, "we need to get together and go over everything. How about I come over later and we can get you ready for court?"

"I think we better. There are things I have to tell you that no one knows and won't know until court," Amber said, turning from her friends and cradling the phone in both hands. "So, when you come here, if you don't mind, I'd like us to talk up in my room."

"That's not a problem," Brenda assured her. "I'll be over in a little while.

See you later."

"Bye." Amber hung up the phone. "Tim, Brenda will be coming over in a little while so we can discuss the case. I hope you don't mind if we discuss everything privately upstairs. I'm just not ready to tell you yet. It would humiliate me. I hope you understand," she said, taking his hand. "I do love you and trust you, I'm just very embarrassed."

"I understand. I'll know soon enough anyway, and then you can be set free of your past."

"Thanks for being so understanding. I appreciate it. It's one of the reasons I love you so much, because you are so understanding and caring and loving." She reached out and grabbed one of Carol's hands too. "You too," she said to her friend. "You guys are the best."

Chapter Thirty-Seven

A few hours later, Brenda showed up. "I see the reporters are still here," she said as she walked into the foyer.

"Yeah, I don't think they'll ever leave," Amber said, pursing her lips.

"They will, don't worry," Brenda said reassuringly. "They'll get bored of sitting out there and not seeing you. But when we go to court, they'll be waiting for you. You can talk to them when your trial is all over if you want."

Amber nodded thoughtfully. "I probably will make a statement or give a warning to other women out there who are in the same situation I was in."

Brenda turned to Tim who was sitting on the couch. "Hi Tim. How are you?"

Tim stood and walked over to them. "Good, and yourself?"

"Good, thank you," Brenda said with a smile.

Amber grabbed his forearm gently. "Tim, we're going to go upstairs."

"Okay. See you in a little bit," he said softly as he kissed her on her forehead.

When they got settled upstairs, Amber's first question was, "When do I go to court to finalize the divorce?"

"In two weeks. Divorce court is simple. You'll be out of there within a half hour."

"Does Jim have to be there?"

"No, just one party has to show up," Brenda said, leaning over to pat her arm. "Since he's in jail, he won't have to attend. It's not necessary. He already signed the papers."

Amber smiled with relief. "Good."

By the time Amber and Brenda went through everything, two hours had passed.

As Brenda gathered her things up to leave, Amber asked, "Brenda, will he *for sure* get life in prison?"

"He should. He's had three prior drug convictions. He's been arrested for abuse several times, and one of those times, he spent thirty days in jail and was on parole because you ended up in the hospital. Then we have attempted murder, rape, conspiring to kidnap and kill. If he had no priors and nothing violent in his past, he'd probably serve eleven years for each offense. The other possibility is that he could get maximum penalty for each, which would put him away for about sixty years without the possibility of parole. That would make him about ninety-five years old. He would die in prison anyway. Either way, he will be there forever."

"That's good to hear. Brenda, thanks for coming over and going through everything with me." Amber held out her hand, but Brenda leaned forward and hugged her.

"That's what I'm here for. Amber, I can't wait until the verdict is read. He sure put you through hell and back. When this is done, your life will be a lot better."

"I know," Amber said with a smile.

"Well, I have to get going."

"I'll show you to the door," Amber said, walking Brenda downstairs. "Thanks again for coming over. I'll see you in a couple of weeks at court for the divorce."

"It'll be here before you know it."

"Oh, before you leave, did you find out anything on whether we can have a closed court?" Amber asked, her hand on the doorknob.

"Sorry, I forgot to tell you. It's going to be an open court. Amber, I'm really sorry about that. I tried everything I could."

"Thanks for trying," Amber said, her spirits dampened. "I'll just have to deal with it."

"You'll be okay, trust me," Brenda said as she walked out of the house.

"Thanks again, Brenda."

Chapter Thirty-Eight

The days passed and before she knew it, Amber's day in court to divorce Jim was only a day away. She was still nervous, but she was excited at the same time.

"I can't wait until I'm divorced from him!" she told Tim the night before. "Then the only thing holding me to him is the trial, and after that, I am free of him forever."

Tim smiled and poked her playfully in the arm. "I think after court tomorrow, we should celebrate," he said in a sing-song voice.

Amber's eyes lit up. "That's a wonderful idea."

"What would you like to do, honey?"

"I think we should have a nice, romantic evening alone. Dinner, drinks in front of the fireplace, and you. That's all I need," she said genuinely.

"You are so easy to please. That's one of the things I love about you," he said, sitting down. "I think that's a great idea. What would you like for dinner?"

Amber squinted her eyes and thought for a moment. "Surprise me."

"Okay, I can do that." He gave her a flirtatious look.

Amber walked over and sat on Tim's lap. "Tonight I'm going to turn in early, since we have such a big day tomorrow."

"Yeah, me too."

"I think I'm going to read for a while, then go to bed," she said as she laced her fingers through his hair.

"I have to prepare for tomorrow evening," he said, raising his eyebrows exaggeratedly, "so I'll be out there in a couple of minutes."

"I can't wait to see what you come up with."

Amber went out into the living room, and Tim called Chuck.

"Hi Chuck, I need a favor. Do you think you can help me out tomorrow?"

"Sure, what's going on?"

"Amber has court in the morning for her divorce, and we want to celebrate afterward. I was wondering if you could come over in the afternoon and be with Amber while I run some errands."

"Sure, what time?"

"I'm going to take her out to lunch afterward, so we should be back by one. My errands should only take a couple of hours."

"I will be there at one then."

When Tim went out to the living room, Amber had already fallen asleep. Tim picked her up to carry her upstairs, and she woke up. She looked at him with sleepy eyes. "Oh, honey, I can walk, but thank you anyway. Are you tired?"

"Actually I am, I'll come up with you."

They both headed upstairs. Tim tucked Amber in and went to his own room.

"Tim," Amber called across the hall.

"Yes, Amber?" he answered.

"You know, you can sleep with me if you like."

"I would like that."

Tim came back into the room undressed down to his briefs and climbed in. Amber snuggled right up to him and kissed him good night, and shortly after drifted off to sleep.

Chapter Thirty-Nine

The next morning was cool and crisp. Amber awoke full of energy. "Today is going to be an excellent day," she stated confidently.

Tim agreed with a nod. "Are you nervous?"

"Yes, but excited to be done with it."

"I feel the same way and I'm not the one getting the divorce." He climbed out of bed. "Well, I'll leave you alone to get ready."

"Okay, I'll be done shortly."

Before they knew it, it was time to leave.

They arrived at court right on time. A few minutes later, Amber was called to approach the judge. The judge leafed through the information that was provided to him and granted her divorce. Brenda had told her the divorce was going to be easy, but she had no idea it was going to be this easy. She had to answer a few questions and that was it.

Amber was amazed. "Tim, can you believe how easy that was?"

"No, I had no idea it was going to be that simple," he agreed, taking her hand. "Do you feel any different?"

"Actually I do. I feel as if a great weight has been lifted off my shoulders."

Tim gave her a big hug. "Amber, when we get home, Chuck is going to be there. He's going to stay with you for a few hours until I get back. I have to do some shopping for tonight."

"I'm so excited for tonight!" Amber exclaimed. "Is Carol coming with Chuck?"

"I don't know. It depends on if the girls can cover for her. Let's grab some lunch."

When they arrived back at home, Chuck was there, just as he said he would be. He sat waiting on the front porch swing.

"I'll let you guys in, then I have to go," Tim said, running up the steps and unlocking the door. He turned and gave Amber a big hug and kiss. "I'll see you when I get back. Have fun."

Amber and Chuck walked into the house. "So Chuck," Amber said as she took off her shoes, "Carol couldn't come?"

"She couldn't get Joan to work for her. She had other plans."

"Oh, that's too bad."

"She sends her love," Chuck said, gesturing toward the living room with his arm.

Amber nodded and they both moved in that direction. "She's so sweet. Are you two still acting like newlyweds?"

"Yeah, it's been wonderful," Chuck said with a smile as he sat down on the couch. "Carol has had a glow that I haven't seen in a long time."

Amber settled into the recliner. "That's so wonderful."

"So, when are you and Tim getting married?"

"Married?" Amber asked, laughing. "Well, he hasn't asked me yet, if that's what you mean, but between you and me, if he asked me today I would say yes. But I don't think that's going to happen."

"Why not?"

"Well, it's kind of soon, and there's a lot going on right now, and who knows if he would really want to marry me."

"I can tell he's totally crazy about you," Chuck said, shaking his head. "I've never seen him act like this around anyone. You two are perfect together. In fact, I've never seen you so happy before either."

"I know," Amber said, staring dreamily out of the window and smiling. "He's very special to me. He's so wonderful and sweet."

Chuck and Amber talked so much that before they knew it Tim was home.

Tim opened the door and motioned to Chuck. "Go distract her while I bring these things in."

"Okay."

Chuck asked Amber if he could see the garden and she happily obliged him. It gave Tim just enough time to get everything put away, so that Amber would be surprised. A few minutes later, they headed back in.

"Thanks so much for coming over and keeping Amber company," Tim said as he heartily shook his friend's hand.

"That's alright," Chuck responded with a smile. "We had a nice talk while you were gone."

"Good."

"I better get going, though."

Amber walked over and gave Chuck a hug. "Thanks, Chuck. I enjoyed our talk."

They both saw Chuck out. Tim shut the door and turned to Amber. "So, what did you two talk about?"

"A little bit of everything, but mostly you."

"Me? What about me?"

"Just how good you've been to me, among other things."

"Okay, I know how to take a hint. I'll quit asking." He put his arms around her and kissed her gently. "Amber, why don't you go relax in the tub while I get things going down here?"

"That sounds good," Amber said, squeezing him around the middle.

As Amber went to soak, Tim got things ready for the evening.

When she got out of the tub and walked into her room, she was already impressed. He had laid out a flowing, low-cut, peach-colored gown on her bed with matching shoes with crisscrossing straps. It was like something out of a magazine. He even had jewelry to go with it. She immediately fell in love with it.

Amber stayed upstairs for an hour and a half. She wanted to look just perfect for Tim. She walked slowly downstairs and found him in the dining room by the fireplace. Tim stood there in a tuxedo, his hair cut short with a sexy wet look to it. They looked at each other with amazement.

Amber spoke first. "You look absolutely handsome. Better than handsome. Gorgeous."

"I have never seen anyone more beautiful than you," he replied sincerely. "You look amazing."

"Thank you. You went through so much trouble for me. You didn't have to do that."

"I know, but I wanted to. You deserve it."

Amber looked around in awe. There were flowers everywhere. On the table and throughout the room he had lit candles. He had champagne chilling, and the table was set elegantly. There was soft music playing.

He walked over to Amber and gave her the softest, most gentle kiss she had ever felt. "Amber," he began, "I love you. You are the greatest thing that's ever happened to me. I can't imagine never knowing you. I may not have known you for very long, but I've known you long enough to know that a life without you wouldn't be complete. You have made my life so rich. I know in my heart that you are the woman for me, the woman who makes my heart sing, who makes my spirit soar free. I'd love nothing more than if you would be my wife." He got down on one knee and looked up at her with sparkling eyes. "Amber, will you marry me?" he asked, opening a velvet box that held the most beautiful diamond ring she had ever seen.

Tears rolled down her face. "Yes, I will be your wife. I would love to marry you. I have loved you from the moment I laid eyes on you."

He lifted her hand and slipped the ring onto her finger. He said, "I promise to love you always and forever."

She pulled him to his feet and put her arms around him. "I promise to always and forever love you too. You have made me so proud and happy. Thank you, Tim."

"No, thank you."

"The ring is so beautiful," she said as she stared at it through tear-filled eyes.

"I was hoping you'd like it."

"Like it? I love it."

"Would you like a glass of champagne?"

"Yes."

After he popped the cork and poured two glasses, he toasted, "To us."

Amber lifted her glass. "To us, and a happy life together."

"Amber, come have a seat," he said, walking over to the table and pulling out a chair for her. "It's time to eat."

"What are we having?" she asked as she smoothed her dress and sat down.

"Crab legs, shrimp fettuccini, and salad."

"Sounds delicious."

"Thank you."

He brought everything out. Dinner seemed to last forever. They were both happy and talkative. After they ate, they lay in front of the fireplace and held on to each other as if they would never let go. They stared at the fire for a few moments, mesmerized by it, before they turned to each other and kissed.

"I love you," Amber said. "It feels so good to finally be able to say it so freely."

"Yes it does," Tim responded, kissing her again. "I love you too."

Tim got to his feet, then bent over and picked Amber up and carried her upstairs, not to her room, but to his own. In his bedroom, candles flickered everywhere and rose petals were strewn over the bed. He laid Amber down and began to kiss and suckle her. He wasn't going to just have his way with her, he was going to make love to her. He slowly undressed her. She took down her hair. He lightly rubbed rose petals all around her erect nipples and slowly past her tummy to her soft wavy hair. She began to moan, "Please take me."

But he wasn't going to give in so quickly, he was going to tease her and get her close to the point of climax before he gave in. He placed his tongue on her nipple, then slowly wrapped his lips around. He ran his hand down and gently stroked her, only penetrating every so often, just enough to drive her wild.

He kissed her, his tongue darting in and out of her mouth. He moved his lips to her neck and then back down to her nipples, licking his way down. When he reached her warm spot, he began to suck and lick ever so gently, yet firmly, just the perfect pressure.

She moaned, "Please, please take me." She sat up and began to undress him. She couldn't wait any longer. "I must have you." After he was undressed, he lay her back down and slowly penetrated her. He kissed and thrusted at the same time, their bodies becoming one. He reached his hand down and stroked her some more until one last deep penetration, and they were in ecstasy as their bodies shook together.

The last thing Amber said that night was, "This was the most perfect, wonderful day I have ever had," right before they both drifted off to sleep.

Chapter Forty

The next day, Amber had a glow about her. She felt better than she ever had before in her life. She lay there watching Tim sleep. She felt as if she was in a dream.

Tim woke with a big smile on his face. "How long have you been awake?"

"Only a few minutes. Just long enough to know that I wasn't dreaming about last night. I truly am in heaven."

"So am I, honey. Never have I felt so wonderful."

"Me neither."

"Amber, you have made all my dreams come true," he said, running his large hands down her long, thick, beautiful hair.

"And so have you. Thank you. I can't wait to share an entire life with you. And to think, this is only the beginning of our life together. It's all very exciting. I can't wait to call Carol and tell her the news."

"Go ahead and call her."

Amber reached over, picked up the phone, and dialed Carol. "Carol, I didn't wake you, did I?"

"No. I was awake," Carol answered.

"Good," Amber said, her voice shaking with excitement. "You're never going to believe it, Carol."

"What?"

"I have the greatest news ever. Tim asked me to marry him!" she shrieked out.

"Oh my God! Amber! That's wonderful. I'm so happy for you two. You're perfect for each other! I can't wait to tell Chuck. After all you've been through, now you will finally get the chance for a happy life. I'm so excited and happy for you."

"One more thing. Carol, would you be my maid of honor?"

"Amber, I would be honored. Thank you for asking me."

"No, thank you for always being there for me. You are a true friend, and I love you."

"I love you too. I better let you go. I want to call Chuck and tell him. Oh yeah, have you set a date yet?"

"No, not yet. Hold on, maybe Tim has one in mind," Amber said, turning her head on the pillow to look at her fiancé. "Tim, do you have a date in mind?"

Tim reached over and put his hand on her shoulder. "Yes, after court is done would be the best time, so I was thinking September 9 would be perfect."

Amber got back on the phone. "September 9, so we have a lot of work to do."

"Can I go with to pick out your wedding dress?"

Amber smiled and started to giggle. "You sure can, and then we'll find your bridesmaid dress."

"I can't wait. When should we do this?" asked Carol.

"How about today?"

"Sounds great."

"Tim will have to come, so I better ask him first." She turned back to Tim, her face aglow. "Tim, can we go shopping for my wedding dress today?"

"Sure. Then we can pick out my tuxedo too."

"Carol, we can do it today, so get ready and come over!"

"Okay, I'll see you in a little bit. Bye."

As she hung up the phone, Amber was so excited she could barely contain herself. "Thank you, Tim! You've made me the happiest woman in the world," she said as she kissed him over and over.

"You're welcome," he giggled, kissing her back.

"We're going to pick out Carol's bridesmaid dress too."

"I should call Chuck and see if he can get someone to cover his shift. Then he can get fitted for a tuxedo also."

"That's a good idea, here's the phone," Amber said, handing him the receiver.

Tim dialed the station and asked for Chuck. When Chuck got on the phone, Tim didn't waste any time. "I was wondering if you would be the best man in my wedding?"

Chuck was silent for a moment. Then he said, "You're kidding me, right?"

"No, I'm not."

"Hell yeah!" Chuck exclaimed, then broke into excited laughter.

"Here's my next question: do you think you would be able to get someone to cover your shift today?" Tim asked, smiling at Amber.

"Actually, I'm on desk duty so it shouldn't be a problem. Let me go ask, hold on." When he came back to the phone, he said, "Yes, and the captain said congratulations. I'll be over in a little bit, I just have to finish what I'm doing. And Tim, congratulations! I'm very happy for you. You got yourself a wonderful woman."

"I know, thank you. See you in a bit," Tim said, putting the phone down and wrapping his arms around Amber.

"This is going to be so much fun! Thank you, Tim. You're so wonderful."

"So are you," he said as he gave her a big kiss. "Amber, while you're getting ready, I'm going to go make some arrangements. I know the perfect caterer. You don't mind if I set those things up, do you?"

"No, not at all. I wouldn't know the first place to start."

Tim cradled her face in his hands. "I'll take care of everything," he said, kissing her nose. "You don't need to worry about a thing."

"How did I get so lucky?"

"That's what I keep asking myself. How did I get so lucky?"

❦ Chapter Forty-One ❦

The weeks passed, and suddenly court was only a few days away. Everything was set up for the wedding, even the invitations had been sent out. Amber was very excited about the wedding, but very nervous about the trial.

"Tim," she said one morning, "I keep going over everything that happened with Jim. It just seems like it was a nightmare, and now I'm living in a fairy tale. It doesn't seem possible that my life could change so drastically. I usually pick the wrong type of man, so I was going to stay single for the rest of my life, but then you came along. I feel so blessed. I just thank God you came along. I love you."

"I love you too, honey." He pulled Amber into his lap.

"I can't believe how fast you got everything ready for the wedding. You're a genius," she said, weaving her fingers through his hair.

Tim laughed. "Far from it. I just happen to know a few people."

"Well, I just wanted to thank you for everything," she said, nuzzling his neck. "You've made it so easy for me."

"You're welcome. Honey," he said as he stroked her hair, "I hate to bring this up, but are you mentally prepared for the trial?"

"As prepared as I can be. Having you by my side has really helped. I feel a lot stronger. When Brenda gets here and we go over everything again, I'll feel a little less nervous about everything. And then Dr. Dahl will be coming over later, so we can talk too."

"What time did you say they were coming over?"

"Brenda's coming at one o'clock, and Dr. Dahl is coming at four."

"Good. I think that will help to get rid of some of your anxiety."

"Yeah, I think so too."

Brenda arrived a few minutes after one o'clock. Tim answered the door. "Hi Brenda. Come on in. Go ahead and have a seat. I'll go get Amber up. She took a little nap to calm her nerves."

"I can understand that, this has to be very hard on her," Brenda said as she walked into the living room and sat down.

"Yes, it has been." He turned and headed upstairs to Amber's room. "Amber, get up, honey. Brenda's here."

Amber stretched and yawned. "Oh, I slept that long?"

"Yes," he said, sitting on the edge of her bed, "but you needed it."

"Tell her she can come up."

"Okay. I'll see you when you're done," he said, kissing her forehead. "I'm making spaghetti tonight. Is that alright with you?"

"Yeah, sounds great."

"So I'll be down in the kitchen. If you need me, give me a yell."

"I will." He looked at her adoringly, reached down and gave her a kiss, and then went back downstairs. "You can go upstairs. Amber is ready to see you."

Brenda climbed the stairs and went into Amber's room. "Hello Amber," she said, pulling up a chair by the bed.

"Hi Brenda, how are you?" Amber asked as she sat up and arranged some pillows behind her.

"Good and yourself?"

"Nervous."

"Well, you just get as much rest as you can before the trial. That will help you get through some of your nervousness. You'll need all the energy you can save up to get through the trial." Brenda pulled out a file and leafed through it quickly. "So, we're going to go over some of the same things we've already talked about. It will just help to refresh your memory. It will also help you feel more confident. I know it's hard to talk about these things, but we have to do it one more time."

By the time they finished talking, Dr. Dahl was there, waiting to see Amber. Tim came upstairs and let them know.

Brenda gathered up her things. "I'll see you at the courthouse, Amber. Everything will be fine."

"Okay. See you then," Amber said, smiling and taking a deep breath.

A few moments later, Dr. Dahl walked in and sat in the chair that Brenda had just vacated.

"Hi Dr. Dahl," Amber said pleasantly. "It's nice to see you."

"I'm happy to see you too," she said, crossing her legs and leaning forward.

"I have been so busy lately. I haven't had much of a chance to see or talk to you."

"That's okay, Amber. You've got a lot on your plate right now, so I understand. How have you been doing with everything? Are you managing okay?"

Amber sighed and collected her thoughts. "I'm doing better than I expected, but I think it's due to being so busy with the wedding. That's helped to keep my mind off the trial, at least a little bit."

"Well, I'm happy to hear you're managing okay," Dr. Dahl said, sitting back and pulling out her notepad. "In the end, after the trial, what would be your goal? What do you want to have happen in your life?"

"Besides marrying Tim, I want to be able to move on, put the past in the past, and move forward one day at a time. I want to live life to its fullest," Amber said, nodding confidently. "I've been thinking a lot about a career."

"Really? What do you think you want to do?" Dr. Dahl made some notes on her pad.

"I was thinking of becoming an advocate for abused women. If I could help just one person get out of the situation she's in, then I'm making a difference. I want to make a difference in this world. I'd like to go around and give speeches and tell my story, maybe write a book."

"Amber, I think that's wonderful. You would be the perfect person for it. You've been through so much, and yet you've managed to stay so strong. I think it's wonderful that you want to help others. That's just like you, even when you're in need, you are there for everyone else. I'm very proud of you, Amber," she said. She flipped her notebook shut and put it back in her briefcase. She studied Amber's face for a moment. "I don't think you need to make appointments to see me anymore."

"Are you sure?" Amber asked, raising her eyebrows.

"Yes, I'm sure."

"Thank you, Dr. Dahl. I'm glad you were part of my life. You've really helped me so much. I can't thank you enough."

"I'm happy you were part of my life too. Since this will be the last time I'll see you before the trial, I want to wish you luck. You'll do just fine. I'll be there every step of the way." Dr. Dahl stood and gathered her things.

"Thanks for your support," Amber said, shaking her hand. "I appreciate what you have done for me."

Chapter Forty-Two

"Good morning, honey," Tim said, gently stroking her cheek.

Amber yawned. "Good morning," she said, smiling at Tim.

"How are you feeling?"

She was silent for a moment, gauging her mood. "Nervous and anxious, but ready to get this over with. The sooner it's over, the better off I'll be."

"I know what you mean," Tim said, nodding. "I can't wait until we can move forward with our lives."

"Me neither. I have so much to look forward to."

"I know. We both do." He kissed her softly.

"Tim," Amber said, stretching luxuriously, "what do you think of me becoming an advocate for abused women?"

"I think that's a wonderful idea," he responded, his eyes lighting up. "You would be very good at it."

"You think so?"

"I *know* so."

"I was talking to Dr. Dahl the other day and she thought so too."

"Well, she's a smart lady."

"I'd like to give speeches and I may have to travel. That will take some time away from us. Is that going to be a problem?" she asked, her face filled with concern.

"Not at all," Tim said, shaking his head. "We have our whole lives to be together. You have to do what makes you happy, and that's the bottom line. I think this would be the perfect career for you."

"So, you're okay with everything?"

"I'm more than okay with it. I'm so proud of you and that you've come out so strong from such a horrible life. I know I've said it before, but you are such an amazing woman." He pulled her close and buried his face in her hair. "Well, I think we need to get ready for court."

"You're right."

Amber showered and began to get ready. As she tried to put on her make-up, she couldn't stop herself from shaking. She began to have an anxiety attack. "Tim!" she shouted.

Tim came running at the urgency in her voice. "What's wrong?"

"I'm having an anxiety attack and I'm hav . . . having a hard ti . . . me catch…ing my breath," she gasped, her hands clutching her throat.

"Hold on. Let me get a bag and your anxiety medicine." When he came back a few moments later, she was struggling even harder to get air. "Here, breathe in this bag," he said, putting it over her nose and mouth. "Now concentrate, and slowly breathe in through your nose and blow out through your mouth. There you go. That's my girl. Slow down your breathing even more . . . good job."

She put her hand on his wrist and he lowered the bag. "Thank you. All of a sudden, I just couldn't breathe."

"Here, take this," he said, handing her the anxiety medication and pouring her a glass of water.

"Okay. All of a sudden it really hit me. We're going to court today and I'm scared." She took the water and swallowed the pill.

"There's nothing to be afraid of," Tim said, putting his arms around her. "He can't hurt you."

"I know, but you're going to hear some things that are very horrible about me. I'm afraid you're going to feel differently about me."

"No, that will never happen. Nothing could make me feel any differently about you. Nothing." He took her face in his hands and looked into her eyes. "Do you understand?"

"Yes. I'm shaking so bad, I couldn't even put on my makeup."

"Well, after this pill kicks in, your shaking should improve. Amber," he said, still looking intensely into her eyes, "everything will be okay. Pretty soon it will be all over, just remember that. You need to focus, so that you don't fall apart in court. I'll be there to protect you. It's okay if you fall apart, but I know you wouldn't like to be like this in front of anyone else. And just in case, I'll bring a bag and your medicine."

"Good idea," Amber said, breathing deeply as she met his gaze. "There, my shaking is better. I think I can finally put on my makeup. Thank you, Tim, for helping me."

"Anytime, honey. Don't you worry about it."

Amber finished putting on her makeup. It took longer than usual, but she was finally ready. She headed downstairs.

Tim sat on the couch waiting for her. "Are you okay now?" he asked, standing up.

"Much better, thanks to you."

He went to her and put his arm around her. "Can I get you some breakfast?" he asked, leading her over to the couch.

"I don't know if I can eat. My stomach is so upset," she said wearily as she collapsed into a seated position.

"I understand, but I think it's a good idea to try to get some food in your stomach, so you don't get sick."

"Yeah, you're probably right. Maybe I'll try to eat some toast."

"I'll go make it you just try to relax."

Tim came back a few moments later with some toast and a glass of orange juice on a tray. He set the tray down in front of her.

"Thank you, honey," she said, looking up at him with a weak smile.

By the time she finished eating, it was time to go. On the way to the courthouse, all she could think about was what was going to happen. She knew that the other lawyer would try to make her look bad and that he would do a good job of it, too.

When they arrived at the courthouse, she saw Brenda and Dr. Dahl waiting for her. She looked around. There were people everywhere. She knew some of them were members of the press. She began to feel a little panicky again.

"It's okay, honey," Tim said, grabbing her hand. "Remember to focus. Don't pay attention to the people or anything else, just concentrate on your testimony. You will get through this just fine, I promise."

They parked and headed up the steps. The press ran toward her asking all kinds of questions. "What do you think the outcome will be?" "Is there anything in your past that will come out today?" There were questions coming from everywhere, but Brenda handled it.

The four of them walked through the crowd. There were lots of women there to support Amber. When Amber realized that, she was able to walk with her head up instead of feeling shameful. Women were shouting, "We love you Amber! We support you! Put him away forever!" There was so much yelling that she wasn't able to take everything in. They finally made it into the courthouse. Tim and Dr. Dahl took a seat right behind Amber.

Tim hugged and kissed her. "Hold your head up high."

Dr. Dahl hugged her. "You'll do just fine. Remember the things we talked about."

A few moments later, Carol and Chuck arrived and sat next to Tim. Pretty soon the courtroom filled up. Amber stayed focused to the front. She didn't want to see all the people. She needed to stay focused. She didn't look over at Jim. The courtroom was filled with talk and whispers until the judge walked in.

"All rise for the honorable Judge Mallord," the bailiff said, and then there was silence. The judge sat down. "You may sit," he said, and everyone sat.

"Please bring in the jurors." The jurors came in and took their seat. "We are here to hear the case of Amber Labell versus James Labell. Go ahead with your opening statements."

Brenda started first. She walked over to the jury and gripped the wooden rail with both hands. "Ladies and gentlemen of the jury, we will prove beyond a reasonable doubt that James Labell is guilty, but not by reason of temporary insanity. He has subjected Ms. Labell to years of abuse—mental, verbal and physical. He has, through the years, drugged and raped Ms. Labell.

"On the frightful day of March 6, when Ms. Labell arrived home, she found Mr. Labell cutting up her clothing. He was enraged because she had arrived home late. He lunged at Ms. Labell, grabbing her from behind, and cut her neck, hoping to kill her."

The jurors gasped. Brenda nodded solemnly, then continued. "That evening, he gave her what he said was a painkiller. When she woke the next morning, she felt different, as she had many times in the past. When Ms. Labell yelled for him, he was gone.

"She managed to make it out of the house and stumbled to her place of work, where the ambulance was called. After Ms. Labell's stay at the hospital, Mr. Labell, from jail, hired his cousin Dan Deliano to kidnap and kill her."

Brenda paused dramatically, and looked at each juror. "Does that sound like temporary insanity to you, ladies and gentleman of the jury? I think not. This was a malicious act planned out by Mr. Labell. Ladies and gentleman of the jury, Mr. Labell needs to be found guilty for attempted murder, rape, and conspiring to kidnap and kill Ms. Labell. He needs to be punished accordingly. Thank you."

Judge Mallord spoke. "Mr. Stone, your opening statement, please."

Mr. Stone stood and walked grimly over to the juror. "Ladies and gentleman of the jury, we will prove that James Labell was temporarily insane. The events of March 6 were borne out of temporary insanity, and not planned as Mrs. Johnson would like you to believe."

He paused and adjusted his round, wire spectacles. "Ms. Labell repeatedly had sexual relations with other men." He ran a hand over his bald head, shaking it in disbelief. "When Mr. Labell arrived home from work, there was evidence of Ms. Labell's infidelity, which drove Mr. Labell over the edge. He found men's briefs. Ms. Labell was not home, and when she arrived home late, he knew she had been with another man. He became enraged and lost it. This was not a planned event. It's that simple. I am asking that you find Mr. Labell guilty by reason of temporary insanity on that day in March. Thank you."

"Thank you, Mr. Stone and Mrs. Johnson. Mrs. Johnson, you may call your first witness," the judge said.

Carol was the first witness. She explained that Amber had worked late on March 6. She then recounted—almost in tears—Amber's arrival at the café the next morning.

Dr. Anderson, Dr. Miller, and Dan Deliano—in handcuffs—were all called and delivered their testimonies. Dan admitted that Jim had hired him to kill Amber, and the prosecution was set.

❦ Chapter Forty-Three ❦

Brenda cleared her throat. "Your Honor, I would like to call Amber Labell to the stand."

Amber stood shakily and slowly began to walk up to the stand. She felt as if her legs would give out at any moment. When she took the oath, her hands were shaking. She finally sat. She looked up at Tim and found her strength to go on.

"Ms. Labell," Brenda began, standing directly in front of Amber, blocking Jim from her view, "could you tell me what happened the day of March 6?"

By the time she finished answering the question, there wasn't a dry eye in the courtroom. Amber had to take several sips of water. She shook horribly as she recounted the events of that day.

"Now, Ms. Labell," Brenda said kindly, "we're going to go back and discuss the events that led up to this incident. Have you ever been hit by Mr. Labell?"

"Yes, I have. On many occasions. In fact, so many times I can't even count them."

"On those occasions when he hit you, did he hit you just once or multiple times?"

Amber took a shaky breath. "He beat me. I can only remember a few times where he hit me only once and that was in the beginning of our marriage."

"Amber, have you ever fought back or hit Mr. Labell?"

"I fought back once." She paused. "That was the first time I ended up in the hospital. I didn't hit him, though. I kept trying to push him away, but he was too big and strong. After that, I never fought back. I just tried to protect myself by covering my head with my hands."

"Did Mr. Labell just hit you with his hands?"

"No. He would kick me, he used wooden spoons," she recounted, her voice becoming monotone and detached. "He bit me. Basically, whatever you can think of, he used. One day, when I made a dinner he didn't like, he went outside and got a switch from a tree and beat me with it. He hurt me so many times, I don't think I can remember them all."

"Did he ever use a weapon on you, aside from March 6?"

"Yes. He would hold a gun to my head if I wouldn't . . . perform certain . . . sex acts." Amber stared at the floor as she spoke. "He also liked to use knives; he would hold one to my throat. During these sex acts, he would never set down the weapons. One day, he accidentally cut me a little on my throat, and that's when he decided to put the weapon next to him, instead of hanging onto it."

"Ms. Labell," Brenda said, walking over to the jury, "did he ever rape you?"

"Yes. When he used the weapons, and also I found out when I was in the hospital that when he drugged me, he raped me."

"How many times have you had the feeling you were drugged?"

"I can't say for sure, but I know it was a lot of times, more than fifteen. I always felt different the next day. I didn't understand why until they figured it out at the hospital."

Brenda nodded gravely as she studied the faces of the jurors. "Has Mr. Labell ever been arrested for beating you?"

"Yes, he has. The first time he put me in the hospital, he ended up serving some time in jail."

"Has Mr. Labell ever had any other felony convictions?"

"Yes, three drug convictions." Amber kept her eyes trained on the floor. She knew what was coming.

"Ms. Labell," Brenda began, walking over to stand in front of her again, "I know this isn't easy for you to talk about, but there are some very personal things I have to ask you about. I know you have never shared these things with anyone else because you felt too ashamed, but we have to discuss them." She paused and took a breath. "Okay. Did Mr. Labell ever make you have sex with other men for money?"

Amber swallowed. She was silent for a few moments before she was able to speak. "Yes," she said finally. "He made me do it. He said if I didn't, he would kill me. I believe he would have, so I did what he told me to do." Her face became red as she tried to maintain control of her emotions.

"Who were these people he made you have sex with?"

"His friends and other people he would bring home." Amber's voice broke as her emotions overtook her. She started to cry. She shook uncontrollably.

Brenda looked over at the horrified faces of the jurors before she continued. "Was this just done once in a while or did he make you do this more often than that?"

"He made me do it all the time, like it was a regular job."

"I know this is a horrible question, but was this something you wanted or enjoyed?"

"No!" Amber exclaimed adamantly, crying even harder. "I begged him not to make me do it, but he would beat me and threaten to kill me. I hated it!

It made me feel dirty and ashamed. I would scrub myself over and over to get the dirtiness off of me."

"You're doing fine," Brenda said, looking into her eyes reassuringly. "Are you okay?"

"Yeah," she said, fighting back the tears. She took several deep breaths and regained her composure.

"Ms. Labell, what kind of sex acts did Mr. Labell make you act out?"

"All different kinds of things, including S and M. He liked to pretend we were in a porn movie, and I had to do what the girls did. He would have his friends watch . . . and then . . . join in."

"Did he ever videotape you during these acts?"

"All the time."

Brenda turned to the judge. "Your Honor, can we please mark these movies as exhibit C." The judge nodded, so Brenda continued. "Did Mr. Labell make you wear outfits that you didn't want to wear?"

"Yes. He had me wear outfits, wigs, everything."

She turned back to the judge. "Your Honor, I would also like to have these items marked as exhibit D." Brenda glanced at the jury, then at Amber. "What about sex toys? Did he make you use them?"

"Yes . . . I didn't want to, but he would make me in front of him and others."

"Ms. Labell, did Mr. Labell ever beat you in front of these people he brought home?"

"Yes, when I would try to refuse having sex with them."

"I know this is hard for you, but it is important that these facts are brought to light. Did Mr. Labell ever beat you because you refused to have sex with him?"

"Yes. I refused a lot, but I never won. If I cried when he brought people home, he would beat me for that, too."

Brenda paused for a minute. She managed a weak smile at Amber to show her she was doing well. "Ms. Labell, what did he do to humiliate you in front of these people?"

"He would grab me in my private areas. He would have his friends do the same. Then they would all laugh. He would call me a whore and a lousy lay," she said shakily. "Everything he ever did to me or had me do was humiliating. It all made me feel like I wasn't a person anymore, I was just an object he could do whatever he wanted with."

Brenda nodded sadly. "Did you ever accept money for having sex with these people?"

"Oh no, that was Jim's job," Amber said, still staring at the floor. "He made it very clear that it was his money. He would sometimes steal from these people when I was having sex with them. He used to have people pay to watch, then join in."

"Did Mr. Labell ever take pictures of you?"

"Yes. Then he would show them to his friends."

Brenda leaned over and whispered to Amber, "Hold your head high. This is not your fault."

Amber slowly raised her head. She was afraid to look up and see Tim, but she did, and he was crying, along with the rest of them.

Judge Mallord spoke. "That will be it for the day. I think Ms. Labell has had enough. We will adjourn until tomorrow at eight o'clock."

Amber stepped down from the stand and went to Tim who held onto her as tight as he could. "Come on, honey, let's go home."

On the way home, there was an uncomfortable silence that Amber couldn't take. "Tim, please say something!" she said finally. "Do you wish you hadn't asked me to marry you?" She spoke quickly, firing questions at him. "This is too much for you to take, isn't it? Do you want to break off the engagement? I would understand if you did." She didn't give Tim a chance to answer, she was so nervous about what he thought now that he knew everything.

"Amber, Amber, slow down! Really, it's okay. I love you the same as I did before. I don't want to break off the engagement, I want to marry you. What happened to you, Amber, is more than horrifying. I'm so sorry you had to live through that. He deserves to be punished. I hope he burns in hell." He wrapped his arm around her shoulders and she leaned her head against him. It didn't take long before Amber finally calmed down.

"Come on, honey," he said as they pulled into the driveway. "Let's go in. You've had a hard day. You need to rest."

When they got in the house, Tim went upstairs to run bath water for Amber. "Come on, honey," he said when the bath was ready. "Let's go upstairs and you can soak in a nice bubble bath."

"That sounds good. Tim, would you please get me a glass of wine, so I can relax?"

"Sure, honey. I'll be right up."

Tim walked in with the wine while Amber was undressing, and that was when he first noticed it. "Amber, is that where he hit you with the switch?"

"Yes, right on the back of my legs."

"Oh my God, Amber." He started to cry. "I had no idea. I mean, I knew it was bad, but I never knew how bad it was. I'm so sorry. How could he do that to you? You're such a wonderful woman, so loving and caring. How have you managed to stay so strong through everything you've endured?"

"God," Amber said, putting her arms around him to comfort him. "God has gotten me through it, and the hope that one day I would be able to get out of there and start a new life."

"Amber, I understand now why you kept what happened to you a secret, but just so you know, it doesn't change things between you and me. And now that it's out in the open, I just want you to know, if you ever feel you need to talk about it, I'm willing to listen. And if you never want to talk about it again, I understand, and I will never say anything about it."

"You're so wonderful to me," Amber said sincerely. "Thank you for being so understanding."

"I love you. You don't have to thank me. I understand now why you thank me so much, because you were never treated very well before," he said, shaking his head.

"You're right. I'm not used to it, and I appreciate it so much." She thought for a moment. "Tim, I think I will take you up on the offer to never talk about it again. I know I will never forget what happened, but I want to leave it in the past and move into the future. With you by my side, life will be wonderful. You are my dream come true."

"And so are you. I love you."

"I love you too." They hugged each other as if they were never going to let go.

"Amber," he said, pulling back from the hug so that he could look into her eyes, "I'm sorry about the car ride home. I didn't mean to be so quiet. I was just trying to take it all in. I didn't mean to make you think that I thought any differently about you. You're still my angel."

"I understand."

"Tomorrow is going to be another long day, and a tough one at that. Amber, you do realize that lawyer Anthony Stone is going to try to make you look horrible. You just need to remember to hold your head up high." His eyes were focused intently on hers. "You know the real truth, and you need to be firm about it."

"I will," Amber said, nodding seriously. She stepped into the tub with a sigh and stretched out.

Tim sat on the edge of the tub. "Amber, was it hard for you to see Jim today?"

"Yes, I looked at him once and it really shook me up. Then I remembered that Brenda had told me not to look at him, so I turned away."

Tim shook his head angrily. "It looked like he was enjoying it. Other times you could see how angry he was becoming. The jurors saw him. They know what kind of man he is. There is no way he's going to get away with this. Amber, you have nothing to fear anymore."

Chapter Forty-Four

The next day, her gang sat behind her again, and that made Amber feel more secure. The courtroom was filled with people chattering and whispering to one another. Amber focused her attention elsewhere. She knew if she thought about all the people she would have a panic attack. She concentrated instead on the verdict, and how happy she would be when it was read.

"All rise for the honorable Judge Mallord," the bailiff announced, pulling Amber out of her thoughts.

"You may be seated. Mr. Stone, do you have any witnesses you would like to call at this time?"

"Yes. I would like to call Ms. Labell to the stand."

Amber walked shakily back up to the stand, took her oath, and sat down.

The lawyer peered at her menacingly over the top of his spectacles. "Ms. Labell, isn't it true Mr. Labell never beat you?"

Amber's brow furrowed in shock. "No, that is a lie."

"You stated he used weapons on you before. Isn't it true the only time he ever used a weapon on you was the night of March 6?"

"No, he used weapons on me before that night."

"Ms. Labell," Mr. Stone said in a stern voice, "aren't you the one who prostituted yourself?"

"No!" Amber said, becoming angrier.

"Aren't you the one who liked to perform certain sex acts and wear outfits?"

"No, that is a lie." *Be strong,* Amber thought. *Hold your head up high. Look to Tim for strength. The defense is weak. They have nothing on me.*

"Weren't you the one who liked to have your picture taken and you also liked being filmed?"

"No!" she exclaimed in disbelief.

"Isn't it true," Mr. Stone said, walking over by the jury, "that you have had many affairs on Jim?"

"No, that's an outright lie."

"If it was so bad, why didn't you just leave?"

"It's not that easy. Like I said before, I was saving up money to get out of there. I knew it was only a matter of time before he would end up killing me."

"What about the pair of men's brief's Mr. Labell found in your bedroom on the day of March 6? Who did those belong to? One of your lovers?"

"No! I have no idea what briefs you're talking about. I was working at the café all day on March 6. And I never had any 'lovers.'"

Mr. Stone pursed his lips and stared at Amber for a moment. "That's all the questions I have. You may step down."

Judge Mallord said, "Mr. Stone, do you have any other witnesses?"

"No, Your Honor."

Jim stood up, veins sticking out on either side of his neck. "Wait a minute, Your Honor. Against my lawyer's advice, I've decided to testify anyway."

The judge turned to Mr. Stone. "If he wants to testify he has that right, even if it's against your better judgment. Mr. Labell, please step up to be sworn in."

Jim angrily stalked up to the stand, took his oath, and sat down.

"Mr. Labell," Mr. Stone said, approaching the stand, "did you abuse Ms. Labell?"

"No," Jim answered, his eyes flashing.

"Besides the night of March 6, did you ever use a weapon on Ms. Labell?"

"No."

Mr. Stone paused and looked at the jury. "Did you drug and then rape Ms. Labell?"

"No," Jim said, never taking his dark, furious eyes off of Amber as he spoke.

"Did you ever make Ms. Labell have sex for money?"

"No, I never forced her to do anything she didn't want to do."

"Did you ever film Ms. Labell during sex?"

"Yes," Jim said, pushing his dark hair out of his eyes, "but she liked it. She wanted me to tape it. She asked me to."

"Did you ever beat Ms. Labell because she refused to have sex with you?"

"No."

"Thank you," Mr. Stone said, turning to Brenda. "Your witness."

Brenda rose slowly and walked to the stand. She hadn't prepared any questions because she didn't know Jim would testify, but she was quick on her feet. "Mr. Labell, have you ever beaten Amber before?"

"No," Jim said, shaking his head adamantly.

"Have you ever hit her before?"

"Only if she hit me first."

"How many times would you hit her?"

"Maybe five or six times."

Brenda's eyebrows rose and she looked over at the jury. "You don't consider that beating her?"

"No, I was only defending myself."

"A big man like you and a little woman like her?" Brenda asked with a smirk. "You needed to defend yourself? She must be really strong?"

"All I'm saying is, she hit me first and I had to defend myself."

Brenda nodded slowly. "I see. You say you never used a weapon on her, except for on March 6. Why should we believe that? You cut her throat and almost killed her, and this was the first time you used a weapon on her?"

"Yes, it was." Jim was hunched forward in his chair, his eyes still trained on Amber's face.

"You said you didn't drug and rape Ms. Labell. How is it they found your semen in Ms. Labell and roofies in her bloodstream?"

"Well, we had consensual sex, and as far as the drugs go, I don't know where they came from, if they were hers or what."

"So what you're saying is, after you cut her throat, you two had sex?"

"She wanted it, so yes we did," he said, his eyes narrowing.

Brenda paused to let that sink in. She glanced at the jurors. They looked at Jim with disgust. "What drug did you give her the night of March 6?"

"I gave her a pain pill called Vicodin."

"How come that didn't show up on the drug screen?"

"I don't know," he said, shifting uncomfortably in his seat. "I can't answer that."

"Have you ever put Ms. Labell in the hospital from beating her?"

"Yes."

"Oh, I know, it was self defense, right?" Brenda asked condescendingly.

"Yes."

"The night of March 6, did you cut up Ms. Labell's clothing, as she stated earlier?"

"Yes, so she wouldn't be able to go anywhere and be with other men."

Brenda walked up and stood in front of Jim, blocking his view of Amber and forcing him to make eye contact. "But weren't you the one making her prostitute herself?"

Jim cleared his throat nervously. "No."

"I'd like to remind you that you are under oath, Mr. Labell. And Your Honor, again, I'd like to remind you of exhibits C and E." Brenda continued to stare directly into Jim's eyes. "Did you cut her throat?"

"I guess so," Jim said, shrugging. "I don't really remember."

"Have you ever beat–Ms. Labell because she refused to have sex with you?"

Color slowly crept up Jim's neck. "No," he said forcefully, anger flashing in his eyes as he met Brenda's gaze.

Brenda smiled slightly at his obvious anger. "So what we see on the videotape I'm about to show the jurors never happened?"

"It was for show, that's all."

"Ladies and gentleman of the jury, what you are about to see is very graphic. Start the tape, please."

The tape began. It showed Jim beating Amber while she cried and men in the background cheered. After a few minutes, many of the jurors couldn't watch it anymore and looked away. By the time the tape had finished, it was very clear to everyone in the courtroom what was going on in the Labells' house. "Thank you," Brenda said finally. "You can stop the tape." She turned her unwavering gaze back on Jim. "Mr. Labell, lastly, did you conspire to kidnap and kill Ms. Labell?"

"No, I certainly did not."

"So what Dan Deliano, your cousin, said was all a lie?"

Jim banged on the rail of the stand with his fist. "Yes, it was. Him and I had a falling out a while back, and ever since then, he's had it out for me."

Brenda stared at him for a moment longer before turning and walking to her seat. "Thank you. No more questions."

The judge stood. "At this time, we will take thirty minutes for lunch, and when we come back, I will hear your closing arguments."

"All rise for the honorable Judge Mallord."

The judge sat. "You may be seated. Mrs. Johnson, you may start with your closing statement."

"Thank you, Your Honor," Brenda said, getting up and walking over to the jury. "Ladies and gentleman of the jury, this is a rather simple case, due to all the evidence. We have the court records of his past criminal history, the hospital records, the tapes, the blood test results and swabs taken from Ms. Labell proving that Mr. Labell drugged her and raped her. We also have the weapon which was used to cut Ms. Labell's throat, police reports, and the clothing he cut up before he cut her throat. Then we have his testimony, which shows he lied, because we have the tapes to prove it. We also have his confession, which you saw earlier."

Brenda paced slowly back and forth in front of the jury, looking solemnly at each juror as she spoke. "So there is no question that he didn't do this. The only question we're stuck with is: was James Labell temporarily insane? We know that Dan Deliano was hired by Mr. Labell to kidnap and kill Ms. Labell. Does that sound like he was temporarily insane? I think not. We have the fact that he has told her many times that if he can't have her, no one can. He repeatedly threatened to kill her. We have all the facts right before us. Now it's up to you to return a plea of guilty, but not by reason of temporary insanity. Thank you." Brenda looked at the jury for a moment more, then took her seat.

"Mr. Stone," the judge said, "your closing statement."

"Thank you, Your Honor." Mr. Stone stood and approached the jury. "Ladies and gentleman of the jury, I'll go along with the fact that Mr. Labell did cut Ms. Labell's throat, but I won't go along with the fact that he planned it. Ms. Labell is an adulterer, and Mr. Labell became very jealous. Wouldn't you? If your wife was seeing other men, or your husband was with other women, wouldn't you be jealous? Well, when he came home and Ms. Labell was not there yet, he knew that she was with another man again." He paused and shook his head. "He found briefs in his bedroom that did not belong to him. He just went over the edge. It was the last straw. He lost it. In fact, he doesn't remember a lot of what happened. You see, this was not a planned-out murder, this was spur of the moment. You must see this for what it is and return a verdict of guilty, but by reason of temporary insanity. Thank you." He took his seat.

"That will be it for today," the judge said, standing. "Come back tomorrow at eight o'clock in the morning to see if the jury has made their decision yet. Jurors, you may go to the meeting room and discuss what the verdict shall be. We will be back tomorrow and hopefully you will have reached a decision by then."

Chapter Forty-Five

When Amber and Tim got home, they were both exhausted. "Today and yesterday seemed to be the longest days ever," Amber sighed, stretching out on the couch.

Tim nodded. "Eight hours at court seems like fifteen hours."

"I know what you mean."

"Would you like to pop in a movie and order out later when we're hungry?"

"Yeah," Amber said, her voice weary.

The rest of the evening they spent lounging. They didn't talk about court or much else.

On the way to court the next day, Amber was so excited she couldn't stop talking. Tim began to laugh.

"What's so funny?" she asked, turning to him.

"You are," he said with a smile.

"Why?"

"I can tell you're excited. You haven't stopped talking since we got in the car. But that's okay. I like to see you this happy."

When they arrived at court, there was the biggest crowd yet. They were all waiting for the verdict. They found the gang waiting for them in their regular spot. By the time they made their way through the crowd and into the courtroom, they only had to wait a few minutes for the judge and jury to come out.

The judge began to speak. "Ladies and gentleman of the jury, have you reached a decision?"

One of the jurors stood. "Yes, Your Honor, we have."

"Bailiff, please bring me the decision." The judge read it to himself, and then handed it back to the bailiff. "Bring it back to the jurors. James Labell, please stand to hear the verdict. You may read the decision."

The juror read, "We the jury, on the case of Amber Labell versus James Labell, in the matter of first-degree attempted murder, find the defendant guilty. In the matter of first-degree sexual assault, we find the defendant guilty. In the matter of conspiring to kidnap and kill, we find the defendant guilty."

"Thank you, jurors," the judge said. "You have done your job to its fullest. You may be seated."

Amber looked at Jim. His mouth was hanging open. He looked shocked, like he had thought he was untouchable. Then she noticed his face turning red and the veins in his neck starting to bulge. He started yelling, "I'll get you! Every last one of you! You don't know who you're fucking with! Amber, you're dead! Dead! Do you hear me?"

The judge yelled, "Remove him immediately!"

When Jim was out of the courtroom, and not without a struggle, Judge Mallord announced, "Sentencing will be held on August 8, at eight A.M. We are adjourned."

Everyone began to cheer as they rushed out of the courtroom.

When they stepped outside, the press ran up to them. "What was the verdict?"

"Guilty on all three charges," someone shouted, and then there was even a louder cheer from the crowd outside. They wanted to hear what Amber had to say. For the first time, Amber could reply.

"I'm just glad it's over with and he got what he deserved. That's all for now. I just want to go home. Thank you."

Chapter Forty-Six

For the next couple of days, Amber and Tim felt as though they were floating around the house. They were both so happy.

Finally, it was the morning of sentencing, and they were both ready to go. They couldn't wait to hear his sentencing. When they arrived at court, everyone looked so happy.

"Shall we go in?" Tim asked, opening the door with a flourish and bowing to Amber.

"Yes, I can't wait until this is done," Amber said, skipping happily into the courthouse.

Tim followed her in. "I don't blame you there."

"All rise for the honorable Judge Mallord."

"You may be seated," he said abruptly. "Mrs. Johnson, Mr. Stone, I need to see you in my chamber immediately."

Amber turned around and looked at Tim. "I wonder what's going on. Where's Jim?"

"I don't know, but something's going on."

Brenda returned about twenty minutes later. Her face was drained of color.

"Amber, we need to talk," she said, sitting down next to her. Tim, Chuck and Carol leaned forward. "You're never going to believe this, but Jim escaped during transportation to the courthouse. They had him handcuffed with his hands behind him. At some point during transport, he got the handcuffs in front of him, probably by slipping his hands under his feet. When they pulled up to the courthouse, the officer had his head turned. When he opened the door, Jim jumped out and grabbed for the gun. There was a struggle as they both fought for the gun. Jim got shot in the leg, but unfortunately he overpowered the officer, and during their struggle, he shot the officer in the stomach." Brenda paused her rapid speech and took a deep breath. "He took his keys, unlocked the cuffs, and sped off in the officer's car. They found the officer's car abandoned. The officer that was shot is getting ready to go into surgery. He's still alive, that's the only reason we know what happened. They haven't found Jim yet. I'm sorry, Amber."

I can't believe this. How could this happen? Amber thought. *I think I'm going to be sick.* "I need to use the restroom," she said. "I'm not feeling so good."

They all got up and headed to the bathroom. Tim put his arm around her to comfort her the best he could.

"Honey, don't worry. They'll find him," he said soothingly to her. "It's going to be okay. He won't be able to find you. He doesn't know where you are." Tim turned to their friends. "Chuck, Carol, you can't go to your home until he's found." He turned back to Amber. "Besides, he's wounded. He'll need help sooner or later. I'm sure the police are already checking every hospital around. Who knows? Maybe he'll show up there. And they'll put extra security outside the house."

They finally reached the bathroom. Amber went in with Carol and Brenda following behind her. Amber went into a stall and became violently ill.

"Amber, honey, you need to sit down," Carol said, putting her arm around her and leading her to a bench. "You look very pale. Are you feeling any better?"

Amber swallowed carefully several times. "No, I'm not. But I don't think I'm going to get sick again."

There was a knock on the door.

"Amber, honey, are you okay?" Tim asked through the door.

"I'll be right out. We better go out there. I need to talk to Tim. What are we going to do?" she asked as Carol helped her up and out of the bathroom. "Do you think it's going to be okay to go back home?" she asked Tim.

Tim nodded. "We're going to go home. He doesn't know where we live. We'll be safe there. Look at me," he said, taking her face in his hands. "We'll be safe. I will protect you."

Amber breathed deeply. "I need to calm down and think rationally. Okay, you're right. He doesn't know anything about you. He doesn't know where I live. Chuck and Carol aren't going home, so they will be safe. I need to get out of here."

"Amber, if I hear anything I'll call you," Brenda said, squeezing Amber's arm.

On the way home, Tim looked in the rearview mirror constantly to make sure they weren't being followed. Amber laid her head on Tim's shoulder. "I'm so exhausted."

"Amber, when we get home, you go take your anxiety medicine and get some rest." He had his arm around her, trying to comfort her the best he could under the circumstances.

When they got home, they went in, turned on the alarm, and made sure everything was locked up tight. Tim brought Amber her medicine, helped her up to bed, and tucked her in.

"Don't worry, honey," he said, smoothing the sheet over her. "I will stay awake. You go to sleep and everything will be fine. Do you want me to stay with you until you fall asleep?"

"Would you please?"

"Sure."

He stayed with her until she was asleep, then went downstairs.

After Jim abandoned the officer's car, he found a car that he shimmied open and hot-wired. He went to Chuck and Carol's first, but no one was there. He had to think. *Where could she be?* Then he came up with an idea: her lawyer. *I'll look her up*, he thought. *She'll bring me to Amber's house or I'll kill her.*

When he saw a phone booth, he stopped, went to the booth, and opened the phone book. There it was: her address. He drove the car to a place near her house. He walked the rest of the way.

When he got to Brenda's, he broke in through the back door. He slowly and quietly walked around the house looking for her. Then he heard the shower going. The door was open. He threw the shower curtain open, and held the gun to her head.

Brenda started screaming, "What do you want? Please don't kill me!" She grabbed the shower curtain with both hands and tried to cover herself. Water sprayed everywhere.

"That depends on you," he said menacingly.

"What do you mean?"

"You're going to lead me to Amber's house."

"I can't do that," she said in a high-pitched voice.

"If you want to live, you will do as I say. Otherwise, I will just look around. I know you have her address somewhere. I just need money to get out of here." He left the bathroom and looked around until he found her briefcase. Amber's file was in it with all her information, including her address. "Now you're going to drive me over there."

"Please, no," Brenda said, hurriedly pulling on some clothes. "You got what you wanted . . . just let me go." She was so frightened, she didn't know what to do.

"No, you're coming with me." He continued to hold the gun to her head. "Here's what we're going to do. We're going to get in your car and you're going to drive us there. Don't pull any fast tricks. I have a gun and I will use it."

"Okay, no tricks. I don't want to die, please."

They got into the car and drove to Tim and Amber's.

"I'm going to duck down," Jim said. "I'll have the gun on you the whole time, so don't do anything stupid. I'm sure they have an officer out front. I want you to pull around back. If you see an officer, keep driving. If there isn't an officer out back, pull up and we'll go through the back door. You're going to knock on the door. I'll be off to the side. You better act as if nothing is wrong."

"I will, I will do what you say," Brenda said, her voice shaking. "There's no officer in back."

"Pull in." He sat up and looked. "So this is the house. That little bitch is shacking up with someone else already. That whore. I'm going to get her."

"You said you just needed money!" Brenda exclaimed, shaking and crying uncontrollably.

"Shut up! Get out of the car go up to the door. Don't try to pull a fast one. I have the gun right at your back."

When they reached the door, Brenda knocked.

Tim came to the door and yelled, "Who is it?"

"It's me, Brenda."

"Just a minute. Let me shut off the alarm system."

Brenda and Jim heard the sound of leaves crackling. Jim turned around, just as the officer came around the corner and Tim opened the door. Tim pulled Brenda in. The officer had his gun drawn, but it was too late because Jim was ready for him, and he shot him. While Tim tried to shut the door, Jim pushed it open. Jim shot through the door. He heard the thump of someone hitting the floor, and then footsteps running away. He made his way in just in time to see Tim escaping.

"Stop right there, or I'll shoot!" Jim yelled. Tim stopped and put his arms up, then slowly turned around.

"Where's Amber?" There was silence. "Where is she? Tell me or I'll shoot you."

"She's not here. She's staying at a hotel on the east side."

Jim's face grew red with rage. "Where in the hell is she?"

"I already told you."

The gun went off. Tim hit the floor with a loud crash. Jim shut and locked the door and began to search the house. He made his way upstairs. He went toward Tim's room first. When he went into it, it was empty. He turned and headed toward Amber's room. No one was there, so he headed into the bathroom. Nothing. He opened the shower curtain. There was no time for him to react. Amber, using Tim's gun, shot, then shot again. He fell to the floor.

Amber ran downstairs, scared that Tim had been killed. She saw him lying on the floor, not moving. Her eyes were wide open in alarm, then they filled with tears. She ran to him, throwing herself on the floor. "Tim, Tim, please. . . don't die on me . . . no!" she yelled as she laid her head on his chest.

Then she heard a soft whisper. "Amber, I love you," he said, then passed out again.

"Oh Tim! You're not dead! I love you too." She collapsed in tears.

A minute later, policemen filled the house. The police officer out front had called for backup. Tim was taken to the hospital in an ambulance. Amber went with him. Brenda however, did not make it; she was killed instantly. Jim was also dead.

A police officer came down to the hospital and questioned Amber while Tim had surgery on his stomach.

One of the officers had called Chuck to tell him what happened. He and Carol rushed to the hospital. They ran up to Amber. "Are you okay?" Carol asked as they both hugged Amber, trying to console her.

"I don't know. I don't know if Tim is going to make it," she sobbed. "He's up in surgery right now. That's about all I know."

"Amber," Chuck said, "he's a strong man. He'll pull through."

"I hope you're right," Amber sniffled. "Brenda . . . didn't make it." She collapsed into tears again.

Carol squeezed her tightly. "Oh, I'm so sorry to hear that."

"Yeah, me too."

"One of the officers told me that you shot Jim," Carol said, taking Amber's face in her hands.

"Yes, I did, and now I really will never have to worry about him because he's dead. I hope he burns in hell."

About two hours later, the surgeon came down. "Amber, he's going to make it. We got the bullet out. It didn't hit any major organs. The bleeding is under control, and he's in recovery right now."

Amber jumped up, her face flushed with relief. "Can I go see him?"

"In about an hour or so," the surgeon said, smiling.

"Okay." Amber lunged toward the doctor and hugged him. "Thank you, thank you so much." Amber turned toward Chuck and Carol. She was crying. "Did you hear that? He's going to make it! Thank you, God."

An hour later, Amber was by Tim's side, holding his hand.

"Honey, I'm so happy to see you," she gushed. "You had me so scared. I don't know what I would have done without you in my life. I love you so much."

"I love you too," he said, his voice very quiet and raspy. "Amber, you saved my life. Thank you so much. Most of all, I'm so happy he didn't kill you. You did good, honey. The doctor says I have to stay here about a week before I can go home."

"Well, I'm not leaving this hospital until you are." Amber kissed him, and it was the best kiss ever because he made it, he was alive.

❦ Chapter Forty-Seven ❦

A week later, Tim arrived home. He was much better and able to move around again.

"Honey, it's so nice to be home," Tim said once he had settled in.

Amber's face shone with happiness. "Yes, it is."

"I asked the doctor about the wedding, and he said by then I should be practically healed, so to go ahead and stick with the date we set up."

Amber threw her arms around him. "Great! That's so wonderful to hear!"

"Amber, you are the light of my life. You are truly an amazing woman. I feel proud just having you by my side. You are the one for me, my soul mate, the one I was meant to be with forever."

"That's exactly how I feel about you," Amber said, kissing him gently. "Chuck and Carol will be here in a few minutes. Do you need help getting ready?"

"No, I actually can do it by myself now," he said with a smile.

"That must mean you're healing well."

"The doctor said I would be doing well by the time we get married, and that's only a week away. I guess he's right because I'm feeling much stronger compared to last week. Look, I can actually bend without having any pain," Tim said, bending his waist from side to side.

"Good," Amber said proudly. She went to the window. "Here they are now. They just pulled in. I'm glad we're getting together to go over the last-minute details of the wedding. I'm so happy, but I can't help but feel guilty at the same time with Brenda being killed. I know she wanted us to get married, but it still bothers me."

"Honey, it will get better in time."

"I know, it's just hard to deal with."

"I know you think it's your fault, but it's not. When we went to the funeral, her family even said they didn't blame you." He put his arm around her. "Honey, things will get better. Don't worry so much."

"I'll go get the door." Amber opened the door and let Carol and Chuck in. "Hi, how are you guys doing?"

"We're doing good," Carol replied with a smile. "The question is, how are you and Tim doing?"

"I'm fine and Tim is doing so much better. You'll see. He's getting around really well, and his appetite is back, that's for sure. Come on in and have a seat."

Tim came out from the kitchen eating an apple. "Hey guys."

"See what I told you? His appetite is back," Amber said with a laugh.

"I see that," replied Carol. "So you guys must be getting pretty excited about the wedding."

Amber went to Tim and put her arm around him. "I'm just glad Tim is doing so well."

"Oh Amber," Tim said, "I will pick up the flowers the morning of the wedding. They called and said they would be ready by eight o'clock."

"Good, I was getting nervous about it when they weren't calling back."

"Yeah, me too."

"Oh, and the caterers called," Tim said, smiling. "They're all set to go also."

"Oh, when did they call?" Amber asked, leading him over to sit next to her on the couch.

"They left a message yesterday." Tim turned to Carol and Chuck. "I don't think we really needed to have a meeting about this, but Amber was getting nervous."

"That's okay, we understand," Chuck said.

"I just figured it would be a good idea," Amber said.

Sometime during their conversation, Tim and Chuck quietly disappeared into the kitchen.

"Well," Carol said, "those two snuck off pretty quietly."

Amber nodded. "They sure did. I guess I can't blame them."

"To guys, this is a boring conversation," Carol said with a chuckle. "Amber, instead of meeting at the church, you know what would be fun?"

"What's that?"

"How about the night before the wedding, I spend the night here, and Tim spends the night with Chuck. That way, you two don't see each other until you meet at the altar."

"That's a great idea!" Amber said excitedly.

"We'll tell the guys later," Carol said, reaching over to hug her friend.

Chapter Forty-Eight

The day of the wedding, Amber woke up to the sound of the phone ringing. She picked it up. It was Tim calling from Chuck's house. "Hi honey, how did you sleep?"

"I had such a hard time sleeping last night!" she exclaimed. "I couldn't stop thinking about today. How did you sleep?"

"I slept great. I fell asleep with such happy thoughts. Anyway, I just wanted to call and see how you were doing, and to say I love you and I can't wait to see you."

"Honey, I love you too," Amber said, sitting up in bed. "I'm so happy, and I can't wait to see you either."

"I'll be at the church around twelve thirty. You're going to be the most beautiful bride ever."

"Thank you. See you at the altar."

"I'll be waiting for you."

Amber went to get ready. When Carol returned from picking up the flowers, Amber was just putting her hair up.

"You look beautiful," Carol said, her voice full of emotion.

"Thank you, so do you."

"We better get going to the church. We can finish getting you ready up there."

When they got to the church, Amber was filled with emotion and excitement. "Carol, I can't wait until I see Tim at the altar. I'm so happy Chuck is going to walk me down the aisle, since I don't have anyone to do that. I'm not sure if a best man has ever done that before, but I am so happy he agreed to it."

Carol put her arm around Amber. "He would have never said no to walking you down the aisle. In fact, he feels honored to do it. Well, should we finish you up?"

"Yeah, we better."

By the time Amber finished getting ready and putting the last touches around the church, it was time to start the ceremony. Amber went back to her room so Tim wouldn't see her before she came down the aisle.

The music started, and Carol began to walk down the aisle, then stood off to the side of the altar. Next came Amber and Chuck. All the guests stood in admiration of the bride. Chuck kissed Amber's cheek at the altar and whispered, "You look beautiful."

Tim took her arm. He couldn't take his eyes off her. "You are so beautiful."

Amber took a look at him, and she too couldn't take her eyes off of him. "You look so handsome."

It was as if nobody else was there. They proceeded up the steps of the altar, where the pastor stood smiling at them. He announced to the guests, "Amber and Tim have written their own vows."

Tim began first. He cleared his throat and took both Amber's hands in his own. "I, Tim, take you, Amber, to be my wife. You are the wind beneath my wings, my heart, my soul, my soul mate. And my one and only true love. On this special and holy day, I give to you, in the presence of God and these witnesses, my sacred promise to stay by your side, as your faithful husband, in sickness and in health, in joy and in sorrow, as well as through good times and bad. I promise to love you without reservation, honor and respect you, provide for your needs as best I can, protect you from harm, comfort you in times of distress, grow with you in mind and spirit, always be open and honest with you, and cherish you for as long as we both shall live. This is my solemn vow."

Amber wiped a tear from her eye as she began her own vows. "I, Amber, take you, Tim, to be my husband. You are the wind beneath my wings, my heart, my soul, my soul mate. And my one and only true love. On this special and holy day, I give to you, in the presence of God and these witnesses, my sacred promise, to stay by your side as your faithful wife, in sickness and in health, in joy and in sorrow, as well as through good times and bad. I promise to love you without reservation, honor and respect you, provide for your needs as best I can, protect you from harm, comfort you in times of distress, grow with you in mind and spirit, always be open and honest with you, and cherish you for as long as we both shall live. This is my solemn vow."

"May I have the rings please?" the pastor asked. Chuck handed them to him. "Do you, Tim, take Amber to be your lawfully wedded wife?"

"I do," Tim said, looking deeply into her eyes.

"Place the ring on her finger," the pastor said, and he did. "Do you, Amber, take Tim to be your lawfully wedded husband?"

"I do," Amber said, returning Tim's gaze.

"Place the ring on his finger," the pastor said, and she did. "I now pronounce you husband and wife. You may kiss the bride." Amber wrapped her arms around Tim's neck as he put his arms around her waist and kissed her.

Epilogue

After Tim and Amber came back from their honeymoon, life was the best it had ever been. Amber no longer lived in fear, and Tim no longer felt he had to constantly protect her. Life was perfect. After all Amber had been through, she still had so much of an innocence about her. There had been so much in her life she had missed, and now Tim was making sure she got to see everything.

Amber quit working at the café to go to the university and take classes. She started her own women's advocacy group. Amber appeared on many talk shows to tell her story and urge women to come forward, and many did. Amber's goal was to help as many women as she possibly could. She set up private safe houses for women to go to where their husbands wouldn't find them. She helped them with whatever they needed help with. Amber traveled across the country to give speeches. Tim went with her when he could. Tim continued to work as a police officer, and enjoyed every minute of it. Even with everything Tim and Amber had going on in their lives, they were always each other's first priority.

Tim and Amber and Chuck and Carol remained best friends. In fact, the following summer, Amber became pregnant and so did Carol. They had planned to have their children as close in age as possible, and it worked. They had their babies two weeks apart. Carol had a boy and named him Tyler Lee, and Amber had a boy named Nicholas John. Two years later, they both had another child. Carol had another boy named Joseph Paul, and Amber had a girl named Pamela Joan. They spent as much time together as they could. Tim and Amber were happier than ever.

Brenda was born and raised in Minnesota. She grew up in a very loving family and has three older brothers, Joe, Dan and Dave, who throughout the years have showered her with love. She still lives in Minnesota with her two sons. One of Brenda's favorite hobbies is writing poems, because they come from the heart.

Through the Eyes of a Woman is Brenda's first novel. Although this book is fiction, the author knows all too well about abusive relationships. She lived through one herself and understands, fully, that after one first gets out of an abusive relationship, life is confusing and difficult. Through counseling and loving family and friends, one can rise above it and push on, day by day, until finally one day life becomes easier, and better, and one can be thankful for what one has and the love shown by one's supporters. Then the stars look brighter than ever!

I pray for all the women who are going through or who have lived through an abusive relationship and I want you to know there is life afterwards—a better, more fulfilling life. Just push on and you'll get through. Life is wonderful and too short to waste. Enjoy it while you can. I hope you enjoy this book as much as I have enjoyed writing it.

Brenda Latourelle
April, 2005